A DEATH MOST COLD

A DEATH MOST COLD

JARSOLAV (JERRY) PETRYSHYN

IGUANA

Published by Iguana Books
720 Bathurst Street, Suite 303
Toronto, ON M5S 2R4

Publisher: Meghan Behse
Editor: Allister Thompson and Heather Bury
Front cover design: Meghan Behse
Front cover illustration: Melissa Novak

ISBN 978-1-77180-438-7 (paperback)
ISBN 978-1-77180-439-4 (epub)
ISBN 978-1-77180-440-0 (Kindle)

This is an original print edition of *A Death Most Cold*.

Dedicated to the memory of my brother Mike
(April 22, 1957 – June 26, 2019)
'Always and Forever'

CHAPTER ONE

Monday evening

Oliver Spinner sat down, his face a puzzled frown. He had been informed that the board of governors just finished an extraordinary "in camera" session and he had not been invited. This in itself was perplexing considering that, as the institution's chief financial officer, he attended all such meetings as a matter of course. Bewilderment deepened into concern when he saw the board chair in the president's office as well, looking bleaker and more severe than he usually did. Sheldon Blythe was clearly discomforted, his high forehead profoundly creased, the mouth etched into a pucker as if tasting something thoroughly unappetizing and the eyes averted, studying the hands clasped in his lap.

The only individual who seemed herself, which was to say in control, was the president; Vanessa Dworking shifted slightly in her seat, took full measure of the two men before her, and, seemingly satisfied that they were sufficiently attentive — in the case of Spinner, riveted to the edge of his chair — decided she might as well get it over with.

"I'll get right to the point, Oliver. This is an exit conference. You are being released from your position as dean of financial and administrative services under the dismissal clause in your contract."

Spinner blinked blankly at the woman behind her mammoth desk, then glanced sideways at Blythe, who was now preoccupied with straightening his cuffs. To be sure, his working relationship with the president had been strained lately, but he hadn't anticipated this scenario at all.

"Why?" he finally managed to croak.

"I've lost confidence in your ability to perform your duties."

Met by a stunned silence, Dworking continued, "Late last week, I placed your name before the Board Personnel Committee with two options — either you go or I go. The committee has chosen."

Dworking stated this with a hint of smugness, nodding slightly in the direction of Blythe, who also happened to chair the Personnel Committee. "There was a special meeting of the full board earlier this evening. They ratified the committee's decision. The only avenue available to you, if you so choose, would be to tender your resignation; it might be advantageous to do so — save public embarrassment. This, of course, will not affect your contractual benefits in any way," she added gratuitously.

Spinner cleared his throat a couple of times, trying to comprehend the full scope of his situation and gather his thoughts. "Excuse me if I seem somewhat overwrought…I have been caught by surprise — in fact, I'm shocked and bewildered to find that there has been a serious problem with my work. I would like to know whether this action is a result of my performance or—"

The president's gravelly voice cut him off. "There's no use going into details. The decision has been made, and that decision is not debatable and in any case will not be overturned." Turning again to her board chairperson as if for confirmation, she proceeded, "Now, I suggest we stick to the purpose of this meeting. Do you wish to tender your resignation?"

Struggling to keep his composure, Spinner scarcely knew how to respond. "I…I regret that events have reached this stage and that I wasn't given any indication that there was a serious problem between us. But I don't appreciate this kind of pressure and such short notice. I would need some time to think as to what is my best course of action—"

"Oliver," Blythe spoke for the first time, perhaps sensing his cue, "the dismissal is a reality. After today, you will no longer be employed by Great Plains College. I'm sorry. If you do choose to resign, there will be a generous package; however, I...er...we would need a letter to that effect after this meeting."

***

Vanessa Dworking stood low to the ground, with a good centre of gravity. She had black, closely cropped hair and a wide Slavic face with a generous mouth — features well proportioned to her stature. In the corridors of the college, she was instantly recognizable by the dapper fur coat and the formidable handbag/purse that swung rhythmically from her side. She walked with a measured cadence, not quite a swagger but still as someone who knew who was in charge. Not that she was an overly familiar figure in the main building; she chose to perform her duties from a solitary edifice that formerly housed the college's extension services (made defunct by budgetary restraints in her first year). Refurbished inside and out, the squat structure perfectly served her detached administrative style. The sign in front read "President's Office"; to most, however, it was simply known as "the bunker."

At the time of her appointment, she had been the vice-president of a large polytechnical institute in Toronto. Undoubtedly, she would have remained there had she been able to move up that last rung of the ladder. And for a while, she thought she might actually do it. Indeed, for one heady year she served as acting president while the incumbent lay in hospital recuperating from a bad traffic accident (even big Buicks didn't react well to broadsides from TTC buses). Alas, he recovered sufficiently to resume his post, and her career advancement was temporarily halted. Then she spotted the ad in the *Globe and Mail*: "A dynamic, growing college in a progressive Northern Alberta community is seeking a Chief Executive Officer." Well, why not! As it turned out, Great Plains College was looking for a no-nonsense money manager to lead it out of a huge deficit. Being a good bean counter, she fit the bill.

But not without resistance. The fact of the matter was that when her application arrived, Dwane Pubber, head of the Presidential Selection Committee (and Sheldon Blythe's predecessor as chairperson of the board of governors) set it aside on the grounds that she couldn't be seriously considered because of her gender. Not that he was a sexist, mind you — as he explained — it was just that some women at certain times of the year became emotionally distraught on account of "hormonal eruptions" and couldn't be trusted to make the proper decisions.

This line of logic did not go over well with other members of the committee. Most members wanted to replace the incumbent, whose contract was not renewed after due deliberation, with a competent, financially responsible administrator with gender considerations irrelevant. One particular female student (the committee was an enlightened one, with student and faculty representation) took the chairperson to task in no uncertain terms for his remarks. It was the mid-1980s, after all, and times were changing, with little tolerance for such misinformed views. Besides, it was discreetly pointed out that given Ms. Dworking's age — north of fifty — chances were she was beyond "those" kind of potential problems. Accordingly, her application was quickly reinstated, and on the finalist list at that. Suitably chastised and chastened, Pubber kept any further opinions to himself, and matters, for better or worse, took their course.

For her part, Vanessa knew exactly what she wanted; she had long ago decided on a career above all else, and she pursued it with the tenacity of a born-again Christian. Her only diversion occurred early in her university days. The young man's name was Jules Weinstein. A flighty, unorthodox personality, Jules was proved to lack all those characteristics that Vanessa possessed: sober judgement, practicality, and a hard-headed appreciation of reality. But then opposites were supposed to attract.

At any rate, their relationship was brief and in retrospect doomed. One day, Jules handed her a letter to give to the sociology professor with whom they were both taking a course.

"I won't be coming to class anymore," he announced. "It's all explained in the note."

Jules, as it turned out, was a dedicated Marxist–Leninist. His mission in life was to replace decadent Western capitalism with revolutionary socialism. As fate would have it, the "class struggle" took him to a political rally at Maple Leaf Gardens. During the course of the demonstration that followed, he was accosted (his version) by a fascist pig (code name for one of Metro's finest). Now, he was being incarcerated and therefore could not attend classes.

"What happened?" she asked.

"I hit the cocksucker with a two-by-four."

After that, Vanessa declined to fraternize any further with Jules, or with anyone else, for that matter.

***

With the meeting concluded and the parties involved gone, Vanessa took a long, satisfying drag on her cigarette. There, that was done! She felt a kind of intoxication at having triumphed once more.

And triumphed she had. It had been, after all, a bit of a gamble, calculated and weighted heavily in her favour, but a gamble nevertheless. "I've lost confidence in the dean of financial and administrative services," she told the board, "and I want his services terminated."

There had been some raised eyebrows, and a couple of the more strident members voiced fairly strenuous objections. Spinner had been with the institution for quite some time — in fact, much longer than she. But in a test of wills she won, as she had been doing from the day they hired her. The clincher, and hence the gamble, required that she lay it on the line — either he goes or she goes. The board chose her, as she knew they would.

Vanessa decisively crushed her cigarette butt into the overflowing ashtray. Enough for one night! She glanced at her watch. Almost nine — she rarely stayed this late. Indeed, except for the occasional meeting, she adhered to a nine-to-five routine. The quintessence of a good administrator: do what needed to be done in the time allocated and escape to your own sanctum. In her experience those who chained themselves to their desks or brought excessive work home with them were likely inefficient and were apt to suffer from premature burnout. She guarded against both.

Vanessa got up and stretched. Shrugging into her coat, she paused at the window, parted the blinds, and peered out with a shiver. Great Plains had been enveloped in one of those Arctic cold fronts for three days now; the parking lot was shrouded in ice fog, with her encrusted red Olds sitting forlornly under the pale glow of a street lamp. Must have been minus thirty with no relief in sight, but at least it hadn't snowed in some time. She didn't mind the temperature extremes so much but loathed the snow, or rather driving in it, since she lived a good twenty kilometres outside the city.

Her thoughts were momentarily jarred when she heard the outer doors of the "bunker" creak open. Now who could that be at this time of night? The custodial staff had already made their rounds, and it was still too early for the security check. Picking up her handbag, she emerged from her office.

"Oh, it's you!" she exclaimed, raising an eyebrow in surprise.

∗∗∗

As he wheeled the John Deere into the parking lot, Merle Morgan thought about his warm bed and how he wished he were still in it. Hauling your arse out at 5:30 a.m. and then freezing it off sanding sidewalks and roads wasn't his career ambition, but then neither was being unemployed.

The issue wasn't so much the nature of the job, which he didn't mind (and the pay was good), but his behaviour that night that had led to his "out of sorts" morning. He had gone to the Great Plains Inn to catch the hotel's latest attraction, none other than the Rhythm Pals from the *Tommy Hunter Show* that he used to watch on CBC.

Merle liked his country music, but these guys were a cut above; he considered the trio more than just a house band for Tommy Hunter but rather great Canadian performing artists like Al Cherny or Juliette, whom he often enjoyed after the hockey game. For him, they transcended the usual nasal, twangy sounds with more elaborate vocal harmonies and instrumental backup. He was particularly partial to the mellow moans of the accordion during their sad ballads. And it was a welcome break from the mid-February cabin fever blues.

He sat in the corner of the lounge, subsumed in the shadows, a lone lump — at least these days — nursing his beer and tapping his right big toe to the beat. Sparse crowd, he had noted, but it was Monday night. During the intermission, he wandered over to the Rhythm Pals' display table just off the stage, picked up their latest album, *Just for You*, and briefly chatted with the musicians. They thanked him, after which the album cover was duly signed by Mike, Marc, and Jack under their respective photos.

No complaints — that part of the evening was all good… It was later when he arrived home that he got derailed. Hurtin' songs did that to him, and the album had a couple that made him break his rule about overindulging during the work week. He sat, listened, and drank well into the night, feeling more and more maudlin as the hours wore on. With the strains of "Illusions of Love" stoking his sorrow and sips of Canadian Club dulling his resolve, he thought of his brief time with Maggie and what might have been had she not packed her belongings and left him without so much as a goodbye note.

That was just over two months ago, and although he was getting over her (after all, there was no formal commitment, and he knew that she was a bit of a free spirit) and had started to move on, there were moments of pain. The Rhythm Pals, or rather their music, had inadvertently caused him a relapse.

With a deep sigh, Merle drove the tractor cum snowplough/sand spreader alongside the only vehicle in the parking lot; he recognized it as the president's car. And so he should, since he'd been in charge of its maintenance for the last two years! Part of the perks of office, he supposed; every three years, the president was entitled to a new car, and it was serviced as an integral part of the college fleet.

The '86 Oldsmobile Delta 88 Royale was a sharp, substantial conveyance, as befitted the institution's chief executive officer. Nicely squared off, with an imposing presence — although a bit forlorn at that moment — it was just the kind of automobile he'd love to own, if he could afford it. He wondered what happened to these presidential cars when the time period expired. Were they leased and thus returned (he didn't think so, if he had to perform the maintenance)? More likely, it was traded in for a new version or sold — possibly auctioned off. He'd take it if the price was right. His old Malibu would be ready to rust in peace in another year or so when the prez was due for a new one. He made a mental note to ask around, get the scoop, and stake out his interest, so to speak.

Judging by the thick layer of frost on the windows, it hadn't moved all night. Dworking mustn't have gotten the thing going, Merle surmised.

"Probably the battery," he muttered. Maybe he should give it a boost. But he didn't have the key, did he? And she wouldn't leave them in the ignition, would she? On the other hand, you never know, do you? What the hell — might as well check it out anyway.

He put the tractor in neutral and eased himself out of the warm cabin with a shiver, his boots crackling on the crystallized snow as he approached the driver's door. He tried it and was surprised that it wasn't locked.

As the door swung open, Merle Morgan staggered backward, almost gagging on a deep, involuntary intake of sharp, pristine air.

"Holeee thundering Jesus!"

Not only were the keys in the ignition, but the president was there too, securely fastened in her seat belt, staring straight ahead, about as stiff as a body could be.

CHAPTER TWO

Tuesday morning

Myron Tarasyn stared out his apartment window; all he could see was the misty dullness of the ice fog and the diffusion of lights from Great Plains College shrouded in various shades of grey in the distance. It promised to be another frigid, surrealistic day.

"Minus thirty five and dropping," announced the slightly nasal voice on the radio, "a real Northern Alberta February. So much for global warming…"

So much for a hell of a lot of things, thought Tarasyn, pulling out a battered Brigham pipe from the inside pocket of his limp tweed jacket. He went through the ritual of stuffing tobacco into the pipe, tamping it down with his index finger and finally igniting the mixture. It was a bit early to begin puffing, but these days he didn't much care. What did one of his old mentors say about the vice? A woman is just a woman, but a pipe is a good smoke. Well, not quite right. Both could burn you; it was a matter of degree. One scorched only the tongue; the other could blacken the soul.

Through the veil of rising smoke, he surveyed the latest manifestation of his blackened soul: an empty living room. Nadia had come by unexpectedly last evening with some of her cohorts and more or less cleaned him out.

He was a bit aghast but didn't want to contribute to a scene, considering that Ted Mack and Benson McDougall had stopped by to cheer him up. Besides, he was through with histrionics; best to let her take what she wanted and be done with it. So while he and his college colleagues sat around the kitchen table, talking shop in muffled tones, his grim-faced wife marched in with her "movers" (*Where'd she find Curly and Moe?* Tarasyn vaguely wondered) and proceeded to take things out. The sofa (it was ugly anyway), the two side chairs (no great loss), the stereo system (ouch! that hurt; it was a Telefunken), a lamp, the coffee table, and generally anything else that she had presumably grown attached to at some time or other during their five years of acquiring chattels together.

"Are you going to just let her walk out with all that stuff?" asked Ted Mack as he watched Curly and Moe doing their heave-ho routine.

Myron shrugged and stared into his beer. "Sure, why not? I'm a little short on bullshit repellent just now."

"Bad move," replied Ted. "She'll walk all over you."

"I'd say she already has," offered, Benson shaking his head.

In retrospect, he should have protested the carting off of the Kurelek pencil sketch that had hung above the stereo. It was a delicate piece of a boy lying on the grass in an open field, chewing on a blade of straw, looking up at the prairie sky. True, she had picked it out (which in her mindset meant that she was entitled to it — end of discussion), but he too had grown rather fond of it. Days of long lost innocence and all of that...not to mention that it was valuable art, which would only appreciate with time. But he felt too hollow, distracted, and distressed to do anything but watch with a kind of numb detachment as she took it down, tucked it under her arm, and resolutely spirited it away.

When at last her work was done, she paused at the door, bit her lip thoughtfully, and evidently having made up her mind, declared, "Since you have guests tonight, I'll come back later for the dining table and chairs."

With that, she was gone.

***

They met at York University in Toronto. Myron was a teaching assistant/marker and in the throes of writing his doctoral thesis. Nadia was an English major who chose history as an elective, and his seminar section was the only one that fit into her timetable. She was enthusiastic; he was intrigued. They hit it off but prudently restrained themselves until the semester ended.

"I'm happy!" she exclaimed the day after she moved into his ratty one-bedroom apartment near Jane and Finch.

"A course in Canadian history will do that to you," he mused.

"No," she said, "only certain profs—"

"I'm not a prof. I'm a mere graduate student, simply doing what profs do but for a pittance. I may become a prof, though, whereby I can continue to do what profs do for a whole lot more — if I can ever finish my thesis."

"Oh, you'll finish," she proclaimed confidently. "You're one of those plodders — and plodders always finish."

And he did: a thick tome on the rise and consolidation of prairie radicalism, 1914–1921, overstuffed with footnotes (which thesis advisors loved and which drove Nadia nuts typing). Meanwhile, he raided a couple of his more meaningful chapters to produce a paper, which became a "useful" article in a respected academic journal. This was considered obligatory to get his career launched in higher education. Shortly thereafter, he was ready for the fast-track lane on the "sessional circuit," an accepted route for those aspirants to an eventual permanent university position. Sessional lecturers were hired on a limited-term basis (usually eight months with a chance of renewal), often to replace a tenured professor gone off on sabbatical. Every year, there were numerous such positions advertised across the country.

Myron's CV went nationwide, with a long string of nays, until he was lucky enough to be hired by the University of Edmonton sight unseen. Subsequently, he learned that indeed a senior member of the History Department had perused his "useful" article and thought him a deserving candidate. It was an eight-month appointment at subsistence wages. Both he and Nadia were elated. They decided to get married before driving west together to seek their fortune.

That presented some complications, however. Nadia's mother was none too keen to see her daughter whisked away in matrimonial bliss by a strange man to God knows where — even if he was from the right ethnic background.

Myron and Vera Karpovich didn't exactly hit it off. From the moment he arrived at Karpovich's modest bungalow near Myrtle Station just north of Whitby, Myron felt the suspicion and resentment of an outsider who dared to come into Mrs. Karpovich's tightly run matriarchal world to claim for himself her most treasured prize.

Part of it was that Mrs. Karpovich was a widow; Stan Karpovich had died about two years before. To be sure, he left her with a paid-up mortgage and a relatively comfortable existence thanks to an insurance policy and a tidy pension from GM, where he had worked for almost thirty years. Still, she was alone and anxious that her flesh and blood should not abandon her in her twilight years. Aside from that, Mrs. Karpovich had another trait that Myron found all too evident in Nadia; she was possessed of great reserves of nervous, volatile energy, which, coupled with the immutable conviction that she knew what was right for everyone concerned, inevitably produced emotional eruptions. Through some fathomless deductive process, she concluded that he wasn't good for Nadia. And she proved correct, after a fashion.

"So...Nadia picked you," she finally acknowledged to Myron when he had shown up for the sixth or seventh straight time — some sort of record, Myron imagined. They were sitting around the kitchen table with Mrs. Karpovich's shrewd black eyes appraising him once more. Evidently, she decided that he was one apparition that wasn't going away easily.

"We picked each other," Nadia amended, giving Myron a quick smile.

"Yes...yes...and now he wants to take you far away to Elberta!" She shook her head indignantly.

"That's where he got a job… It's a good opportunity for Myron's career," Nadia argued.

"Can't he find a job here?"

"University positions are scarce just now. I'm lucky to get this one," Myron contributed, trying to be more than the silent third person in the conversation.

"And it's not forever," added Nadia, all too aware of his limited-term appointment. "In a year or two, Myron might get a job in Ontario…closer to home. But before we go, we want to get married," Nadia pressed on. "It would only be right."

"Yes…I s'ppose," Mrs. Karpovich sighed.

"A small wedding — just family and close friends before we leave," suggested Nadia.

Mrs. Karpovich appeared to acquiesce, albeit reluctantly (Myron later discovered that mother and daughter had a donnybrook over her proposed marriage to him and the subsequent plan to move west, with Nadia tearfully prevailing). Now, with ruffled feathers apparently smoothed, Mrs. Karpovich insisted that the marriage take place in her church and that the reception be held in her home. Myron agreed in the full knowledge that his side of the family would not object.

Speaking of which…the Tarasyns had much in common with the Karpovichs. To begin with, both came to Canada in 1949 as part of the 30,000 or so "displaced persons" that the country allowed in from the postwar refugee camps in Germany. And while adjusting relatively well to life in the new land, each family carried its share of old world cultural baggage.

No less than Vera, Myron's mother, Marta, was the linchpin of the Tarasyns, but for entirely different reasons. Myron's father, Bohdan, was one of those incredibly useless individuals who never accomplished much on his own, had no evident skills, and would have drunk away whatever the family had were it not for the firmness and resourcefulness of his wife. Bohdan was an illiterate, ignorant, self-serving man who abused the trust of those around him, and Myron wondered why Marta married him. But it was wartime

Germany, she was a peasant girl plucked from the steppes of Ukraine and he, twenty years her senior (also transported to Germany as part of the Nazi labour requisition campaign in 1942), was one of the first individuals she encountered who took an interest in her. They met at her assigned village farm about an hour's drive west of Bremen.

"He wasn't always so bad," Marta told Myron one time, "but the drinking pickled his brain."

Although Bohdan more often than not exhibited poor judgement (he wanted to go to Brazil rather than Canada until Marta interceded with immigration officials and straightened him out), he did have an innate peasant cunning and instinct for self-preservation. And, after all, he did have enough good sense to woo and marry Marta.

Once in Canada, Marta slowly liberated herself from his boorish, overbearing ignorance; she strove to adjust and embrace her new environment while her husband drank with his cronies and stagnated. She went to school to improve her English, obtained a driver's licence after many painful attempts, and finally, with the children grown older, secured employment in a furniture factory in Pickering. The family bought a small farmhouse on a few acres about ten miles northwest of the city.

Marta gave up on Bohdan, who was for the most of his life only sporadically employed, and concentrated her energies on bringing up her three sons, of which Myron was the oldest. Although she never really understood Maroslav's (which somehow got transcribed in the Canadian documentation as Myron) academic pursuits, she was nevertheless proud of his success. When he introduced Nadia, she was delighted, taking an instant liking to her. And when he announced that he had gotten a job in Edmonton at the university there, she said, "Good for you," followed in the same breath, "is Nadia going too?"

"Of course…but before we do, we want to get married."

"That's good too! When?"

"End of June. We want to leave early in July so that we're settled in before I start work August 1."

As Myron anticipated, where they were to be married was of no consequence to his mother as long as she could be there.

The wedding went off fairly smoothly (although privately, Nadia and her mother continued to argue). There were a few moments of anxiety when Myron and family got lost on their way to the church, but the ceremony did proceed on time and without any hitches. The reception at Mrs. Karpovich's house also seemed to go well. The two mothers-in-law were polite to each other, albeit restrained in their conversation — particularly Mrs. Karpovich, who found it difficult, given her reservations.

The two women did make quite a contrast, Myron observed, not only in their personalities but also in appearance and interaction. Vera was an angular, bony woman with the skittishness of a doe ready to bolt; Marta was smaller, rounder, with a more relaxed, placid manner. One scurried about worried that something was amiss; the other hardly raised an eyebrow, letting the flow come to her. Bohdan, meanwhile, along for the ride, so to speak, simply melted into a corner, drank a continuous stream of beer, and looked sheepishly on Mrs. Karpovich's small living room congested with a plethora of milling people.

Not that there were really that many — no more than thirty. Aside from the immediate family members, there were a number of aunts and uncles from Nadia's side that Myron had never met until the wedding. The remainder were an assortment of friends, mostly from university, on either side. All told, a very small, inexpensive, and relatively intimate affair that left both Myron and Nadia profoundly relieved.

***

For a time it appeared they would live happily ever after. Myron successfully completed his eight-month contract with the university and was retained for another year. Meanwhile, he moonlighted at a city college one evening per week and taught a summer session to supplement his meagre income. Nadia, who had a BA in English, obtained an administrative position in the university's older adult outreach programme.

Alas, Myron's time ran out. Since he wasn't on a tenure stream, two years was the max. Once more, he sallied forth in search of employment in academia. A promising opportunity presented itself one day on the Department of History bulletin board. Great Plains College, located some three hundred miles northwest of Edmonton, on about the same latitude as Smolensk/Moscow (Myron looked it up on a map), was in need of a history instructor in its "university transfer programme."

Upon further research, Myron discovered that unlike in Ontario, the Alberta college model allowed for a direct connection to the province's universities. As part of a "comprehensive postsecondary education," many colleges (including Great Plains, as it turned out) offered two years of university courses directly transferable to degree-granting institutions. The idea was to create "university places" for students who would otherwise (usually for economic and/or geographic reasons) not be bound for the hallowed halls. To Myron, it was an enlightened policy. Not only did it ease the problem of access to higher education, but it also provided another institutional pool for employment of academics like himself.

He forthwith sent in his application and in due course received a reply. He had made the short list and was invited for an interview. The Department of Humanities & Social Sciences Selection Committee, consisting of two English instructors — one of whom was the departmental chair — and a psychologist greeted him most pleasantly on his arrival in the city, took him on a tour of the facilities, and then out to a Chinese restaurant, where the main topic of conversation centred on the pleasures of the Great White North and if he was an avid cross-country skier or moose hunter. Myron was neither but got the job anyway.

He was somewhat puzzled as to why the history instructor that he presumably was to replace was not on the committee. Normally, she would have been, he was politely told, but she was in Calgary on pressing family business, and the committee felt the need to get on with the interview/hiring process. Myron nodded in understanding; he would have wanted to meet his potential predecessor and engage in some shop talk, but he appreciated the committee's evident resolve to hire as soon as possible.

Early that spring, Myron and Nadia took an exploratory drive to Great Plains. It was a sprawling, squat city, which, despite its relative unattractiveness, did seem to have the appurtenances of urbanity: a decent-sized mall anchored by a large Zellers and a newly erected Tim Horton's on the major road leading into the heart of downtown. The highlight, in fact, was the college, an impressive curvilinear brick structure located alongside the city bypass. The edifice seemed to arise from the landscape like an amoeba, replete with eccentric curves and conjoining edges.

"I think I'm going to like it here," Myron remarked.

Nadia was less certain. She was saddened that she had to give up her position at the university and leave the provincial capital for the raw frontier. Myron assured her that there was more to Great Plains than gussied-up pickup trucks, grubby mobile homes, and slightly moronic cowboys. Exactly what, he wasn't sure — yet. Nadia, to her credit, took it in stride and indeed, as the time came closer, she became excited about the "challenge" of living in Great Plains.

Later that summer, they moved permanently. Great Plains, already an established regional administrative centre, was in the midst of an oil-and-gas boom, and accommodations were tight. Fortunately, as fate would have it, there was a vacancy in Mackenzie Towers, a vacancy created by the retirement of Ms. Hazel Knolls, whom Myron just happened to be replacing. He never did get to talk shop with his predecessor as he had hoped; by the time he and Nadia arrived, Ms. Knolls had retired to warmer climes in Kelowna, BC.

For over a year after, it appeared that Myron and Nadia's marital bliss would remain intact, despite the occasional flare-up. Nadia, however, showed signs of becoming…unhappy. She was an extroverted creature who could become quite agitated when she felt that all was not right in Camelot. Myron couldn't pinpoint precisely (although he wracked his brains trying) when things started to go seriously wrong.

Perhaps it began when she got a job as a journalist with the *Great Plains Daily Reporter*, a chain publication that scoured the community for noteworthy (and sometimes not so noteworthy) news. Myron began noticing that when he came home Nadia was either out or in the process of going out to cover some event or other. It wasn't that she was avoiding him but rather simply the nature of her job, or so he assumed. When he finally pointed that out, she reacted.

"You're a sedentary slob, do you know that?" she screamed.

True, he was a mite lethargic at times, and he had developed a little paunch, but that was due to her good cooking. Of course, that was then; since, he had lost over thirty pounds — a testament to what marriage stress can do.

That fact was brought home to him when he met an acquaintance he hadn't seen in a number of months. Williams was astonished. "My god, what prisoner of war camp did you emerge from... You're emaciated! Have you been sick?"

"Been on a diet... It's my new gaunt look," Myron joked.

But it was true. His face, once round and fully packed, had developed distinctly angular features; the eyes sank deeper, the cheeks were shallower, and the neck seemed...stretched. And his clothes, he realized, hung on him like drapery, at least two sizes too loose. Indeed, he was, as the phrase went, but a mere shadow of his former self. And this was not to mention that his hair was turning grey at an alarming rate for a thirty-two-year-old.

The final crunch between him and Nadia came one evening when on her way out the door, pen and notebook in hand and the ever-present Pentax slung over her shoulder, she announced with considerable force that she couldn't stand the way he walked, the way he talked, the way he did things — in fact, she couldn't stand *him*!

Later that same night when she returned, in more subdued tones she laid it on the line. "I want to be alone for a while — sort out my life. I'm getting my own apartment."

Myron was hurt and bewildered. He pleaded, he cajoled, but she would have none of it.

"But Nadia—" he tried one last time.

"Just piss off!" Her mind was definitely made up.

And evidently it remained so. First, she whisked away her personal effects, and now the furniture.

In hindsight, Myron wondered what Nadia had told her mother about her pending breakup. He had no doubt of Mrs. Karpovich's reaction: "I told you so," and "when are you coming home?"

For his part, Myron had not yet informed his mother. No sense in unduly disturbing her until he was sure that the marriage was unsalvageable. Then, he would announce the news as gently as possible.

***

Morton took another puff from his pipe and glanced at his watch. Enough brooding: time to go to work. He was almost out the door when the phone rang. It was Ted Mack, whose office was next to his. "Myron…ah…you coming in soon?"

"Right away. I've got a nine o' clock class."

"Good…ah…there's a couple of students here who have been banging on your door wondering where you are."

"Hell…" Myron suddenly remembered. "I told them I'd be in early today…talk about their essays. Totally slipped my mind."

"Okay then. If they're still camped outside your office, I'll tell them you're on your way. By the way, we've had some excitement at the college this morning." Ted's voice suddenly oscillated to a higher frequency.

"Oh?"

"Yeah. It's like a Mountie convention here. They've cordoned off the bunker and the parking lot — yellow tape all over the place."

"What's going on?"

"Can't be sure, but apparently Dworking is dead."

"What!"

"That's what I heard — froze to death."

CHAPTER THREE

On his way to the college, Myron tried to absorb what Ted had told him but discovered nothing dramatic came to mind. Dworking's passing created no emotional upheaval or great void to be comprehended or bridged. Indeed, he felt disturbingly hollow, but then he had been feeling that way for quite some time now. It wasn't that he did not care; he did and was shocked, as anyone would be who had known and worked with a person who suddenly died. But that was the extent of it.

Oddly enough, he had gotten to rather like Dworking, although that wasn't always the case. He clearly remembered his first encounter with her and the turmoil she caused with him inadvertently caught in the middle. It was about a year after he replaced Knolls; being relatively naive and trusting, he let himself be talked into running for president of the Faculty Association, a thankless position, he soon discovered, with no time release or remuneration. He won (by acclamation, it turned out, since there were no other candidates) and soon thereafter had to confront "Attila the Hen," whose deficit recovery strategy included the termination of five faculty members.

They had a number of tense meetings, to the point that when he was summoned to her office one late afternoon, he thought: *This is it! I've aggravated her enough! She's going to get rid of me, a junior, untenured instructor foolish enough to be on the firing line representing his increasingly frightened and belligerent colleagues.*

Dworking's door was open; she sat staring out with a distinctly dour expression, a lit cigarette in her in her right hand menacingly beckoning him to enter. *Said the spider to the fly*, he mused grimly.

Myron wasn't sure what came over him at that moment, but he stopped resolutely in the doorway and solemnly declared, "If you're going to fire me, I'm not coming in!"

She blinked twice at him and let out a huge guffaw, then she went into a smoker's coughing/laughing fit. For a moment he had visions of having to perform mouth-to-mouth resuscitation to save the president from her coughing/laughing/possibly choking spree. Quite unexpectedly, Myron had made her day! And somehow, the ice between them had been broken; they came to an unspoken understanding that each would make the other's life easier, within limits. Thereafter, Myron had gotten along about as well as one could with the very private president.

"Your students didn't stick around," Ted informed Myron as soon as he arrived at his office.

"Just as well," replied Myron, hanging his parka on a hook behind the door and slinging his briefcase sideways onto his battered, paper strewn desk. "I've got a class in fifteen minutes. I noticed the cop cars and the flags at half-mast."

Ted Mack, MBA, CA, was a large teddy bear of a man in his midforties. He possessed thick, reddish hair attached to a roundish face dominated by a lumpy nose. These detracting features, however, were more than compensated for by lively brown eyes and a toothpaste commercial smile. He had a booming voice, which, when matched with an imposing physical presence and quick intellect, made him a formidable instructor who could dazzle or cause to cower commerce students and colleagues alike.

Myron and Ted hit it off, so to speak; certainly, Myron got to know Ted extremely well. Aside from adjoining offices and frequent conversations, they had during the "good" months — spring through summer and fall — when on campus, taken to going on extended walks as sort of reprieves from the workday routine. Usually, they'd stroll out the college's south doors and make their way through an older (some would say seedier) part of the neighbourhood dominated by tiny, mostly rundown homes. The area was known unofficially as College Park. Their destination invariably was Robin's coffee shop.

Like the Walrus and the Carpenter, on these walks they spoke of many things, mundanely on the most profound and sometimes quite profoundly on the most mundane. From office politics to global affairs, they'd voice opinions, dole out wisdom, inject caustic wit, and even solve a long-percolating problem or two besetting the human race. Ted gave as good as he got in the repartee, always with an interesting insight or observation. Moreover, he actually possessed genuine corporate/financial analytical skills that he could summon with considerable force and alacrity.

By any measure, Ted was not your average number cruncher who pored over indecipherable ledgers, chewed on pencils, and played with adding machines; his interpretative knowledge of Canada's byzantine tax rules and regulations made him a high-demand item come tax return time. People lined up to consult with Ted, Myron included. Nowhere were his skills more appreciated than in board–faculty collective agreement negotiations. He was a relentless negotiator who at one moment could be a demure, understanding facilitator and in the next an unleashed junkyard guard dog. He had an explosive temper and didn't suffer fools gladly, particularly government bureaucrats, colleagues riddled with stupidity, and college administrators.

But perhaps his least appreciated quality was his ability to ferret out information; he was a walking sponge who could absorb, digest, store, and regurgitate all manner of communications. He especially thrived on gossip and rumour collection. It didn't bother him that what he gathered sometimes had a reliability problem. For him, that was a separate issue; he just reported the news, true or false. All things considered, though, he had a good track record; generally, where there was smoke, there was a fire in the making, and Ted was a good smoke detector.

Myron became cognizant of Ted under less than auspicious circumstances. He had just arrived at the college and along with Nadia was attending his first "welcome back" barbecue, an annual event put on in late August by the board of governors. The college concourse was packed with new and returning employees, their spouses and significant others. Suffused with food, liquor, and an upbeat selection of canned music spun by a local DJ, a merry party was in progress.

Suddenly, a few feet from where Myron and Nadia were mingling, a disturbance broke out. Myron couldn't see who was doing what to whom other than a short little guy (an artist from the Fine Arts Department, as it turned out) taking a wild swing at someone in the middle of the crowd. A further brief scuffle ensued before all parties were restrained. The little fellow was led away, slightly dishevelled and obviously distraught. Ted emerged from the milling coterie minus his shirtsleeve, torn away from the shoulder.

"Sheesh!" Myron heard Ted's distinctive voice. "All I said was that it might be herpes."

"Yeah, but you said it to his wife!" someone retorted.

Nadia took in the scene and shook her head ruefully. "So…these are your new colleagues. What do they do for an encore…"

Now, attired in a powder blue jacket and red polka-dot tie, Ted plunked his large frame into the visitor's chair in Myron's office. His voice had lost some of its excited edge. "They just packed her off."

"Any more details on what happened?"

Ted shifted in his seat and scratched his bulbous nose. "I'm just a rumour monger, so I really don't know anything for sure, but I heard that the Mounties are suspicious. Maybe she didn't freeze on her own."

"Who told you that?" Myron stopped leafing through his lecture notes; he assumed that Dworking's death had been an accident, a cardiac arrest or something of that nature.

"That's what's floating around the corridors."

"I can't believe that."

"I kid you not. Old Wesley in maintenance overheard one of the cops talking over his walkie–talkie about foul play being involved."

"But no one knows for sure?"

Ted shrugged. "Not yet, but they're obviously suspicious. I certainly would be. She wasn't exactly Mother Teresa around here, you know."

"But for someone to kill her."

"Could happen. You have to admit peoples' careers, maybe even their personal lives, have been screwed by her decisions. Who knows? Someone might have gotten really ticked off and decided to settle the score once and for all. Read about it all the time — fired employees walking into their bosses' offices and blowing them away."

"You've got a point there," Myron reluctantly conceded.

Hurrying to his class, Myron grappled with the thought that someone — someone he knew — could have bumped off the president. Premature…yes, but in theory, Ted was right; there were plenty of potential culprits. Dworking miffed a lot of people, but surely not to such a drastic extent. Those things happened only in whodunits.

Myron observed that the college personnel generally seemed to be coping admirably with the tragedy. Individuals went about their business — not even the classes had been cancelled!

Still, the atmosphere had changed. There were huddled groups sombrely conferring in reverent tones and shaking their heads. It wasn't like the Vatican after a pope expired, but there was a palatable expression of regret nonetheless.

Evidently, not everyone shared this sentiment. Myron rounded a corner and almost collided with the institution's profoundly eccentric mathematics instructor, Orville Wishert. Myron couldn't help but notice that Orville, a short, sour, pudgy man in his middle fifties, who normally walked as if both feet were encased in cement shoes, had a gleeful spring in his step and an ecstatic glaze over his face that matched the shine on his bald head. What gave it away, though, was the song he was singing under his breath: "the witch is dead, is dead; the wicked witch is dead…"

Orville was an original. From a distance, his bespectacled face usually carried a pained expression, as if his pet turtle had died or he was suffering from an acute hemorrhoid attack. Up close, he liked to park himself directly below your nose and with hands on hips spit out sharp, precise sentences.

In conversation, he was the type that talked at you, not to you. There was a subtle distinction, since the former implied a sermon and the latter suggested an exchange of views.

Since he tended to ignore those around him, people tended to ignore him, which in a perverse way caused Orville great distress. He acquired a persecution complex and was constantly on the lookout for dastardly administrators and wayward colleagues who were out to get him. Orville was the classical misfit — a person of great mental ability, well-read but narrow in vision, limited in scope, and totally incapable of dealing with his fellow man on a rational level. A dangerous man to have in any position of power for, quite unintentionally, he would abuse it. Nevertheless, he was well suited for the teaching profession.

It was no secret that Orville despised Dworking. He came to believe that the president conspired with local businessmen and the Chamber of Commerce to eventually do away with the academic divisions of the college and promote vocational and trade programmes. As he explained to Myron shortly after his election as head of the faculty association, "Businessmen want a cheap labour supply in this area… They want to keep the young people here and not go off to university. Dworking is helping them; she's anti-intellectual, you know. For her, academics are overpriced redundancies…"

Orville did tend to exhibit signs of paranoia at the best of times, and his logic seemed a trifle dubious. Great Plains' boom had burst in the early eighties, along with the gas and oil prices, and there wasn't a labour shortage per se; in fact, bankruptcies were up and people were leaving town. Still, he did have a point of sorts. The president's attitude toward the academics had been less than generous, and not only when it came to salary negotiations. She essentially saw them as rapacious eggheads who were always bitching and snapping at the hand that fed them. But she learned to tolerate them because they attracted the most student numbers that translated into FTEs (full-time equivalents), which was how the provincial government statistically measured institutional enrolment, a crucial factor in the government's grant calculations.

Myron was aware that there had been bad blood between Orville and Vanessa, especially since she tried to get rid of him, ostensibly because his student evaluations were below the accepted average. Orville, however, was well entrenched. Moreover, he was independently wealthy; he had a significant interest in his two brothers' lucrative chain of motels across Western Canada. Thus, when he threatened to unleash a battery of high-priced lawyers on both the president and the board, Dworking prudently backed off.

"A marvellous day, isn't it?" was all Orville said, continuing his jaunty strides down the hall.

Myron frowned; Orville's behaviour was in bad taste, if not worse.

***

Through his first couple of sessional years of trial and error, Myron discovered the art of delivering a good lecture. The key was in packaging it, presenting a concise, digestible topic, which focussed on three or four points, underscored by humorous footnotes. Today, however, the technique did not quite work. The subject was appealing enough — gin, sleaze, and Canadian politics, more specifically, Sir John A. Macdonald and the Pacific Scandal — but Myron wasn't into it, and he flubbed some of his more poignant punch lines. The students too appeared restless and preoccupied. Of course, they had heard of Dworking's demise, which, along with his own skewed thoughts, Myron surmised, produced an unsettling effect. Still, not to worry; he'd recapture them next class.

Afterward, Myron checked in at his mailbox. Academics received enormous amounts of internal communications: notes, notices, minutes of meetings, memos, messages, and other generally unsubstantial but annoying epistles. He scanned the pile and promptly deposited the bulk into the nearest trash receptacle; the rest would go onto his desk to be further evaluated and disposed of. There was one item that got his attention. It came from Ms. Whitford, the secretary to the board of governors, informing him of a special "in camera" meeting of the board to be held that Wednesday evening. Myron, who was the duly elected faculty representative on the college's governing body (a reward of sorts for his work as president of the faculty association), pondered this for a moment. No doubt, this special meeting related to Dworking's untimely earthly departure. The board, he reasoned, would need to get a handle on the situation and make some decisions, the most urgent of which was putting in place a new chief executive officer.

The rest of Myron's day was uneventful. He encountered more "have you heard about Dworking" conferences, drank coffee, and commiserated with other colleagues. He gave his late afternoon class in "world history" — the new trend replacing the standard Western Civilization course, which was deemed too self-centred and parochial in a period of emerging "globalization" — and decided that it was time to head back to his empty apartment. There was still some pizza lingering in the fridge.

On his way out, he spotted his first tangible evidence that indeed the college had been the scene of a possible crime: a long-legged RCMP officer. She wore the typical blue parka and blue trousers with the wide yellow stripes down the side; her polished black boots were moving with a sense of purpose.

On closer inspection, Myron figured she was about thirtyish. Peeking from beneath the regulation short-beaked cap were rich, dark strands of hair, some of which curled on her shoulders. Amber eyes, a slightly upturned nose, full lips with a hint of rouge and a nicely rounded chin completed the picture. Altogether an attractive face that drew an arresting stare from Myron. He had seen her somewhere before, although he couldn't quite place where. He was one of those individuals who couldn't always remember a name but never forgot a face. As she walked by, a clipboard solidly grasped at her side, he gave her a curt nod, and she responded with a smile, hesitated momentarily, and proceeded on her way. Myron had the distinct feeling she had recognized him as well.

Chapter Four

Tuesday evening

Myron had his door slightly ajar, peeking out like a tentative tortoise from its shell.

"Myron Tarasyn."

"Yes?"

"I'm Corporal Freta Osprey. I saw you earlier at the college today but didn't get a chance to speak to you."

"Oh yes…" Rather sheepishly, he swung the door open and stepped aside. He had become reluctant to answer unsolicited knocks on his door, particularly when he had not been forewarned via the intercom at the front entrance. His tepidness was easily explained; after all, it could have been Nadia returning with her minions to claim the dining table and matching chairs. And he didn't wish to eat his future pizzas and Kraft dinners propped against the kitchen counter.

Corporal Osprey was without her parka (which puzzled Myron), but otherwise she was fully dressed in her regulation Mountie costume. The dark-blue shirt strained across her chest, and he spent a lingering second or two examining it before he elevated his sight and thoughts to a higher plane.

"You look spooked!" she remarked. "Not hiding a body in the closet, are you?"

"Pardon?" His jaw dropped.

"Never mind, I couldn't resist," she said, stepping in. She took an encompassing survey of his empty living room. "Did I catch you at an awkward time?"

"Ah…no, not at all," he assured her. "You can help me dispose of the body."

"Touché!" She laughed. "I'm your neighbour — of sorts," she continued. "I live a floor below you, and rather than tracking you down at the college, I thought it might be more convenient to reach you at home."

No wonder she looked familiar; he'd probably seen her a time or two in the building without the uniform but took no real notice when he was happily married. It explained the absence of a parka.

"Would you have a few moments," she pressed on, "to answer some questions?"

"Tonight…I'm free…all evening," he babbled, still off guard and trying to collect his thoughts. And indeed, he hadn't any plans but to digest his pizza and feel sorry for himself in front of the TV, which, thankfully, Nadia appeared to have overlooked. "I've just made coffee; can I get you some?" He gestured to the gurgling coffee maker. "Should be enough for two."

"That'd be great — if it isn't too much trouble."

"No trouble at all." He directed her to the dining portion of his abode. She sat with her back to the frost-laced sliding balcony door where she had another perspective on his unadorned living room.

"What happened to your furniture?"

"It got taken away."

"Were you burglarized?"

"Oh no…nothing like that! Umm…my wife took it," he said quickly but didn't elaborate further.

After an awkward pause, she chose not to pursue it but got to the subject at hand. "I'm here, of course, about the tragic incident at the college."

He nodded, setting two coffee mugs on the counter. "Cream and/or sugar?"

"Black, thanks."

Myron poured the brew, placed a mug in front of her, and sat opposite.

"At this time, I'm interviewing those who dealt with President Dworking on a fairly consistent basis. I've spoken to a number of individuals, and your name was mentioned."

"Oh?"

The corporal produced a small notebook from her back pocket and quickly flipped to a section. "You are the faculty representative on the board of governors this year?"

"Yes."

"And until recently, you were president of the Faculty Association — for two years running, someone mentioned?"

"Right — until last year."

"So in those positions you would have had the opportunity to interact with the deceased on a fairly regular basis?"

"I wouldn't say regular — but yes, on numerous occasions I spoke to her."

Taking a pen from her shirt pocket, she asked, "How long had you known President Dworking?"

"Since I arrived at the college — almost four years now."

"And your interaction with her was on a professional basis?"

"Yes."

"Never got to know her on a more personal basis?"

"No, not really."

"So you wouldn't know if there was anyone that she may have confided in — a close friend, relative perhaps?"

"No one that I know of… Don't think she had any relatives out here. She was from Ontario originally," *as is a goodly portion of the faculty*, he mused. "And she was a very private person."

Freta nodded. "So I've gathered. In general, was she liked by the faculty?"

"Not liked exactly," Myron said diplomatically, "but certainly respected and feared, I suppose. She ran a tight ship."

"In what way?"

"Finances, for one. She took the college from a huge deficit to pretty well a balanced budget. That was the hallmark of her administration. She made sure we lived within our means."

"An efficient administrator, then, who didn't mind stepping on people's toes?"

Myron shrugged. "There was a price to be paid — cuts to staff and services whenever there was a fiscal shortfall from Advanced Education. The prez could be quite ruthless."

Freta jotted a line or two in her notebook. "Do you recall anyone she may have personally slighted or offended?"

Myron stifled a cough and reddened; the coffee went down the wrong way. "Who didn't she offend is a better question," he said, regretting his rather trite remark as soon as he said it. "I didn't quite mean it that way—"

"I get your drift," she said. "I've heard much the same from others today. What I mean is were there, to your knowledge, any threats made against her, publicly or privately?"

"No…none that I am aware of. There's always disgruntled talk in the halls, but that's the extent of it. Ah… Can I ask you a question?" Myron's curiosity was getting the better of him, especially since Freta's line of questioning was suddenly aligning with what Ted had told him earlier that day.

"Go ahead." She gave what Myron perceived was a bemused expression, a curt smile with the eyebrows arching up.

"Your line of inquiry seems to suggest that President Dworking met with foul play." *God, that sounded like a clichéd line from a cop show I saw the other night!*

"Not necessarily. That is yet to be determined," Freta responded in a clipped, professional manner.

"You're not a homicide detective?"

"No. The Major Crimes Unit has not been called — yet."

"You're in charge of the investigation?" It seemed a dumb question, but then she seemed relatively young to be handling what he presumed was potentially a murder case.

"That's right," she said, taking a sip from her mug. "For now. The officer first called to the scene gets to investigate — at least initially. Standard procedure."

"Oh," he said, sounding disappointed; somehow he thought she might be from a special squad like on TV. "So when do the detectives come?"

"When the death is deemed suspicious."

"And President Dworking's death is not?" Myron persisted thinking about Ted's passed on rumours that the cops were, indeed, suspicious. Certainly, the corporal's questions seemed to suggest that she was "suspicious."

Freta pre-empted any follow-up questions with a very direct and pointed one of her own. "For the record, where were you last night?" She looked straight into his eyes, her pen poised. *Suspicion is definitely the operative word*, thought Myron.

"At home," he responded, somewhat taken aback by the sudden question.

"Can someone verify that?"

"You mean do I have an alibi?" *This is sounding like something from a cop show after all...*

"Yes," she said blandly. Myron thought he detected smirk lines at the corners of Freta's benign smile.

"Two of my colleagues from the college were here last night for most of the evening — didn't leave till after midnight." Myron mentioned Ted Mack and Benson McDougall, which she duly recorded.

"When did they arrive?"

"About eight thirty... Also, my wife, ah...dropped by around nine thirty with her, ah...friends to take some furniture and the like. We've recently separated," he added almost apologetically.

"I see." Her tone softened. "I had to ask — routine." She gave him a sympathetic smile as if to say, *Sorry, but asking these sorts of questions is part of the job.*

Myron cleared his throat. "Exactly how did the president die?"

"She froze."

"What I mean is — do you think foul play was involved?"

Freta stopped writing and gave him that "nice try" look. They had covered the topic already. "We'll know more when the forensic team finishes its work, but that will take a while."

"Oh…" Myron had no idea about such things.

"Yes, the body was pretty well frozen and needs to be warmed up gradually before an autopsy can be performed. That may take up to a week."

"Oh," Myron repeated numbly, digesting this piece of information.

"In the meantime," Freta continued, "I'm taking statements from individuals such as yourself and establishing your whereabouts — just in case." Myron thought he saw those smirk lines again and frowned.

"You mean in case of foul play?"

"Right."

"For curiosity's sake," *and the sake of my alibi,* "at what time did she die?"

"That hasn't been determined yet. We have to wait for the autopsy report. In any case, it will only be an estimated time, but given what you told me, you and your guests are probably in the clear." She gave Myron an upgrade from smirk to small smile. "I'd say it was some time between early evening and midnight but—" she shrugged, "then again, these things are tricky to determine accurately and depend on many factors. The process of freezing complicates time of death even further by inhibiting the usual markers. So…who knows?"

While Myron pondered that, Freta turned a page in her notebook and abruptly changed focus. "You are, of course, acquainted with Mr. Oliver Spinner?"

"Yes, yes I am."

"What is your assessment of his capabilities as…" she flipped to another page, "dean of Financial and Administrative Services?"

Myron frowned, perplexed. "I presume he's doing a good job. Certainly, as far as I know, he's well regarded — by the faculty, at least. Why?"

"You didn't know that he was dismissed from his position last night?"

"Dismissed? No…no, I didn't." Surprises never seemed to cease at the place. This was news that even Ted's sensitive antenna tuned to whispers in the halls didn't pick up.

"And you're the faculty representative on the board?"

A rhetorical question, no doubt, Myron surmised, since she knew the answer. The truth of the matter was that he hadn't gone to the "special" board meeting early last evening because of his preoccupation with other recent activities in his life. Evidently, he missed an important development.

"Well," Freta continued, not waiting for a response, "apparently, with the concurrence of the board, President Dworking fired him a couple of hours before her death. You didn't attend the board meeting then?"

"No…I decided not to go."

"Too bad," she said, pursing her lips. "I'd be interested in knowing what was said. The meeting was in camera, as I understand it, so no official minutes, other than the key decisions, were recorded."

Myron nodded. He would like to know as well, for his sake, and that of the faculty to whom he reported. It was pretty bad when he couldn't even fulfill the proverbial fly on the wall role. *That will teach me.* The muddle of his own domestic affairs had affected his duty as a duly elected board member. He should have attended; instead, he moped about his apartment for a couple hours until Ted and Benson arrived to "cheer" him up. And, of course, they were on hand to witness Nadia take away "her" possessions.

"You missed a busy night at the college," she remarked dryly.

Freta continued to enquire about a few more people at the college, emphasizing that his interview was, as with others she had conducted, in strict confidence. Myron asked again whether she thought that Dworking's death could be construed as suspicious, but she declined to elaborate or speculate further. "I'm just doing some preliminary leg work at this point. No doubt in a day or two more information will be released. Right now, I'm interested in general impressions of the deceased and what individuals thought of her. Your observations are appreciated…"

About forty-five minutes later, Freta closed her notebook. "Thank you for your cooperation."

"No problem…care for more coffee?"

"No, thanks. I better be off."

At the door, she took one more glance at his vacant living room. "I hope things work out for you. Refurnishing the apartment can be expensive." She gave him a becoming smile, which made Myron wonder vaguely if she was attached.

"Er… thanks. And good luck in your investigation. If I can help in any way…" He really didn't know why he said that, but it seemed kosher to offer.

"Well, perhaps you can at that." She left with the thought hanging.

***

After Freta left, Myron tried to digest what he had learned. One thing for sure, good ol' Ted was closer with his speculations than even he probably realized; the president, in all likelihood, did not die of natural causes, an accident, or misadventure. Freta didn't directly say so, but the case could very well as not turn out to be a homicide. And then there was the secondary bombshell, for him at least, of Spinner's dismissal. Well, that would teach him to miss a board meeting; he would definitely be at the one scheduled for tomorrow. And the lead investigating officer — his thoughts meandered to Freta and her cryptic parting comment about him helping her out. He would not be averse to getting to know her better…

The beginnings of a reverie about his uniformed neighbour a floor below was suddenly shattered by the sharp ring of the telephone. It made him jump.

"Get a hold of yourself, old boy," he muttered as he picked up the receiver. It was his mother.

"Is there something wrong?" she wanted to know. "I have hard time reaching you — you never home!"

"I've been busy lately, Mom."

"Nadia too?"

"Yes, Nadia too," he answered lamely.

"I haven't talked to her in a long time."

"It's her work — the hours are unpredictable."

"Well, don't you see each other?"

"Yes…we do," he said, wincing into the mouthpiece. If he told her that Nadia had left him, she'd probably be out on the next flight.

"She busy…you busy… Is there trouble between you and Nadia? She not happy?" *Mother's intuition is as sharp as a bat's radar.* "We're having a spat at the moment," he said defensively. *Better to tell her something.*

"Spat?"

"Disagreement… Hopefully, we'll work it out."

"Disagreement? Over what?"

"Oh…a number of things — Nadia's job, my habits — domestic things. Nothing to worry about." Myron tried to keep his tone light. Although he lied in terms of the magnitude of what was happening in his personal life, it was for a good cause; he didn't want to unduly upset her. She would know soon enough if it were really finished between him and Nadia. But for the time being, while there was still a chance to patch their relationship up, Myron thought it best to minimize, if not conceal, his marriage difficulties.

Still, Mother was persistent and the topic could not be so cavalierly dismissed. "Myron, something smells feeshy there?"

"I'll be fine," he tried to reassure her.

"Do you want me to come for a veesit?"

"No…no. It's cold and miserable here. Been forty below for a week. I'll be back east as planned in June." *With or without Nadia,* he added.

They went on to talk about the usual fare of long distance family phone calls. Myron learned that everyone was doing fine, that his youngest brother, Andrew, had gotten a job with an insurance company after receiving a diploma in computer technology; that the dog had a litter of six; and that their neighbour of twenty years, Dennis Holick, was dying of cancer. It was a capsule panorama of the life and times of the Tarasyn clan, as interpreted by Marta Tarasyn. But beneath the flow of information, Myron realized that he hadn't fooled his mother. She knew now that something was up; she just didn't know how serious. For that matter, neither did he really, although all the signs of a permanent breakup loomed large.

CHAPTER FIVE

Wednesday

In general, Myron's mid-afternoon class in world history compared rather poorly with his early morning section. The students appeared overly listless and less interested in the subject matter. He attributed this collective behaviour to the deadly time of day (3:00 to 4:20) and the fact that most took the course not because they wanted to but because it was the only arts requirement that they could fit into their schedule.

Normally, the evident apathy didn't bother Myron. He considered himself a professional who worked hard on his preparation and communication skills. And as long as he did his best in setting the conditions for learning, he had fulfilled his end of the bargain. *After all*, he reasoned, "*nobody can't teach nobody nothing if they don't want to be taught.*" It was a line from an old movie or book (he couldn't remember which) that he had read. Today, however, the overall negative ambience of this particular group was made worse by the addition of discordant elements.

The first came in the form of Ralph Sorrey, a bright but moody eighteen-year-old who had lately exhibited a sporadic attendance record. He sauntered in a few minutes late, took a seat on the far side of the room, and for the rest of the class proceeded to glower at the instructor, hands folded across his chest, his notebook unopened. Although Myron chose to ignore him (at least he wasn't nodding off like a couple of others were threatening to do), after a while it became distracting. *What's his beef?* Myron wondered, casting the occasional glance in Sorrey's direction. *Is it me or something more generic?* He decided to let it pass, but if this were the beginning of a new behavioural trend, in the near future he'd need to take the kid aside and discuss his attitude and body language.

The second problem was more straightforward. Two females sitting together were engaged in an almost whispered conversation while he lectured. It created a most annoying background buzz, which abruptly ceased when he stopped. Myron deliberately paused a number of times and glared pointedly in their direction, hoping they would receive the message, but to no avail.

"Ladies," he finally said, "have you got something urgent to add about Louis the XIV and the Theory of Absolutism, or is your discussion of a more current nature — like what you had for lunch?"

There was a quickly stifled snicker from the middle of the room, followed by silence. Myron finished his lecture without further disruption. As soon as he uttered his last word, Ralph Sorrey unrepentantly picked up his chattels and stomped out of the classroom, obviously unimpressed.

"And a nice day to you too!" muttered Myron, gathering up his lecture notes.

After class, Myron went to the cafeteria and bought a ham and cheese sandwich — his favourite meal at home, besides pizza. In this case, it constituted early supper. Since there was the board meeting "extraordinaire" at six, he hadn't planned to go back to his apartment before. *Not much to look forward to there anyway; might as well hang around the place and do some desk work until the meeting*, he decided sourly, slowly walking up the stairs to his office.

After spending an hour or so updating class lists and preparing a midterm test, Myron's powers of concentration had started to wane. He found his mind wandering off into the gloomy winter landscape just beyond his window. It was dark now — nothing but vague shapes of blackness and a drawn face staring back at him as he gazed out. At least in the summer there'd be a small lake there — actually the city reservoir — but now it was simply a barren, depressed expanse of frozen white under the curtain of darkness, ringed by yellowish street lights in the distance.

The truth was Myron missed Nadia, plain and simple. He wondered where she was and what she was doing; he felt quite disconnected at that moment, as if he had suddenly inherited an alien reality with nothing to ground him except an empty apartment and increasingly melancholy memories. He sighed, placing his pen down. If nothing else, the board meeting would provide a diversion, a reprieve from his very oppressive preoccupation with personal problems.

***

Arriving half an hour early, Myron hadn't expected to find anyone in the boardroom. He was therefore surprised to see the solitary figure of Sheila Penny, dean of Career Studies, occupying one of the rolling executive chairs round the large oval table. Head bowed, her hands clutched around her coffee mug, in the subdued light it seemed that she was in deep contemplation over a weighty matter.

Sheila was a striking woman, in her midforties, Myron guessed, with curled auburn hair, tastefully highlighted with lighter streaks collected in a stylish coiffure, bluish-grey eyes, a wide mouth, and full lips moderately lacquered with a medium shade of red. Her squarely framed face was well preserved, showing but a hint of middle-age looseness under the chin. She kept her body nicely toned and adorned with heavy jewellery and expensive clothing.

Myron had gotten to know her relatively well in the last couple of years. They sat on a number of committees together and had travelled with a college contingent to Banff Springs Hotel late last year for an institutional conference. There, he discovered the social Sheila, one who could play a mean piano and sing Broadway show tunes when in the partying mode. Her pleasant disposition and graceful features, however, belied the cool glint of her eyes and the hard-headedness of an effective administrator. In some sense, for Myron she embodied a kinder, gentler version of the late president. She could be tough, as Myron found out in committees, but by all accounts she was fair and judicious in dealing with the faculty in her division, which was something that could not be said of her counterpart, Charles Leaper, the dean of Arts and Sciences.

Nevertheless, there was no denying that Sheila had a hard side, one that cracked her cordial facade every so often. Myron recalled such an incident at a social gathering in a colleague's home.

A paediatrician who participated in the nursing student experience placement programme complained to Sheila about the lack of beds at the local hospital. The conversation had started with vaccinations during the flu season and drifted to the health care system in general and acutely ill senior citizens, more specifically. While on the periphery, eavesdropping amid other chatter, Myron heard Sheila adamantly pronounce that the existence of the elderly sick should not be unnecessarily prolonged when they occupied hospital beds, especially when there was an acute shortage for those who could still lead productive lives.

Ouch! He winced inwardly.

The soft-spoken paediatrician too was clearly taken aback by these words from a former nurse cum college instructor and administrator who was in charge of the nursing programme.

"So what do you propose we do?" the doctor asked, her face reddening.

"Let them die naturally and in their own beds if possible," Sheila replied forcefully.

From there, the discussion ventured into the choppy waters of too much medical intervention and euthanasia. Myron didn't catch the full exchange, but Sheila seemed uncommonly strident in her comments.

Her uncompromising statements reflected a rigid mindset that chagrined the doctor and bothered Myron (and no doubt others close enough to hear). Myron couldn't quite rationalize Sheila's cold, calculating logic. But then there was a fair amount of alcohol consumed by all, and perhaps interpretations and meanings were skewed by loose words best left on the outer edges and not unpacked.

Myron's initial greeting received no response. It was as if Sheila was in a deep meditative trance or some subliminal state. He presumed it was the president's sudden demise. "Awful business — wasn't it?"

After still receiving no response, he tried for a spot of levity. "A penny for your thoughts," he mused, rolling up a chair near her. Ordinarily, he would not be that familiar given their respective positions in the institution, but he knew Sheila well enough to get away with such informality without her taking umbrage.

"Not very original, Myron. I've heard that one before."

Ah, wherever she was, she's back now.

He shrugged. "Originality was never my strong suit. I leave that to the students..." He cringed inwardly at the creative but uninformed and/or just plain nonsensical history papers he had been marking lately. "You've been away, someone mentioned the other day?"

"For over a week," she replied, "just got back from Vancouver."

"Nice!"

"Not this trip. Visiting my mother. She's been under the weather — rheumatism acting up compounded by a nasty fall."

"Sorry to hear that—"

"She's comfortable and doing much better now. Nothing broken and I've made arrangements for regular in-home care. She's resisting, but soon she may have to move into a senior's residence."

"At least I hope the weather wasn't as brutal as it has been here for the last week or so."

Sheila rolled her eyes. "Drizzled almost the whole time I was there. Don't know which is worse, miserable, damp cold or just this freezing dry cold." She pulled her coat from the back of the chair over her shoulders, shivering slightly.

"Well...you've returned to some interesting developments," Myron noted.

"But not soon enough!" she remarked rather forcefully. "Tell me," she leaned toward Myron, "were you part of the travesty that took place at the last board meeting?" There was a definite edge in her voice.

"I...er..." It took a few seconds for Myron to catch on. "You mean the dismissal of Oliver?" *As opposed to Dworking's sudden demise?* wondered Myron.

"That's exactly what I mean. What the hell is going on here? How could Dworking can Oliver — the bitch that she...was."

Sheila spat out the words so venomously that Myron flinched.

She caught his expression. "I know...I know... Shouldn't speak of the dead that way — even if it's true. But I can't believe that the board would have gone along with her power tripping. On the other hand," she frowned, "maybe I can at that."

"I plead innocence and ignorance on that one," Myron assured her. "I wasn't at the meeting. Haven't got the foggiest what went down."

"Too bad, but you would have supported Oliver?" There was a sudden frisson of doubt in her voice.

"I would have," Myron replied truthfully. He liked Lynch and was absolutely sure that short of some outrageous behaviour or inappropriate actions that came to light (he couldn't imagine what) he would have defended the dean of Finances and Administration.

Sheila nodded, apparently satisfied. "Wish you had been there so that I could pick your brain — see what really went down and what set that old battle axe off. Pardon my disrespect for the dead."

A second person who wishes that I was there, Myron thought impishly. *Pretty soon I might get an "I'm wanted" complex!* "As I said, I wasn't there," he repeated, still digesting Sheila's uncharitable outburst.

She sighed. "The politics of this place...I hate it. Oliver may have stepped on her toes a bit, particularly in the last admin. Budget debate — but to get fired over it..." She paused for a moment, reflecting. "Part of the problem, you know, is that we have such a wimpy board. Most of the appointees are totally clueless about the inner workings of this place — lawyers, businessmen, real estate agents, and aspiring political hacks who know nothing about education. Debits and credits, that's all this institution means to them, and looking good to government bureaucrats. Why wouldn't they support Dworking? She spoke their language and balanced the books, which made their tenure on the board relatively painless — one of them rubber-stamping her bottom-line decisions." She shook her head.

Myron supposed that Sheila's tirade was true, to an extent. In Alberta, when the *Public Colleges Act* was first passed in the mid-1950s, it guaranteed that the board of governors would be comprised of individuals with some interest and experience in educational matters. Members were selected from the participating local school boards to direct college affairs, along with an advisory committee made up of area school superintendents. By the mid-1960s, however, the *Act* had been amended to broaden the membership. Now included were local business and professional types whose chief criteria was not their contribution or acumen in the educational field but rather their connections to the political party in power and/or their clout with the local member of the legislative assembly.

"Well…" she continued when Myron kept his silence, "I suppose they'll have to begin a search to replace her."

"Dworking's death has certainly come as a shock," Myron said lamely.

"Bring me up to speed," Sheila said in a slightly less belligerent tone. "What happened?"

"I really don't know all that much." *Who does?* "Other than she was found frozen in her car."

"What are the police saying?"

"Not a whole lot more. They may be treating the death as suspicious and certainly are asking a lot of questions."

"I see…"

At that moment, the door swung open and Sheldon Blythe appeared. Blythe, Myron knew, was a stockbroker by profession but a politician by inclination, who, it was rumoured, wanted to be the constituency's next conservative Member of Parliament. Although most certainly on the cusp of fifty, he had a youthful face with a prominent forehead, accentuated by a receding hairline and egg-shaped head. His tall body complete with a protruding belly was always tailored in a pinstriped suit — at least anytime Myron saw him.

Blythe stopped and held the door open for Jack Hoar, the vice-chair of the board. Silver-haired with a trace of flabbiness around the jaw, Hoar was the quintessential corporate lawyer, refined, restrained, and expensive. It was no secret that his firm had most of the big government business in Great Plains. Success, however, had not blinded him to his civic duty; as he explained at the time of his appointment, now almost two years ago, he was more than happy to take time out from his busy schedule to offer his services to the institution. The two men quietly conferred near the door before making their way toward Sheila and Myron.

Next to make his appearance was the other lawyer on the board, Anthony Chorney. Narrow-faced, diminutive in stature, Chorney represented the bottom end of the profession; he specialized in divorce. Although not quite a pettifogging sleazebag, he did have a reputation for screwing people (in the legal sense). Myron wondered if Nadia had gone to see him yet!

Barely had Chorney closed the door when it sprang open again with the board's two business representatives: Norm Bowell (Norm's Sports on 100th street, as Myron recalled) and Gordon Prybiewski, proprietor of an independent grocery store in the Northside Plaza. The two men were a study in contrast. Bowell was short, balding, and fat — all that a lifelong couch potato sports freak aspired to be. Prybiewski was tall and willowy, with sharp edges, of which the most notable was the nose. Both were pillars of their community, family men and good Christians with correct political views (while concomitantly supporting the local MLA), which made them excellent choices for the board.

"Sheila...Myron," Blythe said by way of acknowledgement. He focussed on Sheila. "Welcome back! Just wish it could be under more pleasant circumstances. How was your trip?"

"Other than being wet — fine." Sheila rose from her chair, continuing with small talk, and joined Hoar as they, like the others in the room, gravitated toward the coffee urn, which had magically appeared just inside the entrance. This was the work of Ms. Whitford, the efficient board secretary, who entered unobtrusively and just as unobtrusively exited until she was needed. Myron also got up but stayed in the back as the parties gathered around the coffee way station.

After polite inquiries regarding her mother's health, assurances that she was in good hands (a reference to Sheila having been a practising nurse in her former life before becoming a college instructor and ultimately administrator), and some additional small talk about Vancouver's version of a nasty winter, Sheila got to the matter that was on her mind: "I understand that there was a rather important board meeting in my absence?"

"Well, yes..." Blythe cleared his throat uncomfortably. "You are referring to the dismissal of Oliver—"

"I most certainly am. It was appalling, especially to someone who has served this institution so well."

She sure had a bee in her bonnet regarding the board's treatment of Oliver, thought Myron as he circulated closer to the conversation. Not that she didn't have a point!

"Well...there are differing opinions on the matter," began Blythe, a little wary of Sheila's strident tone.

"I gather," Hoar broke in, "that you have some reservations about the board's decision to support the president's recommendation."

"I most certainly do. This college seems to have developed a callous attitude to those who have contributed in no small way to building this place. Oliver deserves better."

"I hope we're not overly unfeeling," Hoar said, turning to Blythe. "We try to be fair to everyone. In the case of Mr. Spinner — well, the decision was made."

"On what basis?" Sheila asked harshly.

"I appreciate that you were absent when the board took the action that it did, but rehashing the reasons wouldn't get us very far at the moment," Hoar responded perfunctorily.

"You mean that the late president's decision won't be reconsidered by the board?" Sheila sounded both surprised and annoyed.

"Well…that may be an item of future discussion," Blythe said soothingly.

At that moment, Charles Leaper came in, looking somewhat less than his usual officiousness personified. It took Myron a few seconds to figure out why or more precisely what was missing: the fancy silver aluminum briefcase that Charles seemed never to be without at every meeting he attended, or at least that Myron was at. Instead, he appeared with a big binder under his arm. After a quick sweep of the room, he quickly zeroed in on the board heavyweights.

If the eyes were the windows to one's soul, then the look Sheila gave Charles was that of Lady Macbeth: a sharp dart of mortification, loathing, disgust, and just main hatred. Charles was much less obvious, observed Myron, no less menacing but better hooded, concealing the full depth of his animosity. It was a brief, stark unveiling as they acknowledged each other before eye contact broke and the curtain came down, but it was unmistakable nevertheless. *These two have a history*, surmised Myron, *a very nasty one…*

"Ah, Charles…" Blythe chirped pleasantly, "you're just in time."

"Sheldon, Jack…Sheila." He bowed his head slightly. "In time for what?"

"We were talking about Oliver. Sheila believes that the board may have been hasty in his case."

Charles Leaper was not an imposing figure. Slightly paunchy, with receding hair slicked back, he had the ubiquitous quality of blending into any crowd. He had been with the college almost from the first. For a number of years he was an instructor in the Business Department; later, he became chairperson of that department and a couple of others. Indeed, he specialized in filling administrative gaps;

"Have vacancy will fill" seemed to be his motto. After a while, he climbed higher up the administrative ladder to registrar and director of Student Services. Finally, he got his shot at the presidency when Dworking's predecessor stepped down (with a little nudge, as it turned out). Alas, the board went external and hired Dworking. Undaunted, he sought and got the consolation prize: the deanship of Arts and Sciences, which became available shortly after the new president's arrival. Charles may have begun in teaching, but administration was his forte. For some in the college, he was viewed as the archetypical mini Machiavellian bureaucrat, the one who ensured his survival by plotting behind a desk. And survive he did, through all the institutional twists and turns that came his way. Myron had heard that his tenure on the Dworking team had become rather tenuous of late, but that was now a moot point.

Charles pretended to give Sheila's reservations some thought before answering. "I'm not sure that we were out of line. After all, it was endorsed by those who were present. Of course, I'm willing — as are others I'm sure — to give the matter a second sober thought, as they would say," he added diplomatically.

Myron again noted a palatable crackle of intense dislike between them. "And so you should," she said tightly. "Tell me, were you a willing party to Oliver's dismissal, or did Vanessa bully you?"

"Now, that's not fair, Sheila," Charles responded with a controlled smile that did not extend to the wrinkles around his eyes.

"Fair? What would you know about fairness?"

"In Oliver's case, are you sure you're being totally objective?" he countered.

Sheila blanched. He'd hit a nerve. "What do you mean by that?"

Charles shrugged. "Nothing untoward, I'm sure." He smiled in a mean, contrite way — almost lewdly.

Myron and others listened to this exchange with stunned, albeit avaricious interest, not exactly sure what to make of it.

After that exchange, both Sheila and Charles pulled back and the conversation drifted to other matters that seemed less contentious, including the "regrettable loss" of Vanessa Dworking. The last word came from Gordon Prybiewski, who, although not noted for his wit, unwittingly remarked something about the chilling nature of the president's death putting the presidency "on ice."

Further comments were cut short when Sarah Libalsmith and Cecil Mackay made their appearance, followed by Dorothy Whitford, the board secretary, which meant that the meeting could now commence with all accounted for. Libalsmith, an earnest local graphics designer, had just been appointed to the board, while Mackay, a wily, leather-faced grain grower, had the distinction of being the longest-serving board member, with reportedly the least to say.

Everyone took their seats, and Blythe called the meeting to order, announcing that both the student and employee reps had given their notices of absence. After a moment of silence in tribute to Dworking, Blythe got down to business. "I remind everyone that the meeting is strictly in camera. The press has been excluded. Afterward, as a result of our deliberations, I will make a suitable public statement. Now, the first item on the agenda is, of course, the presidency. We not only need but are obligated by legislation to have a CEO in place as soon as possible." He paused, studying some scribbled notes in front of him. "Since at this stage the board cannot engage in a full, expensive, and time-consuming national search for Ms. Dworking's replacement, I propose, and the vice-chair has agreed," he nodded toward Hoar, "that a temporary in-house person be selected for the remainder of the term."

There were nods of agreement around the table. Myron certainly had no objections; he had heard about the long, drawn-out process involving the whole college community in selecting Dworking.

"The Personnel Committee had a little huddle before this meeting," Blythe continued, "to discuss and lay the groundwork of how to go about doing this. As I mentioned, the college is under an obligation to appoint an acting president as expeditiously as possible. As you are aware, our administrative structure is a flat one. We have no vice-president per se and no obvious appointee but our deans. The legislation stipulates an individual needs to hold the top position, not a committee of deans. We do, I'm sure, want to be judicious and scrupulous in our decisions, which invites no suggestion of bias — whether justified or not — so the Personnel Committee proposes what amounts to an internal competition of very short duration that would allow individuals here at the institution to put their name forward for consideration."

"How short a time frame?" asked Sheila.

"A week, we thought," answered Blythe. "A document could be prepared and posted internally as early as tomorrow afternoon, inviting potential candidates to apply with the cut-off date, say, Monday, end of the working day. The Personnel Committee would then meet, review the CVs, and make a recommendation for the full board's ratification meeting next Wednesday."

"Still seems a very short digestion period for those interested in making such a significant career move," said Sarah Libalsmith, not so much a question as a comment.

"I daresay," interjected Norman Bowell, "we have two qualified candidates in the room — what do they say?"

Heads swivelled to Sheila and Charles. Myron silently concurred; they were not only qualified but most likely candidates, given their respective positions in senior management. Oliver would have certainly been in the running, but his status was in doubt, to say the least. And the only other individual who had almost the same ranking was Reginald Mercur, the current dean of Student Affairs, but he was a withdrawn, low-profile personality almost invisible to the college community as a whole. There were a number of quite competent departmental chairs who might be tempted to apply, but that seemed a stretch to be catapulted from departmental chair to the presidency, if only as an acting one.

Blythe filled in the awkward pause that followed. "The short timelines cannot be helped. An acting president is required, and normally we would appoint one. But as I said, our administrative structure flattens out below the president, and we don't want to be capricious or arbitrary in our selection. This process, while not ideal, is about as transparent and judicious as we can make it… Should I ask for a formal vote?"

A general consensus was reached without a show of hands. All agreed that it was paramount that an acting president be in place "tout de suite" and that it had to be a selection rather than strictly an appointive process.

There was still to be clarified who exactly decided from the presumed list of candidates. "That should be left to the Board Personnel Committee," Blythe reiterated, "consisting of Mr. Hoar, Mr. MacKay, and myself. We would review the submissions, undertake what other enquiries we deemed required, and make our recommendation to the full board for approval."

There was some discussion in terms of the ranking order of those who applied. Blythe pointed out that not everyone would necessarily wish the college community to know that they had applied, so there had to be some discretion in that regard, and that they would go to the next suitable candidate if for some reason the first had changed her/his mind or the board by a formal vote rejected the Personnel Committee's recommendation.

On the whole, what Blythe proposed seemed quite reasonable, given the circumstances. Myron felt a little uneasy about the top-heavy makeup of the Personnel Committee — excluding Cecil Mackay, who in all likelihood would support any decision Blythe and Hoar reached. Also, he wasn't sure how the faculty would react to being excluded directly from the selection process. But then again, this was the board's prerogative, and to question the Personnel Committee might imply a challenge to its integrity, and certainly he had no basis for that. Sheila, Myron noted, didn't look thrilled about the process but evidently couldn't muster any sound arguments against Blythe's proposal.

"It's settled then," Blythe said with a tone of finality. "The committee will draft an advertisement for internal distribution by tomorrow afternoon."

The second and last item on the agenda proved just as contentious as the first, if not more so. This was the matter of Oliver Spinner, or rather, more precisely his status. Blythe recounted the meeting he had with Dworking and Spinner following the board's decision to terminate their dean of Financial and Administrative Services. He stated that Spinner was given the opportunity to resign but that the letter of resignation had to be submitted forthwith.

"Nothing like sticking a knife into someone and giving it a twist!" grumbled Sheila.

Blythe gave the dean a pained look. "That's an unworthy comment, Sheila. The fact is that Oliver was not willing to sign—"

"I should say not!" exclaimed Sheila.

"Sheila, please. You will have an opportunity to fully say your piece on the affair in due course. I just want to bring the board up to speed on what transpired."

"I'm sorry," she said, clearly anything but. Myron thought that while not necessarily totally out of bounds, she was, a bit uncharacteristically, skirting near the edge and in all probably not endearing herself to Blythe or the Personnel Committee.

The board chair gave her a small smile and a slight nod to indicate that sincere or not, her apology of sorts was accepted. He continued, "Oliver then asked for additional time to more carefully consider his options. At this point, I was willing to use my prerogative as the board chair to allow time to defer the decision of what options were best for him until a board meeting could be arranged. This special meeting was called for that purpose. Of course, no one could have anticipated the tragic event of that evening... And here the matter stands. Oliver and his legal counsel are waiting outside to meet with us now."

Hoar cleared his throat. "That puts us in a rather awkward position... He is no longer employed by the college?"

"No, he is not," replied Blythe. "That has been emphatically underlined. The purpose of the meeting is simply to consider what option he chose or wishes to pursue."

"Then we should at this point stick to that," said Hoar, "hear what Mr. Spinner and his counsel have to say."

"Why not just reinstate Oliver," said Sheila. "May I remind everyone that the college is without a financial director, as well as a president!"

"Wouldn't we look rather silly firing the dean one day and rehiring him two days later?" Bowell asked.

"Quite...I agree with Jack and Norman," offered Chorney, twiddling his pen. "Any reconsideration of Mr. Spinner's status should be dealt with after we have selected an acting president, who, after all, should have input."

There were nods from others around the table. Leaper, perhaps prudently, stayed silent; Sheila too bit her tongue and stared stonily somewhere beyond Blythe's left shoulder. The decision to refrain from taking further action was palatable because it relieved board members from having to make a decision.

Minutes later, Oliver was ushered in by Ms. Whitford. A distinguished-looking man with bushy greying hair and heavy-rimmed glasses, he nodded gravely to everyone in the room and took the seat indicated. His lawyer sat beside him. Oliver had retained the services of Brian Conkle, a well-respected local who, in fact, had been one of the college's charter students. After terse pleasantries, Conkle cited the pertinent clauses in Spinner's contract and proceeded to present his client's case.

Myron only half listened to Conkle's legal language regarding the dismissal clause in the contract and the concomitant severance package provisions; he was more interested in the silent interplay between Sheila and Oliver as their eyes locked and then quickly disengaged to less meaningful objects, in Oliver's case the grain on the oak table. There was something there, Myron decided, something intrinsically intimate. And Charles had shrewdly touched on it...

"Now, in my reading of the contract, the term 'dismissal,'" Conkle punctuated in a sombre voice, "is defined as the 'cancellation of an appointment for cause. On behalf of my client, I would request the board to elaborate on the cause or causes for which Mr. Spinner was let go. According to the relevant clauses in the contract, you have not established, as far as I can tell, the basis of Mr. Spinner's dismissal."

Blythe stole a quick glance at Hoar, the city's most prominent corporate lawyer, before responding. "Mr. Spinner is fully aware of the discussion that took place between himself, myself, and the late president when his termination notice was given. On that I will comment no further. This meeting was called to discuss only the options and compensation which are available for Mr. Spinner, including resignation, and that is all the board is prepared to discuss tonight."

"On that score," Conkle retorted, "let me say that my client has no intention of resigning, precisely because no valid cause for dismissal has been provided. The 'loss of confidence,' which apparently both President Dworking and the board cited, is not cause for dismissal — not without documented evidence. Indeed, Mr. Spinner is seeking reinstatement as dean of Financial and Administrative Services; failing that, he wants to return to the teaching staff in a full-time, tenured capacity."

"Those alternatives are not on the table here," Blythe reminded Conkle. "And although we appreciate your client's position, if there is no further discussion on the specific matter for which this meeting was called, then little more can be accomplished tonight."

Conkle agreed that nothing further could be gained, in that case and he and his client, who had said nothing throughout the proceedings, picked up their notes and left. Myron couldn't help but notice Oliver cast one last forlorn glance at Sheila as he made his exit.

The board meeting carried on for another fifteen minutes or so, in which it was again reaffirmed that Oliver's future with the college would not be resolved without input from the acting president. In fact, that would be one of the first items of business for the person selected. Sheila did not participate; she seemed traumatized by the events that had transpired.

CHAPTER SIX

Every institution has its self-appointed VIPs, and they all don't come from the Fine Arts and Music Department. The next day, Myron ran into Sidney Sage, PhD (Political Science); Sidney predated Myron in the Department of Humanities and Social Sciences, but with each passing year, it seemed, he became more and more isolated from his colleagues. Part of the problem was that he had a foolproof method of antagonizing people through his untiring efforts to manipulate them for his own purposes.

Myron realized this from first-hand experience. About six months ago, he had been approached by Sidney to write him a letter of reference for admission to a doctoral programme at Pacific Olympus University, somewhere near Los Angeles.

Myron had never heard of the place, but Sidney assured him it was a reputable institution that gave credit for the candidate's "life experiences" and allowed him to complete his graduate studies on a part-time basis without the usual residency requirements.

Myron wrote a "to whom it may concern" letter in good faith based on Sidney's presumed good teaching and supplied a list of worthwhile academic achievements and community activities he was involved in. Sidney did, after all, appear to frequently get his photo featured in the paper. And indeed, there was no doubt that Sidney was intelligent, articulate, and knowledgeable. That, in retrospect, Myron came to understand, was his character flaw; he knew all those things and sought to further his personal ambitions at the expense of others, whom, he tended to believe, fell short of those qualities.

At any rate, about a month ago, Sidney had applied to the administration for reclassification on his salary grid because he now had a PhD. Either Sidney was an awesomely brilliant student or there was something fishy about Pacific Olympus U.

An ad hoc committee of the Faculty Association was struck to check out the credentials of the institution (Dworking insisted that this be done before any salary adjustment could be made). The committee duly discovered that Pacific Olympus, while having a license to operate in the state of California, was not an accredited university; in fact, it came close to being one of those mail-order degree mills that for about $3,000–6,000 US would provide one with a degree in nearly any subject one desired. Pacific Olympus was not quite that bad, since it required that some sort of work had to be submitted before a credential was forthcoming. No one was amused (least of all Dworking), and Sidney did not receive his pay raise.

Persistent if nothing else, Sidney readjusted the nameplate on his door to read "Sidney Sage, PhD," and even attempted to get that distinction put beside his name in the next edition of the college calendar. Myron never raised the matter with Sidney but found the whole affair odious. Since it took years of work to earn a PhD, Sidney's actions were tantamount to intellectual dishonesty, if not outright fraud.

Sidney's fox-like face was now in front of Myron, intensely superficial, profoundly vain, making well-rehearsed eye contact. "Just off to class, but I'm glad I bumped into you... There was a board meeting last night?" he asked in his carefully modulated, suspiciously accented voice. Myron was never sure what it was — a cross between English and Irish, perhaps?

"Yes."

"Anything decided about Dworking's replacement?"

"The meeting was held in camera," Myron pointed out, but he saw no reason not to tell Sidney about the internal competition, since by the end of the day the position would be advertised on the Personnel Office bulletin board and other strategic areas around the college, as well as the faculty mailboxes. "On the other hand, it will be out of the bag soon — the board will select an acting president from internal candidates."

"Ah…any names mentioned?"

"It will be a competition," Myron clarified, "so interested individuals actually have to apply. The memo will be out later today."

Sidney nodded earnestly. "I should imagine that Charles will be in the running again. He's been grooming himself for the position for years."

Myron agreed, but he wasn't about to say so or get drawn into a prolonged conversation whereby Sidney would try to ferret out whatever nuggets of information were available. "I really don't know — anyone could apply, I suppose."

"So the field is open?"

"Well…within the institution… One never knows who will come out of the woodwork." Myron gave a small, humourless laugh.

"Was there any further news on what happened to Dworking?" Sidney asked, suddenly changing the subject.

"None."

"The police are still around. Just got interviewed by that lady cop who seems to be in charge. Asking questions about who's who and what we thought of our dearly departed president. Wonder what they're after?"

Myron kept his face deadpan. "Probably routine. Covering all the bases in a case like this."

"They believe she died from natural causes, don't they? I heard talk about foul play…" Sidney's voice trailed off, but his stare was as intense as ever.

Myron shrugged. "They have to ask questions."

"Well," Sidney postulated in a conspiratorial tone, "I wouldn't be surprised if someone bumped her off."

And you were not among her favourites, Mr. PhD. Where were you Monday night?

Before Sidney could launch another question, they were interrupted by Ted ambling down the corridor with an armful of exam booklets.

"Myron!" he boomed. "You've been holding out on me!"

"How's that?"

"You didn't tell me that Oliver was fired!"

"I didn't know when I talked to you last."

"You're on the board—"

"Not that particular evening. I stayed home. You and Benson came by later, remember?"

"Oh...right. It was Monday night... Okay, you're forgiven. It's hot news now making the rounds."

"I can believe that," Myron said.

"Does anyone know why he was fired?" asked Sidney, keeping his conspiratorial tone intact.

"Did she need a reason?" quipped Ted, rubbing his nose.

"Good point!" Sidney let out one of his fake comradely laughs. "You think he did her in?"

"That theory is already circulating," said Ted.

Myron shook his head. "That's outrageous!"

"Can't stop people's sordid imaginations or wagging tongues," Ted proclaimed, shifting his bundle of exam booklets from one arm to the other.

"Got quite a load there," Sidney remarked, eyeing Ted's burden. "A bit early for a midterm, isn't it?"

"Yeah...they'll hate me for this — the mother of surprise tests."

"Tsk, tsk," Sidney mocked, shaking a finger at him. "Socking it to students can have a detrimental effect on your teaching career come student evaluation time. Be nice and nurture them — until at least after the evaluations."

"Is that what you do?" Ted's tone had a touch of sarcasm, which seemed to be lost on Sidney.

"Absolutely!" he replied. "It also helps one to retain students to the end of the term. And I," he emphasized, "like an audience when I lecture. Speaking of which—" he glanced at his watch, "I'd better be off. Talk to you later, Myron."

"I hope not," Myron muttered under his breath as he and Ted watched him march down the hall.

"Sometimes, I think he's unreal... And I like an audience when I lecture," Ted mimicked distastefully.

"Phoney as a three-dollar bill, but you caught his better side. I think he was trying to be collegial."

"You mean nice?"

"That too."

"He's trying too hard then."

"Yeah, well... Sidney probably feels a bit alienated these days with his academic credentials in question."

"Oh, you mean his Mickey Mouse degree. It's all over the college. Wonder what made him do it?"

"Ego, plain and simple, I suspect. He couldn't stand the thought of others in the department having their doctorates, so he had to have one at whatever the cost — and I mean that literally."

"Hmm..." Ted scratched his chin. "You think he did any work to earn it, aside from shelling out a chunk of dough?"

"Oh, I'm sure he did. Those pseudo universities usually require some kind of work, and I think I know what Sidney did. A while ago, he handed me a paper he had written, requesting my comments and suggestions."

"On what?"

"The political elite of Great Plains."

"Is there one?" Ted laughed.

"Of course, every community has its shakers and movers in the political arena. Actually, it wasn't a half-bad piece, delineating who's who locally, their party affiliations and machinations on the municipal and provincial level. I assumed that after he sanitized suitably, he'd want to get it published. With a few revisions, he could be in one of a number of academic journals. Now I believe he had a better use for it. I bet he submitted it for his doctorate."

"Are you saying Sidney actually earned his degree on the level?"

"Hardly. The paper was only about sixty typed pages — perhaps a solid honours BA essay, but nowhere an acceptable Master's thesis, let alone a PhD. No, he didn't earn it; he just tried to short-circuit the system by finding an institution that would accept it."

"Looking for an easy route to status then."

"Something like that. Since no legitimate graduate school would accept such a minimal effort — or least would require much more — he went to a degree mill, hoping that we would accept his degree at face value. In his mind, he probably believes that he really deserves it."

"He miscalculated badly then," said Ted, shaking his head, "not only is he out a bundle, but he may have put his position on the line."

"Oh, I don't think it will go that far—"

"Just some talk I heard."

"Wishful thinking on the part of some of his detractors, I think," said Myron. "At any rate, he's got other things on his mind I think."

"Or up his sleeve," amended Ted uncharitably.

"Or up his sleeve," Myron agreed. Given his experience with Sidney, he had no doubt of that. "But Ted, you should take note of what Sidney said about your midterms."

"Why?"

"Because," Myron replied with a smirk, "it's sage advice!"

***

En route to his mailbox, Myron rounded the corner and almost collided with Freta. "Ah, there you are," she said. "I was looking for you. This place is like a rat's maze — curves and corridors. Having a devil of a time finding people's offices."

"It does take time to orientate oneself, if you don't know the building."

"I'll say…got time for a quick coffee? Want to run something by you."

"As a matter of fact, I do — about an hour before my class. I'll just get my mail. Why don't we go to the cafeteria? I'll buy."

"Best offer I've had all day."

The college's cafeteria was a model of space and brightness thanks to the row of skylights overlooking the rotunda. Most people, of course, assumed that it was planned that way; however, in this particular instance it was a case of architectural error. Somehow, the blueprint had about 600 square metres more than was allowable by the government for the size of the institution. But since neither the college nor government officials in Edmonton noticed this "overage" until construction began, and since nobody wanted to be accused of incompetence, the college's extra-large cafeteria remained as per blueprints. The administration did promise, however, not to apply for additional operational monies.

Freta sat down and sighed, "I've got about five interviews left, and so far I've come up with zilch."

"You can't be doing all the interviews of the college personnel by yourself? There must be over 250 people — not to mention the students."

"Well, it's selected interviews, and fortunately I'm not. Rob, Corporal Rob Rainy, is helping out. We divided a selected list. I do the faculty, and he does the staff."

"What about the students?"

"Forget about the students. We don't have the manpower. Besides, what's the connection? Dworking didn't give a course. Why would a student know or want to harm the president — hypothetically speaking?"

Myron shrugged. "It could have always been a deranged kid who flunked his exam or who was pissed off at his girlfriend and decided to take it out on the head cheese of the place. Stranger things have happened."

"True, but that's like saying it could have been some psycho passing through on his or her way to BC," Freta countered. "To tell you the truth, I can't prove that a crime has been committed. Dworking froze to death, but that's all we know for sure. The only reason we are treating this as anything more than a natural death or unfortunate accident is because — well…it doesn't feel quite right — to me, anyway. I mean why did she freeze to death? She didn't have a stroke or was otherwise medically incapacitated as far as can be determined, and people just don't get into their cars, do up their seatbelts, and sit there in forty below weather until they stop functioning. And from all accounts, Dworking wasn't the suicidal type. Was she?"

"Nope — definitely not!" Myron concurred. "And I agree, it doesn't feel right to me or make any sense."

"There's one other suspicious aspect as well — and I trust that this will not go beyond this table; we haven't released any details regarding her death…" Freta gave Myron a conspiratorial look.

"My lips are sealed," Myron assured her, wondering why she was suddenly confiding in him.

"According to the pathologist's preliminary observation, and it's really early, the body is still literally in a sitting position. There was a definite contusion at the base of her skull. Not enough to kill her but perhaps sufficient enough to render her unconscious."

"You mean someone may have whacked her from behind and left her in the car?"

"That's a theory Rob and I have been throwing around. I don't see how else she would have sustained it after she had strapped herself into the car. But you never know. She may have somehow bumped herself earlier and passed out in the car."

"That's one explanation," Myron said, taking a sip of his coffee.

"But a bit far-fetched and hard to accept — in the realm of your aggrieved student/psycho theory. What I do know is that a lot of people had good reasons for not liking her, but as yet none of them seems eager to confess to killing her."

"So where do you go from here?"

Freta shrugged. "I'll finish my interviews. Compare notes with Rob. See what shakes out, if anything, and file a report. That may well be the end of it. If we do find something more conclusive, Major Crime detectives from K Division will be called in. I'm holding off for the moment."

"So you're definitely suspicious?"

Freta eyed him with a hint of annoyance, which Myron took to mean, *Of course I'm suspicious, but I can't officially say that — so quit asking.*

"Until I can get a more definitive cause of death and/or forensic evidence, the jury is out." Freta pursed her lips in distaste. "A bit of a tough call."

"Maybe the perfect crime," Myron suggested.

"Oh, I doubt that, but the Mounties don't always get their man...or woman." She hesitated, thinking for a moment. "The president may well have got done in, but unless something shakes out quickly, I may not be able to sufficiently establish a crime, let alone identify and arrest the culprit."

"Well...it's still early and you may get a break in the case of some kind?" Myron said hopefully, conjuring up the usual cop show scenarios he'd seen on TV.

Freta seemed to have made up her mind about something. "You're right! There's usually a breakthrough eventually — and you might be able to provide it."

"Pardon?"

"I'm the first to admit that I'm out of my element here. I don't know the individuals involved, the inner workings of this place, and who was doing what to whom or with who like you do."

"So?"

"So you can help find out?"

"How?" Myron was now both intrigued and chagrined. What was this Mountie asking?

"Ask around and give me some real dope, pardon the expression. I need to know more. And people talk to you."

"Admittedly, I know about some aspects but to tell the truth, it's no different than any other institutional environment; it has its share of friction over principles, conflicts of personalities, and issues and just plain animosities, real or imagined, ranging from petty jealousies to profound disagreements—"

"Yes, and you're attuned to them. I'm not," Freta said emphatically. "You can separate the wheat from the chaff or whatever the phrase is."

"What are you suggesting?" Myron was becoming interested, if not excited by this unexpected confidential conversation with an appealing law enforcement officer, despite his protestations. "That I help in your investigation?"

"Yes, unofficially — that's my general drift. You're an insider. Perhaps you may be able to stumble onto something. Be my informed eyes and ears for the duration. After I have concluded my interviews, I'd like to kick around what I've learned with you, see what I've missed; what you can add. It may all end up a big zero, but at least I wouldn't feel like a blind cop probing in the dark."

"Why take me in particular into your confidence?"

She smiled. "As I said, I'm making very little progress here, and you have the most solid alibi, which almost covers the time period of Dworking's death. Besides, you're also the one person that everyone I've talk to seems to like…"

That would certainly be news to Nadia.

"…or least, nobody's saying nasty things about you. So let's say I'm playing a hunch," Freta concluded.

"Well," he said, "that's flattering. Let me think about it. I never fancied myself as a sleuth."

"Sleuths are for whodunits. I just want your impressions, opinions, and any relevant information that you come across in the next few days. You'd be surprised how much the police rely on the public to solve cases. Don't take too long thinking about it."

"Will you be home tonight?" It was an impulsive question brought on by an impulsive thought. He was rather enjoying his encounters with this woman.

"I will," she replied, "after six."

"I'll come by, and we'll discuss this further. I'll give you my answer. You're in the apartment just below me, right?"

"Apartment 304. Come by around six thirty... You like pizza?"

"Doesn't everybody?"

"Good. We'll order one. I know the best place in town."

"Great," Myron said with some relish; he wasn't going to eat alone in front of the boob tube for a change.

Freta glanced at her watch. "Uh-oh, got to go. I have a meeting with Charles Leaper, dean of something or other..." She leafed through her notebook. "Where's B301?"

"Take the stairs to the next floor, turn right, straight ahead."

"Thanks."

As Freta got up to leave, a handsome young man in an RCMP uniform came by. She introduced him as Corporal Rob Rainy. *Tom Cruise lives*, thought Myron as he rose from his chair, shook hands, and exchanged banalities. He watched as the two made their way up the stairs, conferring and leafing through their notebooks.

***

His late afternoon class done, Myron hurried to his office, anxious to pack up and go home for a change. He needed to spruce up a bit and wanted a long, relaxing pipe before stopping by Freta's apartment. He was just about to shrug into his parka when Ted came bounding in waving a copy of *The Voice*, the student newspaper. "You're going to love this," he exclaimed.

The front page featured a photo of President Dworking smiling (in happier times) with a brief caption announcing her sudden death. However, what Ted found particularly interesting was the mock advertisement below. It read:

College has an opening for a full-time, temporary position. Must be intelligent, know how to use a Xerox machine, give dictation, be able to learn on the job, attend a number of evening meetings, and do some travelling (car provided). Salary negotiable. Apply to the Presidential Selection Committee, Board of Governors.

"Well," said Myron, taken back a little, "that was quick and quite clever."

The official notice only got posted that afternoon, and here the student rag had it in print, with some artistic license no less. "Don't know what to tell you Ted — the students are on the ball."

"So give me the scoop. Who's on the list? What's the board's criteria? How is the new president to be picked? Give me some details here..."

"First of all, it's *acting* president," corrected Myron. "He or she will only hold the position on a temporary basis." *I hope*, he added in his mind. "A full-blown presidential search involving the whole college community will be undertaken, probably after the end of term."

"Okay...acting president... Is it a committee as a whole? Will you all sit around the table, bantering about applications and taking a vote — or are you drawing straws? Does anyone have the inside track? What do you know, Myron?"

With his eager barrage of questions, Ted got to the heart of the issue more than he could possibly realize. Temporary or not, the selection process bothered Myron — not that he could change it or present a cogent alternative. But it didn't sit well when he thought about it that night, pulling on his pipe and letting the rich, aromatic mixture infuse his senses. If his understanding of the process was right, essentially Blythe and Hoar (Mackay would be easily swayed and would acquiesce) would determine the institution's new CEO and forward the name to the board for a ratification vote. Some would interpret that as simple rubber-stamping. He hoped that would not be the case played out next Wednesday night...

"Sorry, Ted, I couldn't tell you any more, even if I knew. It was a special meeting in camera."

"A hint, at least?"

"Well...to tell the truth, I was partial to retaining the services of a psychic or astrologer. You know, someone who can see the future, solve problems, make us happy, and in the process remove the scourge of black magic, witchcraft, evil spells, and voodoo, with a 100% guarantee against bad board decisions. Alas, I was voted down... A Franklin stove will be brought into the boardroom before we start, and everyone in the college will have to wait for the white smoke from our conclave."

CHAPTER SEVEN

When the famed explorer Alexander Mackenzie traced the Peace River to its source in the BC mountains, duly recording the wonders of the region (including his brief camp and meeting with the Beaver tribe, some sixty kilometres northeast of Great Plains), he had no idea that his name would someday be taken in vain. Mackenzie Towers was one of the city's older landmarks. A five-storey, elongated brick-and-sandstone box, for the longest time it contained a novelty: it was the only erection in town with an elevator.

Of course, that was a while ago; as Great Plains grew (almost 25,000), so did the Tower's competitors. There arose other, more modern apartment buildings, but still, it had aged well, almost stately retaining, for the most part, its lofty status (relatively speaking) with a discerning, albeit older clientele.

There were a few exceptions; Myron and Nadia weren't exactly geriatric, nor was Freta. She didn't live directly below but close, two doors down. Her apartment was essentially the same as Myron's. One entered into a short alcove; hard right at the end of the hall was the bathroom, with two bedrooms on the left; straight ahead emerged the tiny kitchen beyond which was a small dining area and a sliding door to the balcony. The most inviting space was the living room, a clone of his with beige walls and a shaggy brown rug. The big difference was that it had its usual complement of furniture. Freta favoured the modern decor of Swedish design.

She greeted him out of uniform, wearing faded jeans and a large sweatshirt, which had "RCMP" embossed across the front in large letters. Although it hid some of her more notable features, it didn't make her less appealing. They made their way to her living room, where Myron plopped down into one of her low profile wood/canvas seats.

"Want to try some of that wine you brought, or beer?" she asked, flipping out the ponytailed hair from the back of her sweatshirt. She must have just tied it before he arrived, Myron thought sublimely.

"Beer would be good. It goes better with pizza."

"Beer it is," she said, going to the kitchen. "What do you want on your pizza, by the way?" she called, opening the fridge.

"I'm not fussy. Whatever you like — except anchovies and onions."

"Large deluxe, pepperoni, double cheese, hold the onions and fish it is." She carried in two foaming mugs of brew, handed him one, and sat across from him in a wicker chair, curling her feet beneath her.

"How was your interrogation of Leaper?" Myron asked.

"I'd hardly call it an interrogation. He was very circumspect and politically correct," she said. "Didn't have a bad thing to say about anyone and didn't give anything away."

"That's Charles — slick, hooded eyes, plays his cards close to the vest."

"And like three quarters of everyone else I spoke to, doesn't have an alibi — not a verifiable one, at least. Says he worked late in his office until nine that evening and then went home. He doesn't have a motive for killing Dworking — does he?"

"None that I know of, other than ambition. I understand that he threw his hat into the ring for the presidency the last time around but the board had the good sense to overlook him. But then," Myron added a trifle maliciously (he couldn't help himself), "they spoiled it by picking Vanessa! At any rate, I wouldn't be surprised if he becomes the acting president in about a week from now."

"Oh?"

Myron told her about the board meeting and the board's decision to select an internal chief executive officer at the next special meeting on Wednesday. "I'll bet my Wayne Gretzky rookie card that he'll apply, and chances are he'll get it. After that, he'll be harder to remove than Saddam Hussein."

"You don't like him much, do you?"

"It's not a question of like so much," Myron responded, taking a sip of cold beer. "He's just devious — knows which side his bread is buttered at any given moment and plays both ends toward the middle. A man of a thousand postures. Mr. Chameleon. He could be singing your praises in one breath while giving you the shaft in the other if it furthered his goals or made him look good."

"How did he get along with Dworking?"

"Hard to say. The word is not all that well lately. But he did what he was told. If Dworking asked him to jump, he'd ask how high. She as much as said so, publicly calling him her boy scout."

"Ooh...mean. Low blow!"

"Of course, the late prez could be a bit insensitive to all senior administrators at various times—"

"And he's the type who wouldn't forget but carry a grudge?"

"Knowing the way Charles operates — most definitely," Myron affirmed.

"And he can potentially achieve what he's wanted all along now that Dworking is gone."

"You got it."

"You're a fountain of information," Freta declared, raising her mug in a toast.

"Those are my highly biased and unadulterated perceptions that I'm giving you. I could be totally wrong — although about Charles, I doubt it."

"Well..." Freta stared into her beer, thinking, "my number one person of interest is still Oliver Spinner. He had the most pressing, immediate, and devastating motive, and he too has no alibi. Said he drove home straight away after his meeting with Dworking and the board chair in a total state of shock."

Oliver seemed the number one suspect of the rumour mill as well, according to Ted, thought Myron, but he said, "I can believe that Oliver was in shock. He was almost a charter member of the institution; got hired in the Business Department about twenty-three years ago. Taught for over eighteen years before becoming the dean of Financial and Administrative Services under Dworking's predecessor. I guess she didn't appreciate his fiscal style."

"He seemed bewildered when I asked about his dismissal. Couldn't understand it."

Myron shrugged. "I'm not privy to the inner dynamics of the administrative team. Obviously Dworking finally got fed up with him, for whatever specific reason."

"I'll make a note to check into that a little further. Haven't started to interview the board members yet — excluding you, of course," she said.

"Maybe I can help," Myron volunteered, "and ask some questions as well."

Freta smiled. "Does this mean you're taking up the offer of aiding your local law enforcement officer?"

"Something like that." Myron had thought about it ever since their meeting earlier in the day. He was in a rut and needed a diversion. What better diversion? Why not do a little poking around? Besides, he'd have an excuse to keep seeing this intriguing damsel.

"Discreet checking, mind you," Freta said lightheartedly. "You're not deputized or anything."

"I'll be a model of discretion," Myron assured her.

"I better phone for the pizza," she said, getting up and going to the wall phone in the kitchen. "Flattery's, the best pizza in town."

"If you say so."

"And they're quick — delivery within forty-five minutes. Meanwhile, you can tell me more about the board meeting."

After Freta placed their order and replenished their beers, Myron recounted the undercurrent of animosity between the dean of Career Studies and the dean of Arts and Sciences, Sheila Penny's strident defence of Oliver, and the silent interchange between the two. "I can't be sure, but there was something going on there, and Charles smirked about it.

"Possible ménage à trois?"

Myron stifled a cough and set his mug down on the little table beside him. "Oh…hadn't thought of that, but I doubt it. Of course, who knows? Could be a private matter better left undisturbed."

"A homicide investigation leaves little room for privacy," Freta countered. "I haven't talked to Penny yet."

"So this is a homicide investigation?" Myron asked wryly.

"Nothing has changed. Just assume for the purposes of our discussion," Freta replied with an impish smile.

"Okay, all speculation at this point—"

"But back to Penny…"

"She's hardly a suspect," Myron said. "She's got a better alibi than I have. She was in Vancouver the night Dworking died."

"Still, a chat won't hurt. She's on my list. Don't want to leave any stone unturned," Freta said dryly. "Cheers." She raised her mug.

***

The pizza was most palatable, and infused with a couple of mugs of beer, Myron found himself comfortably ensconced in Freta's abode, enjoying her company and in no particular hurry to leave. Nor did it seem that she was in any great hurry to see him go. A couple of hours, and in Myron's case, two trips to the bathroom later, conversation had drifted to more personal matters. In due course, Myron discovered that Freta had been in Great Plains only about six months and that the Dworking case was her second investigation dealing with a frozen corpse.

The first also involved a Great Plains celebrity of sorts who met his demise in the city's industrial park. Jimmy "Gomer" Banks was a well-known panhandler who lived at the men's hostel. He was usually hanging around downtown in front of the Royal Bank, although occasionally he'd try his luck with the Bank of Montreal customers across the street. His favourite destination was the Alberta Liquor Control store, but of course, he could only go there after he had solicited the necessary funds.

Like other citizens of Great Plains, Myron had encountered Gomer once or twice going about his business. A diminutive fellow with a crooked back but an effusive smile, he was an innocuous sort to whom one didn't mind giving a spare quarter or two.

Panhandling wasn't Gomer's only source of revenue. He kept a sharp eye out for bottles and cans, which he stuffed into his ever-present garbage bag. And when he'd collected enough to make it worthwhile, he followed the railway tracks that ran through the industrial park to the bottle depot. In fact, that's what did him in. Apparently, one cold November day he was making his way to the depot, probably got tired, and sat down in an isolated low area near the tracks. He never got up. His body was spied by a railway repair crew two days later.

"Poor Gomer," Freta recalled. "He was my first stiff — literally, about a month after I got here... By the way, that's how I met your wife."

"My wife?"

"Nadia, right? She's the reporter for the *Great Plains Daily Reporter*."

"Uh-huh."

"She interviewed me. Of course, the case was pretty cut-and-dry."

Myron wondered for a moment how well the two really knew each other and if he was the object of some derisive discourse between them. Places like Great Plains thrived on insidious talk, but he purged any further speculation from his mind. In her job, Nadia had gotten to know just about every official in town, from the major on down, and it was best not to imagine what was said or not...

Instead, he concentrated on Freta; he discovered that she had originally come from Regina, where she received most of her RCMP training. Because the "Depot," as the RCMP Academy was commonly called, was bursting at the seams and couldn't readily handle all the recruits while undergoing a construction phase, Freta and select others were sent to the temporary facility in CFB Penhold near Red Deer to finish their training. On completion, she was assigned to the Brooks Detachment for a couple of years before being transferred to Great Plains. "And here I am plying my trade," she told him spritely.

Freta had a certain alluring appeal, Myron decided. Her body — yes — but also her personality. He couldn't quite put his finger on it, but she possessed a kind of direct vivacity that broke through his cocoon of rejection and despair. He detected a hint, a thread, a pulse of healthy sexual tension between them.

This created a bit of a dilemma, however; he was still committed in a rather old-fashioned, monastic sense to Nadia, whom, alas, he suspected did not have the same reservations. If he was really honest in his analysis, though, the truth was somewhat blunter than that. Nadia was much more adept at attracting men than he was women. Chances were Nadia had a few more temptations, and in all probability more than one monk had forsaken the monastery. It was a moot point, then, he decided, and if anything developed with Freta…well, he'll cross that bridge when he got there — if he ever did.

Throughout their conversation, Freta gave no hint of past or current male attachments and it seemed gauche to ask. Assuming none, however, Myron boldly led with his battered ego, suggesting that it might be fruitful to continue their discourse over dinner the following night.

Freta took a moment to think about that. "Technically, with you at the college and me on the case, that might be construed as a conflict — awkward, at least. On the other hand, I asked for your help, you're not really a suspect, and I'm not sure yet that a crime has actually been committed. I'll compromise," she decided. "How about you coming here again — considering the state of your apartment — say seven thirty tomorrow night. This time I'll bake lasagna and we can continue the 'investigation'."

"You're on." He smiled broadly.

Later, back at his abode, Myron appraised the reflection that stared back at him in the bathroom mirror. Bespectacled, thin, greying hair, slightly stooped shoulders, concave chest but still a fairly presentable pipe-smoking, pen-swinging historian. He went to bed feeling happier than he had in quite some time. He doused the lights and hit the pillow with an old Johnny Rivers tune about a "brown-eyed, handsome man" bouncing around in his head.

Chapter Eight

Friday

"If you can't teach worth shit and your scholarly activity is next to zero," Ted Mack averred, digging into his early morning breakfast special — toast, two very messy eggs, and hash browns — "and you still want to hang around academia, then what choice do you have but to administrate? It's as simple as that — besides, there's a bonus."

"What's that?" asked Myron, peeling away the wax paper from his blueberry muffin.

"You get paid more."

"You're being a trifle unfair. I wouldn't want to be any sort of administrator, least of all a dean. Too many hassles and pressures to deal with. You'd forever be arse deep in high-maintenance faculty, in personnel problems, submitting budgets, engaging in power struggles, and worst of all, you're on a personal contract and can get canned just like that," Myron snapped his fingers, "no matter how long you've been here. Look at what happened to poor Oliver — zapped in the blink of an eyeball with no faculty association to support him."

Ted took a huge gulp of his orange juice. "We all have pressures," he said simply, wiping his mouth with a paper napkin and shoving away the dishevelled remains of his breakfast.

It was 8:30 a.m., and the college cafeteria was starting to fill with most of the action at the coffee station and cash register, where students and faculty filed by with brimming mugs (Styrofoam cups were on their way out, since a growing number of the college community had become environmentally conscious) before hurrying off to classes. Official notice that the institution was seeking an acting president was being widely discussed, and Ted was rendering his latest opinion on what he thought of academic administrators in general.

"Not those kinds of pressures," Myron retorted.

Ted sighed. "I suppose you're right. I admit, administrators are a necessary evil, but Dworking and what she gathered around her are a sorry lot. You don't remember Jonathan Munday, do you?"

"He was just leaving as I arrived, said Myron. "He was the college's first president, right?"

"Yup and Dworking's predecessor, a founding president who stayed for over fifteen years — some sort of record as far as college presidents go."

"He was forced to step down in the end, wasn't he?"

"His contract expired, and the board wasn't all that keen on renewing it, I guess, although it probably would have if he pressed the issue. I heard say that he was getting a bit long in the tooth as far as some prominent board members were concerned. I wish he'd stayed on, given what we got."

"So the board pulled the plug on him?"

"Yeah, I think that's the way it went down. A familiar story, really. People get tired of their leaders." Ted's lips formed a symmetrical scowl. "Many members of the board, and I guess among the faculty too, started to think that after so many years, a change in the style of leadership and direction of the college was in order. Of course, the accumulating deficit didn't help."

"So who could blame them?" said Myron, playing the devil's advocate. "Maybe Munday had his day — lost his edge?"

"Just looking back, in hindsight, he was good. The problem is that no one recognized how good until after he was gone!" Ted seemed to be in a genuine lament mode, although it was sometimes hard to tell.

"No one talks about him much nowadays that I have noticed."

"Ain't that the way," Ted sighed. "Once you're gone, you're gone, and nobody cares what you did. Munday made the college, led the institution in its embryonic stage where seat of the pants stewardship was necessary to get things done. We wouldn't have half the programmes without him. That was his downfall; he had plans for the college, went ahead and did them even if the funding wasn't all approved. He'd always persuaded the government to come through — until the oil revenues dried up, that is. That's what really happened, I think. When the money got tight, he was more or less forced out the door. The board thought that it was being smart — that they'd hire a no-nonsense president who'd tighten the belt and do the necessary things to ensure a balanced budget."

"Well, Dworking did that," Myron said, not sure what point Ted was trying to make.

"But that's just it! At what cost? As far as I'm concerned she wasn't any improvement over Munday — worse, in fact—"

"But you're a chartered accountant, a bona fide bean counter who'd appreciate a balanced budget?"

"Technically speaking, yes, but I'm not sure that the budget was ever unbalanced. Just a lot of numbers on the books. And don't forget, while she was cutting faculty and staff, the government suddenly started coughing up money for capital projects for political reasons — election year and all that."

"That sounds mighty cynical." Although Myron didn't necessarily disagree.

"Not really. Maybe I've become a bit jaded over the last two or three years by Dworking, that's all."

"As compared to Munday?"

"All I'm saying is that as far as educational administrators go, Munday was all right. For one thing he was cherubic like me — and," Ted stuck his index finger in the air for emphasis, "he shafted fewer people in fifteen years than Dworking did in four."

"You've got a point there," Myron conceded.

"One thing for sure," Ted affirmed, gathering up his binder of notes, "around here all the deans will apply; nothing like being the top kingpin, even if it's just temporary."

"The field is rather limited," Myron noted, getting up with Ted. "There's only Charles and Sheila left and maybe Reginald at Student Affairs."

"Sheila would be my choice," Ted said without hesitation.

"She'd be the choice of most faculty, I believe," Myron agreed, but not so the Personnel Committee, he thought, given her belligerent tone at the board meeting and her criticism of the board decision to support Dworking's ouster of Spinner. And she made it clear that she would reinstate him if given the chance. He wondered if she had made a tactical error in her outburst, which was unexpected, if not totally out of character for her, at least from his experience. But then maybe he was reading too much into it, or she had no interest in the president's position, Ted's comment notwithstanding, which would indeed leave the field clear for Charles. Perish the thought…

"Well, I'm off to teach tax," Ted said unenthusiastically. "And take flak over that surprise test, which most failed miserably."

"First, you'd better see if you can remove that egg stain off your tie before it hardens," Myron advised. "It doesn't quite match with the red."

***

Myron had matured as an instructor — at least relative to his rookie and sophomore sessional years at the University of Edmonton. At the time, he was so conscious of what he was going to say in front of class that he'd write "good morning" (or "afternoon") across the top of his earnestly prepared lecture notes, lest he forget.

His one time being radically flamboyant in a lecture hall was almost a disaster. Many of the teaching rooms at the university had sliding vertical blackboards so that a scribbling professor could shove a filled blackboard up and without breaking stride slide another down. That was precisely what Myron did one day; however, the empty board was slightly out of reach, so he jumped with unexpected exuberance and caught his wedding ring on the edge of the ledge (that was when he still wore it). The end result was a huge gash in his finger. With twenty minutes still to go in his lecture, he resolved to carry on, trying not to grimace too much while surreptitiously nursing his wounded and profusely bleeding appendage. Finally, a pretty blonde student in the front row couldn't stand it any longer. "Sir," she said, fishing out of her handbag a wad of Kleenex, "I think you better take these."

Myron gratefully accepted and managed to finish his lecture before hurrying off for repairs.

Now he was thinking of that incident and Nadia's somewhat endearing admonishment that he was prone to occasional klutziness because he had done something equally stupid. At his 10:00 a.m. Canadian history class, he decided to show a film, an old but useful black and white National Film Board production on Louis Riel narrated by Austin Willis. Alas, he was having difficulty getting the reel off the projector so that it could be rewound. In frustration, he gave it a good yank and hit himself in the mouth. Fortunately, the lights had been dimmed and he was at the back of the room because although he had drawn no blood, he did chip a tooth and inadvertently swallowed the fragment. Silently cursing himself, with tears welling in his eyes, he quickly dismissed the class and made an emergency visit to his dentist to assess the damage and make the necessary repairs.

Friday was not turning out to be a banner day. When he arrived at the Co-op Mall, he discovered that his dentist was out to lunch and wouldn't be back until one thirty, when, the receptionist was reasonably sure, he could be squeezed in.

With almost an hour to kill, Myron decided to visit the Co-op coffee shop on the lower level of the mall. Myron didn't go there often, but when he did, he always appreciated its character. It was a farmer's rendezvous where, for the price of the cheapest cup of coffee in town, weather-hardened men in crusty boots, work shirts, goose-down parkas, and dirty John Deere baseball caps would sit and shoot the shit. Presumably, the wives were upstairs doing the groceries.

It was a myth that farmers only talked about the weather, world grain prices, and how they were screwed by their bankers. Deeply ingrained (if one pardoned the pun) was what Myron believed a political mindset going back to the frontier days. "God made the country, man made the town" was still a viable creed to these folks, and it seemed that politicians (city slickers by and large), particularly those with the real power in the "middle east" (Ontario and Quebec) had done the country and them a disservice. As one old farmer from "Poverty Flats," an unofficial name for an area northwest of Great Plains, once pointed out to Myron, "We're the backbone of this country, and they're trying to break us. But we're not broken yet, and I aim to fight back." And they did; many of them became redneck reformers and a force to be reckoned with.

Myron didn't see old Hank from Poverty Flats, but he did spy Conrad Streuve, assistant editor of the *Great Plains Daily Reporter*, sitting alone, rather forlornly over a cup of coffee. Myron had met him the previous summer; Nadia introduced him as a fellow reporter at a hot air balloon tournament they were covering at the time.

Myron never quite understood the lure of hot air balloons that took hold in Great Plains. Everyone seemed to be mesmerized by these gigantic globes floating across the sky — as much as fifteen at a time, he recalled from a couple of summers ago. True, travelling at a leisurely pace (as the wind dictated) a thousand plus feet above across a quilt patch of farmlands and boreal forest no doubt provided a view bordering on the majestic. But he knew very few so fascinated who had actually taken a ride. Most of those who volunteered for the tournament remained firmly rooted to the earth as spotters and chasers. Perhaps it was the uniqueness of it all and the romance. When he first saw the stately rise of these artefacts, accompanied by the periodic whoosh of ignited burners heating the ascending air, he thought of his childhood and of reading Jules Verne's *Around the World In 80 Days*. He really couldn't explain it since, in retrospect, he couldn't remember the mention of a hot air balloon in the novel... Certainly, Nadia seemed captivated, and he idly wondered if she had ever gotten around to a flight. Speaking of which... Buying yet another ubiquitous cup from the coffee maid, Myron decided to say hello and perhaps obtain some information on Nadia's more recent activities.

"Mind if I join you?" Myron asked, running his tongue over the sharp edge of his broken tooth. *Dracula lives*, he thought.

Streuve raised a pair of sorrowful eyes to Myron, hesitated for a brief fraction, then seemed to deflate and acquiesce. "Hi, Myron...have a seat."

Streuve was broad-shouldered, fair-haired, and about his own age, Myron judged, sporting a corduroy jacket and blue jeans beneath his open parka. His angular face had a dejected look. Myron hoped that his dog hadn't died, or something worse...

"How's it going?" Myron inquired, injecting more mirth than he felt at the table.

Streuve shrugged. "It could be better. The job's a drag, and the weather is lousy. But I need it to pay the alimony, and I can't do much about the weather."

Myron recalled that Streuve had gotten divorced a few months ago and that it was a bitter one, with his former wife moving to BC with her new accountant boyfriend and taking their young daughter with her. Myron couldn't be sure from whom he received that information, though.

"Right...ah..." Myron was suddenly at a loss for words. Maybe he should leave and let Streuve figure out his life or whatever it was that appeared to weigh him down.

"I should be asking you," Streuve said, suddenly sitting up in his chair, "what's the latest at the college — with the president. That must have been a shocker!"

"I'll say—"

"The paper ran a very short story today — her background, length of time at the college, that kind of thing, but practically nothing on what happened to her. The police haven't released any information at all."

"It will take some time to complete the investigation," Myron said lamely, not wanting to get into a speculative discussion with a reporter. "I'm sure that they'll release what they know when they're ready."

"I suppose," said Streuve, sounding a bit disappointed at Myron's unengaging answer.

"How's Nadia?" Myron asked abruptly, which both changed the subject and brought his focus back on track. There was no doubt that Streuve knew they had separated. Nadia was one not to restrain herself in matters of the heart. Myron knew that he had been described in evocative and graphic language to anyone who cared to listen.

"Fine," Streuve responded with a decided edge in his voice. "Pretty soon she'll be running the paper."

Myron nodded. Nadia was like that. No half measures — either all in or all out. She was, Myron knew, energetic, efficient, and when she set her sights on something, she pursued it with gusto.

"Say…I'm sorry about your breakup," Streuve said.

"So am I," Myron responded heavily. "One of life's unexpected twists."

"There's nothing you can do about it, either," Streuve lamented, dumping a spoonful of sugar into his coffee. "Women… When they decide its over — then it's over. Take that from experience," he concluded almost wistfully.

God, Myron thought, *this guy is as badly dejected and jaded as me — maybe worse! A great pair we make.* He was getting depressed just listening to Conrad.

"A bunch of us were at a newspaper association convention in Edmonton over the weekend," Streuve rambled on, slowly stirring his coffee. "Your wife knows how to have a good time."

"Oh." Myron frowned; he wasn't sure he wanted to hear this.

"Danced the night away after the banquet."

"Yes, she knows how to dance."

"Expected to see a red rose in her teeth by the end of the evening… No, Myron, Nadia's doing fine," Streuve concluded, shaking his head and staring into his cup as if it offered some solace.

After a few more minutes of general banter, Myron excused himself and made his way to the dentist's office, still trying to sort out his disturbing conversation with a very distraught fellow. It left him with an uneasy feeling that he'd missed something poignant in Streuve's ruminative comments about his wife.

Myron did not exit the dentist's chair until about three thirty. It took what seemed a huge amount of freezing and extensive chiselling by Doctor Federko before he applied the filling. "There," Federko said, smiling and admiring his work. "No food or drink for at least an hour, and try not to bite too hard on that tooth."

After making his follow-up appointment at the front desk, Myron walked out feeling like one side of his face had slipped a couple of inches. He hoped he wasn't drooling. Thank goodness his dinner date with Freta wasn't until seven thirty; by then, the freezing should have worn off. Meanwhile, it was a quick stop at the liquor store for a bottle of wine and home, such as it was, to recuperate. All in all, not a great day, but there was still the night to come.

CHAPTER NINE

Myron arrived at Freta's apartment just in time to hear the pinging of an oven timer going off. The air had the appetizing aroma of cooked meat ragout and tomato marinara sauce; the dining table was set complete with a white cloth, two long-stemmed wine glasses, and a burning candle in the middle. *Rather romantic,* surmised Myron, removing his shoes at the door. Freta greeted him wearing a simple mauve dress designed to show cleavage. He gave her a shaky smile; although the freezing had worn off, he was still conscious of his nerve-dead mouth three hours earlier, which had been most uncooperative, particularly when it came to liquid intake.

"Smells wonderful in here," he said, handing her a bottle of Chablis. *And I hope I'm not drooling,* he added.

"Why thank you," she said merrily, leading him into the living room. "Dinner will be ready shortly… Care for some wine?"

"I'd love some…"

Later, over a cheesy but not too mushy lasagna, Myron told her about his less than sterling day. She couldn't stop laughing. "It must be the wine," she explained apologetically. "I know it isn't funny but…" She brought her hand to her mouth to stifle a further outburst. "I just can't help it!"

"For a moment I thought my face still looked strange," he said defensively.

"You look fine," she assured him.

"This is great, by the way," he said, stuffing another forkful of pasta and cheese into his mouth.

"It's premade, if the truth be known. I just stuck it in and let it bake, as per instructions on the box."

"Works for me... What about your day?" Myron asked, taking another sip from his wine glass. He noted that they had almost finished a bottle between them.

"Well, let's see... I spoke briefly to Sheila Penny, and she confirmed what you told me, that she was in Vancouver during the presumed time period of Dworking's death. Other than that..." Freta stretched her arms behind her head and rubbed her neck, "she sure didn't much care for the president. Called her a power-tripping misanthrope."

"A what?"

"That's what she said — had to look it up in the Webster's dictionary later."

"What does it mean?"

"You're the academic — you should know," she admonished.

"The Queen's English was never my strong suit," he replied.

"Hater of humanity or something close to that effect," she smiled. "Rob didn't know either," she added as an afterthought.

"So you met with Rob... How's his end of the investigation going?'

Freta shrugged. "We compared notes, but nothing jumped out. Well, one small item that may be of interest to you."

"Oh?"

"Let's go into the living room and make ourselves more comfortable. If I sit here any longer, I'll need a chiropractor. Pop open another bottle on route..."

"You were saying..." Myron took up the thread of their conversation as he once again ensconced himself in her canvas over wood chair. "Something about developments related to me?"

"Not to you, personally," she said, tucking her feet under her in the wicker chair opposite him. "Your wife."

"Nadia?"

"According to Rob, she had an appointment scheduled with Dworking. She wanted to do a story about the proposed student residences."

"Nadia was there that night?" Myron's pulse suddenly sped up a notch or two. Nadia was the last name he would have associated in any way with the case. "She can't be a suspect—" he started to say.

"No more than anyone else," Freta said flatly, with a trace of officiousness. "Rob has yet to speak to her directly. The appointment was scheduled in Dworking's calendar — Monday night, he said."

"She's got an alibi. She was at my apartment cleaning me out!"

"Around what time was that again?"

Myron thought for a moment. "Must have been after nine — about nine thirty."

"Okay… When did she leave?"

"She and her…friends didn't stay long. Maybe until ten, a little after — when their mission was finished."

"Given the imprecise time of Dworking's death, there's still before and after time gaps that need to be accounted for."

"Back up a bit," Myron said, frowning. "I'm not sure I've got who's where at what times. I know that the board meeting was scheduled for six…"

"Right, and according to my notes, it lasted approximately forty-five minutes. Spinner then met with Dworking and the board chair at seven. Nadia was pencilled in for eight."

"That's rather late for giving interviews?"

"I would have thought so," Freta agreed. "As I said, Rob will talk to Nadia and verify when she met with the president. It's probably another dead end as far as this case is concerned," she assured him, "but it needs to be followed up. Nadia may have seen or heard something. One never knows."

"Right." Myron nodded uncertainly.

"This hasn't put your evening off, has it?" Freta asked with a note of concern.

Myron shifted uncomfortably in his chair. "No, not at all. It was just a bit unexpected…"

Freta nodded, and the subject was dropped.

***

As the evening progressed and the wine continued to flow, the conversation drifted to their personal lives, and almost inevitably, it seemed, relationships. With his tongue loosened considerably by the alcohol, he inquired if Freta and Rob were an item.

She chuckled at that. "Heavens no… We haven't socialized in any way, and besides, he's happily married."

"As opposed to not so happily married." The rather petulant comment seemed to slip involuntarily out from Myron's lips.

Unperturbed, Freta took it at face value. "Well, I'd say Nadia gave you your freedom when she walked out on you."

"Can't argue with that." He was silent for a moment, staring into his wine glass. "What about you?"

"Me?"

"You know my situation, but I don't know yours. Is there someone in your life?"

"I'm unattached at the moment and rather like it that way."

"Oh…"

She laughed lightheartedly, her eyes suddenly bright. No doubt the wine, Myron thought.

"But," she quickly added, "that could change."

"And what are you looking for?"

"You mean what's my type?"

"If you don't mind me asking?"

"Not at all…" She thought about that for a moment. "Definitely not a Mr. Macho. Other than that…" She shrugged. "I'm open. Someone who is reasonably well-adjusted — normal would be high on my list. And believe me, such individuals are harder to find than you might think."

Myron raised an eyebrow. "I should think there are eligible bachelors where you work?"

"I'm a little wary about mixing romance with business after Gary, my last cop beau."

"Why is that?"

"You really want to know?"

"I'm...curious."

"It was while I was still with the Brooks Detachment. Gary was what might be described as a hunk. I kinda fell for him."

"And?"

"Well, one night we got serious at his place. Midway through our...activities his dog started barking. He had it in the basement for the night, apparently. After a while, the noise really began to irritate him. I guess he couldn't concentrate. He got up from the bed, grabbed a pillow, and disappeared downstairs. Moments later I heard a muffled pop, and the barking stopped."

"What happened — or should I ask?"

"I am pretty positive he shot the dog!"

"Phew... That's a bit extreme."

"You know," Freta said in a chilled voice, "we were talking about psychos the other day. Well, it's not a great leap from shooting an annoying dog to shooting people who are inherently more troublesome. That was it for me with Gary. Fortunately, my transfer came through — you know what's appealing about you?" she asked rhetorically.

"What's that?" Myron said, still trying to process what Freta had told him.

"You're safe."

"I'm safe? Not sure how to take that!"

"Take it for what it's worth. You wouldn't shoot your dog?"

"No. Kick him, maybe..."

"And you deal with people on their own terms. If I got involved with you, you wouldn't complicate my life, would you?"

"I seemed to have complicated Nadia's."

"She complicated it herself. You're probably too safe for her."

"What'd you mean too safe?"

"You wouldn't do anything wild or crazy, would you?" There was what Myron perceived as a mischievous glint in Freta's eyes.

"It depends on — back up a minute. Do you want to get involved with me?" Myron asked. The light bulb suddenly went on and he was feeling warm.

"You're here tonight, aren't you? And since you suggested that we get together again, I figure you're interested too."

Well, that's direct enough, thought Myron. He had hoped to get to know Freta better, and now, it appeared, she was not averse to the idea at all. Their evening was on the verge of taking a most revealing turn.

The only question was would Myron's monastic resolve survive? He thought not; his increasingly tenuous fidelity to Nadia was dissolving rapidly as he came to that bridge.

"You know," he mused, "I can't resist a woman in uniform."

"How about one with no uniform at all — of any kind."

As it turned out, he connected with Freta at least as well in bed as he did outside of it. Their primal urges continued well into the night. Myron felt an unbridled release of erotic power, while Freta demonstrated good athletic form.

The only potentially awkward moment came while Myron was chucking off his clothes. Alas, he lacked Freta's poise, and he inflicted slight bodily harm when the Stanfield's resisted (because of a certain bulging appendage) and the elastic band, briefly escaping his trembling grasp, snapped with considerable force onto his struggling, upwardly mobile erection.

He gritted his teeth and grinned. Freta didn't seem to notice.

"You've lost some weight," she observed as he hastily kicked his pants aside and crawled into bed.

"I had a paunch once," he retorted defensively.

"Oh, but I like trim men."

Well, that's good, he thought, not particularly eager to embark on a crash eating course in order to recreate some semblance of his former, more bulbous self.

"And Mario there," she stared pointedly at his rigid member, "appears ready and very willing."

"Yes, he is," Myron declared emphatically, "but will you respect him in the morning?"

CHAPTER TEN

Saturday

Myron woke up with a headache accompanied by a pronounced dried-out feeling. Small price to pay for the excruciatingly good time he had with Freta the Magnificent. He took a quick peek under the covers, just to reassure himself that everything was still there and hopefully in working order, and glanced at his watch, the only accessory left attached from their energetic activities. Seven thirty. Although a late-night person, Myron was also a relatively early riser, and once awake, he stayed awake.

Stretching out on his back, his hands behind his head, he stole a sideways glance at Freta. She appeared asleep, curled up in a comfortable ball. After a few moments of staring at the ceiling, his thoughts blissfully unfocussed, he gave Freta a gentle nudge.

She stirred. "Huh…"

"Rise and shine," he said brightly.

She shifted slightly, raised her head, peered at her digital alarm clock, and informed him that it was Saturday and her day off. Myron took that to mean that she had no intention of bounding out of bed to start the new day just yet.

"I'll take a shower and make us some coffee," he volunteered.

She rolled over toward him. "Good idea. There's extra towels in the closet beside the bathroom," and she pulled the blanket up to her chin.

Myron was giving his best rendition of "Those Were the Days" when the shower curtains opened and Freta stepped in. "Mind if I join you?"

"Only if you can sing," he lied.

Later at breakfast, Freta had a suggestion. "I've been meaning to go out to Dworking's place all week and have a closer look around. You want to come along?"

"You haven't been out there?" he asked.

"I haven't, but Rob has. He only gave it a cursory once-over, though. He went out when Dworking's neighbour phoned the day after her death. Seems she kept a couple of dogs that needed to be cared for. The caller agreed to take them and sort of look after the place until the next of kin was notified and the estate settled."

"Wonder what's going to happen to it? I understand it's an old farmhouse up on a hill."

"Yeah, near the Hutterite colony. I think I know where it is. Rob gave me the keys. You've never been out there?"

"Are you kidding?" Myron snorted. "I don't think anyone from the college had been out there. She wasn't the kind to invite people for socials. Very private person."

"Well, her sister's coming out from Toronto to claim the body and make the necessary arrangements — as soon as we release the body, that is. And I imagine the property will be put up for sale. So...you want to accompany me and scout out her abode semi-officially, so to speak?"

"Sure. I'm game to see the Dragon Lady's inner sanctum," Myron said, crunching on his last piece of his toast.

The extreme weather had let up. It was a clear morning, with the temperature rising to a balmy minus twenty. They made their way to Freta's yellow Camaro, parked in her designated slot in the rear lot of the building, but it wouldn't start. Two slow groans from the engine, and the battery went dead. "Damn," she muttered, "I need a boost."

"Why don't we take my car?" Myron offered. "It's the only one of its kind in Great Plains. I'll boost yours later."

"Okay... Why not."

Myron had gotten rather attached to his automobile, a stoic, squared-off Audi Fox with a scandalous reputation for unreliability. He had bought it in Edmonton a number of years before, slightly used, and had put over 200,000 kilometres on it. This particular chariot had proved the automotive critics wrong, providing, for the most part, stellar service. And this was no mean feat considering that Nadia took a regular turn at the wheel. It wasn't that she was a bad driver; quite on the contrary, she would have made Stirling Moss proud. Over the highways and byways, she motored with blissful disdain for such obstacles as speed limits and surface irregularities. The little Audi (bless its mechanical soul) seemed to take it all in stride.

With their relationship teetering on the brink, one of the greatest fears Myron had was that she might get possessive about the car. Indeed, she had hinted at it a time or two. After all, she needed wheels as much as he did to get around in her work. But a man has to draw the line somewhere. In due course, she was assuaged with a new, bright-red Rabbit. Myron didn't mind contributing financially; he even suggested spending extra on an extended warranty given Nadia's pedal-to-the-metal exuberance. They were still a couple at the time, and Myron had no conception that it would end up otherwise.

Time does take its toll, and German build quality notwithstanding, the Fox had begun to look its age. The beautiful metallic green had faded, with one fender in particular exhibiting an alarming growth of rust. Fortunately, Myron found a private entrepreneur who offered to repair the damage and repaint the car without grossly exceeding its market value. Now, his "Panzer–wagon" was as shiny as ever, minus the metallic flake. Myron was un-phased, however, because now he had the most distinctive lime-coloured set of wheels in Great Plains.

They travelled northeast on the main road out of town by the industrial park and chain of motels toward the airport. Once they got a few kilometres out of the city, the pristine whiteness of farm fields took over. The terrain also changed, no longer uniformly flat but elevating into a series of gently rolling hills with pockets of conifer stands. Looking back from the first of these post-ice-age knolls, one could see the city spreading out like a growing amoeba on a microscopic slide. At night, coming from the other direction, the city was particularly impressive: a thousand sparking dots of light in an ocean of darkness.

"Wonder why she bought way out here?" Freta pondered as they sped along with hardly a car in sight.

"Reclusiveness — as I said, she liked her privacy. Does have its drawbacks, though. Earlier this winter she couldn't get to the college for three days — snowed in. Not that anyone missed her, I'm sure," mused Myron, giving Freta a sideways glance and still thinking of her earthly charms.

They had gone about twenty kilometres before Freta spotted the turnoff. "There, to your right. Has to be. Rob said to look for a sign directing us to the Bowden Lake Hutterite Colony."

"Righto. I see it." Myron made the turn onto a narrow, snow-crusted road. "Not much of a sign, though," he added, looking at a weather-worn wooden plaque with an arrow pointing east dangling from a telephone pole.

"Hutterites aren't much for advertising," Freta surmised. "Now, it's about four kilometres in, an old stone house set back from the road on the left-hand side."

Myron nodded.

The tires crunched on a layer of snow as the Audi slowly powered its way up a long lane way to a rectangular two-storey structure. Dominating the front yard was an ancient, snarled tree, its bare branches reaching out like a forlorn statue to some druidic deity. Otherwise, no other growth pierced through the snow. Against the house, a couple of unruly junipers sprouted, and what looked like lilac bushes.

"Doesn't strike me as a place I'd like to live in. It's so remote and forlorn-looking," said Freta, making her way to the front door.

"I think that was the idea," replied Myron. "Apparently, she bought it as soon as she arrived."

"Well…let's have a look, see what ghosts we can stir."

Shivering slightly, Freta inserted a sturdy, square head key, and a deadbolt lock clicked open inside. A turn of the knob and the door swung open. They entered into a parlour of sorts, with an antique bureau on one side and a china cabinet set against the wall directly ahead. It contained a good number of Royal Doulton figurines and assorted glassware. To the left of the cabinet was a dark stairwell leading to the second floor. Myron flipped on the light switch.

"Okay," he said, "what are we looking for?"

Freta shrugged. "I don't know… Maybe nothing."

An archway to the right of the bureau led to a fair-sized living room replete with the usual appurtenances: a couple of standing lamps, pine coffee table, two Victorian cameo back loveseats, and a rose-coloured chesterfield and chair. Obviously, Dworking had a preference for early Canadiana. The only evidence of modernity was a Sanyo stereo and VCR attached to an aging Sylvania TV. The walls were beige, with heavily lacquered wood trim and a number of Trisha Romance prints hanging — all of nineteenth-century stone homes, the kind one would find in Ontario. There was also a small bookcase filled with volumes of *Reader's Digest*.

Myron stood in the middle of the creaking hardwood floor, absorbing the surroundings. "A bit like a mausoleum," he remarked to no one in particular.

Freta had walked through a doorway to the kitchen. He followed. It wasn't overly large and hadn't been renovated since Dworking moved in. The plain pine cupboards were old-fashioned, designed for a dwelling with a high ceiling; the appliances were at least a decade old. A microwave oven appeared the only recent update. The most attractive item was an oak table on Jacobean legs with four matching chairs. *It would have been more appropriate to have it in the dining room rather than the kitchen*, thought Myron.

There was another stairway up from the side door to the right, while to the left a second archway led to the study and a tiny bathroom.

The study contained a fine oak desk, on top of which sat a Macintosh SE. It was connected to a printer perched on a two-door metal filing cabinet next to the desk. In one corner was a small Franklin stove with chopped wood piled in a large copper tray beside, while the wall adjoining the kitchen was adorned with roughly made bookshelves. Myron surveyed the titles. Dworking evidently had eclectic tastes in her reading materials: the collected works of Shakespeare, a smattering of sociology, psychology, and education administration texts, and two shelves of what might be classified as popular literary genre, from Le Carré to Margaret Laurence.

"You can always judge a person by the books she reads," he postulated, turning to Freta.

"What do you make of someone who reads romances then?" she asked, peering into a cupboard beside the bathroom door. The cavity was filled with romance paperbacks stacked one on top of the other — the kind with suggestive titles and illustrations of handsome, half-naked men embracing beautiful, full-bosomed ladies against an exotic setting.

Myron pursed his lips and said, "She had a romantic side. Long-lost love? Unrequited love? Yearning for what might have been had her life taken a different turn?"

"Maybe she just enjoyed reading them," Freta said, unconvinced. "Let's go upstairs," she suggested. "Begin there and work our way down."

Myron shrugged. "Why not?"

The second floor proved less interesting. It consisted of four nondescript bedrooms and another bathroom at the end of the hall. The president slept in the largest chamber, front right. In it were the usual personal effects on a bureau with a large oval mirror. Freta quickly went through the drawers, while Myron opened the closet door. Dworking, he noted, didn't skimp on her wardrobe; it was filled with expensive business suits, a couple of formal evening dresses, and matching accessories. She also had quite a shoe and boot collection, although nothing like Imelda Marcos, he supposed.

Turning to Freta, he said, "Find anything interesting? Crotchless panties, laced negligees, handcuffs, whips?"

Freta closed the bottom drawer. "Honestly, I'm beginning to think you're incorrigible."

"Just wondering if she had a secret life — you know — like Walter Mitty."

"No perversions; everything is neat and tidy."

"Sterile and cold," Myron muttered, glancing at the dog-eared historical romance on the nightstand beside the huge brass bed.

Another fifteen or so minutes of further rummaging produced nothing of significance, and Freta and Myron made their way back to the study, the most promising source, they decided, of any information that might be had.

"Which do you want to tackle?" Freta asked. "Computer or the filing cabinet?"

"I'm familiar with the Mac system. It's idiot-proof — almost. Why don't I check it? See what's there."

"Nothing in this world is idiot-proof," she reminded him, "but go ahead."

While Myron fired up the Macintosh, Freta turned her attention to the contents of the grey metal drawers. "At least she didn't keep it locked," she observed, giving the chrome handle a yank.

Myron was impressed that Dworking was keeping up with the new technology. *This has to be the latest model,* he thought. The college was just getting out of the electronic typewriter era in its secretarial science programme; rumours were that computers were to be installed in faculty offices as soon as the tech department got all the necessary equipment and wiring. Myron was a bit ambivalent; he saw their value in terms of efficiency, but he had a little Luddite in him. Besides, with the computer in the office, he would be expected to do his own typing…

The small screen lit up, and he scanned the menu. It didn't seem that Dworking stored any files on the hard drive. He looked around for a disk file box; maybe she transferred her files to disks. He finally spotted one on the bookshelf, propping up a row of paperbacks. Most were unused, but two were labelled. The first he slid in contained numerous spreadsheets of the college's annual budgets over a period of three years and the second, entitled "Official Correspondence," was just that: Dworking's letters to Advanced Education and other college presidents throughout the province. Nothing noteworthy jumped out. Disappointed, he turned to Freta. "I've struck out. What about you?"

Freta closed the bottom drawer and got off her knees. "Dead end. Top drawer contains all sorts of reports on the college; the bottom has files with reams of figures and spreadsheets."

"Probably hard copies of what I found on the disk," Myron said.

"I don't really know what I expected to find," Freta said, sounding a little frustrated, "but it was worth a shot. What about her desk?"

"We'll soon see," responded Myron, opening the top drawer. Stapler, scissors, box of paper clips, some pens, and memo pads. "I wonder if these were college-issued," he muttered, unimpressed.

The lower drawer, however, proved much more interesting. On top of a batch of empty manila folders was a 4" x 6" green hardcover book with the words "Daily Journal" embossed in gold ink. Leafing through it, Myron discovered that it wasn't so much an appointment ledger as a diary. Its two hundred or so pages were three-quarters filled with Dworking's neatly penned prose.

"This looks promising," he said. "Maybe we'll get to know the real Dworking."

Myron settled himself comfortably at the desk and began perusing. What he read were pages of short and to the point sketches of personalities and situations at the college that, judging from her running commentaries, she found cause for concern or at least irritating.

"Anything?" Freta asked after a while. She had finished her reconnaissance of the study and came up empty.

"Yeah... Not exactly the equivalent of the Mackenzie King diaries, but definitely more grist for the suspect mill. Vanessa's personal scorecard of who's who at the college and their various transgressions. Looks like she began making notes about a year ago — at least that's her first recorded incident — and guess whose name pops up?"

"Don't keep me in suspense. Who?"

"None other than Charles Leaper. I had forgotten about this episode, but it did create quite a stink at the time."

"Why don't we go into the living room and make ourselves more comfortable, and you can tell me about it," Freta suggested, straightening her back. "I find this room dark and oppressive."

"Lead the way."

Myron opened the curtain behind the couch to let some daylight in and flipped to where he had stopped. Freta plopped down on the couch beside him.

"It revolved around the termination of an art history instructor, as I recall," related Myron. "What was his name...Primrose — Dr. Barry Primrose. He was a recognized expert in some branch of native art, had been a tenured faculty member for at least six years. Then, presto, he was declared redundant and let go."

"I thought tenure was important?"

"As a concept normally yes, but I don't know the particular details of what went on behind the scenes. Certainly faculty and students were aghast. Primrose was an excellent instructor with more students than the rest of the Department of Visual and Performing Arts combined!"

"So where does Leaper fit in?"

"He engineered it — so goes the story. Chaired a committee that screwed Primrose royally, all under the guise of cutting the department's budget. Now, there was a great deal of animosity between the two — I am not sure over what, exactly, and I guess Primrose had a bit of an ego as well; he liked to see things done his way, so he had his share of detractors in the department. Anyway, Charles stacked the committee with those who wanted Primrose out, and they did him in."

"Okay, but how does this relate to Leaper and Dworking?" Freta asked pensively.

"The proverbial shit hit the fan when about fifty faculty and a hundred students and members of the arts community appeared at a board meeting. I remember we had to move to a larger room to accommodate everyone. They came in protest against Primrose's dismissal. The local press was there too. To make a long story short, Dworking took the flak while Leaper sat there, not saying a word. It was a long night for her. She came out looking none too good publicly. First time I ever saw her flustered — sweat on her upper lip, so to speak. The dismissal couldn't be justified, and everyone knew it; it was vindictive, capricious, and all Leaper's doing. That was how it was interpreted, anyway. But give Dworking credit, she defended her administrator when he overstepped his bounds. Later, a board member let it slip that he heard her ream Leaper out — he sure laid low for a while after that."

"She didn't put all of that in the journal, did she?" Freta asked, eyeing the book in his hands.

"No. She just mentions the incident here — calls it the Primrose Affair and makes a note…" Myron paused and found the passage, "and I quote, 'Charles messed up, a re-evaluation is in order — perhaps when he takes his sabbatical.' She's got a question after that. Come to think of it, Charles did apply for leave, and it was granted for this September."

"In other words, Dworking was planning to pay him back when he wasn't around?"

"Something like that, maybe. Have an administrative reorganization, which excluded his services, perhaps. It's happened before. Of course, it's standard academic procedure now."

"Conveniently so," noted Freta. "Still, seems petty stuff for murder."

Myron shrugged. "People have killed for a lot less."

"Very true. I think Mr. Leaper has reaffirmed his position on the suspect list. Another interview is in order, I'd say."

"Yeah, but before we leap to conclusions — ah, no pun intended — there are others mentioned here."

"Who else?"

"Let's see…" Myron flipped through a few more pages. "She's no fan of Oliver — of course, we knew that. She states here, 'no confidence in Spinner, increasingly argumentative — is resisting the proposed budget — last straw.' She's underlined this: 'went over my head, phoned the deputy minister — undermining my authority.'"

"That all?"

"That's it so far. I haven't finished reading yet. There could be more farther on. It's all in point form, little reminders to herself."

"Well, give me the journal," Freta said, getting up. "Why don't I finish reading it while we drive back to town. I've had enough of this place."

***

Once in the car, however, Freta suggested that they go up the road a ways to Dworking's nearest neighbour, the man who phoned and offered to keep her dogs. "Maybe he's got something useful to say about the late president," she added, sounding not at all hopeful.

The sign on the mailbox read "Frank Haley"; it guarded the entrance to a ramshackle farmhouse built along much the same lines as the Dworking home. Myron pulled in and brought the Audi to a rolling stop behind a battered Chevy pickup.

"Let's see what Mr. Haley knows about Dworking and her country lifestyle," Freta said, fiddling with her seat belt release.

The man who stuck his head out the door was old and wrinkled, with wispy white hair and red, rheumy eyes. He wore a flannel shirt that hung around him like a burlap sack. Somewhere behind him could be heard the high-pitched barking of excited dogs.

"Yes?" His eyes darted between Myron and Freta, finally deciding that Freta was the more appealing object of focus.

Freta introduced herself and Myron, indicating that she was an RCMP officer.

"Did yous come about those yapping dogs back there?" He jerked his head backward in the direction of the barking.

"No, but if they're a problem, animal control—" Freta began.

"Naw — no problem — just yappy... Not sure what they be. Some sort of terriers. Yard mutts they ain't, but house-broken. If they'd be going to a pound, I'd just as soon keep them." Haley spoke in a rush of words, getting them out quickly before reaching into his back pocket for a handkerchief and coughing harshly into it.

"We didn't come about the dogs," repeated Freta, "and there is a good possibility that you can keep them if you want. We just want to ask some questions about Ms. Dworking."

Haley seemed relieved; stepping back, he led them into the musty-smelling mud room ringed on one side with hooks and well-worn coats. "Don't know what I can tell yous. Didn't see much of her in all the time she's been down there in the ol' Miller place. But then why would I?" He gave them a gummy smile, punctuated by two very yellow teeth. Myron ran his tongue along his recently fixed tooth and made a mental note to see his dentist more regularly.

Five minutes later, Myron was backing his car out of Haley's driveway. They learned that Haley lived alone (a widower for many years) and that Dworking pretty much kept to herself. "I'd clear her driveway once in a while when I could get the ol' tractor to start," he told them, "and once she invited me in for a spot of tea — can't stand the stuff, but that was all she offered, and it wouldn't've been neighbourly to refuse... Hardly saw her at all during the summer — she wasn't around..."

"A lonely man," said Freta as they drove down the Bowden Lake Hutterite Colony Road.

"Yeah, and not too healthy, either. Seems to have taken a liking to Dworking's dogs."

"They provide company, I suspect. I'll talk to Rob, make sure he gets to keep them, if he wants. Can't imagine Dworking's sister wanting two pets."

"Probably doesn't know they exist."

"Ironic, though…" Freta said thoughtfully.

"How's that?"

"Gary shot his dog for a few moments of quiet; Haley needs this pair to break his solitude.

"Life's like that…"

Freta read Dworking's diary in silence as Myron wheeled his Audi onto the main highway. By the time they hit the airport cut-off, she had three more suspects with a motive. "'Orville Wishert, an unstable little toad and a detriment to the institution…'" she quoted from Dworking's commentary.

"I agree there," Myron said flatly.

"How about Sidney Sage?"

"What'd she say about him?"

"That he bought his degree, and I quote, 'bad reflection on the college — dismissal warranted' with a question mark?"

"I won't argue with that either, although I think she wouldn't have followed through. These were notes to herself."

The last name that came up was a total surprise to Myron: Sheldon Blythe. "What did she say about him?" he asked, perplexed.

"It's one of her last entries. Just has his name written with a cryptic comment, 'incompetent or a crook — check.' That mean anything to you?"

"Not a thing."

Freta sighed. "Looks like I have my work cut out for me. More interviews to come… By the way, you're mentioned."

"What?" Myron gave her a startled glance, his eyes straying to the book in her lap.

"Along with about seven or eight other names. Collectively calls you the 'untouchables.' That mean anything?"

Myron relaxed and chuckled. "Probably means that she likes us and our jobs are safe — at least while she was alive."

CHAPTER ELEVEN

Sunday

After spending another heady night in Freta's apartment, Myron planned for a boring Sunday. His first chore was to boost her Camaro. Luckily, there was an empty space beside the bloated beast, which allowed his green machine ready access. He hooked up the cables, and the car fired up on the first crank. Freta came out in her regulation attire; he held the door open while she slid in. She'd be off to the cop shop for a few hours, catch up on her paperwork, she had told him earlier. They agreed to take a rest from each other for a couple of days. "Get the batteries recharged," she said. Myron thought that an appropriate analogy as she drove away.

Back in his abode, Myron shaved, changed his clothes, and made another cup of coffee. Half past ten, and all was well, except that the Super Bowl didn't start until four. He didn't feel like cleaning, although the place certainly needed it, and any marking he had was on his desk at the college. Tomorrow would be soon enough for that. After fifteen minutes of sipping coffee and failing to come up with anything that would keep himself gainfully occupied in the apartment for the next three or four hours, Myron felt himself beginning to slip into a morbid frame of mind. Freta notwithstanding, Nadia was still a pressing concern.

What he needed was a diversion, something useful to do to get him through Sunday — or at least to the Super Bowl. An idea slowly wormed its way from his subconscious until a light bulb lit up in his brain. Why not help Freta out a bit by performing some proactive detective work? Why not indeed! And he knew just the place to start. First, he'd take a drive to the Northside Plaza. The grocery store there (Gordon Prybiewski's, in fact) opened at eleven, and he needed to replenish his supply of pipe tobacco. Then he'd drop in on Oliver Spinner, commiserate, see how he was doing, and find out what he could about his falling-out with Dworking and his relationship with Sheila.

Myron and Oliver weren't exactly friends, but when the occasion warranted, they got along rather well. Myron recalled the party he and Nadia had thrown in their apartment almost a year ago in happier times. There was a good sprinkling of college people, including Oliver. As the evening wore on, Myron was persuaded to take out his accordion (what immigrant kid didn't play a squeeze box at some time or other?). Oliver, obviously feeling no pain as well, told him to hang on a minute, and he rushed out of the apartment and returned shortly with a violin case, complete with a fiddle inside. He had it in the trunk of his car; why he carried it there, Myron never got around to asking.

"You lead and I'll follow," Oliver said after tuning his instrument to the accordion.

They probably didn't sound that good, but no one seemed to mind as the evening wore on. They even took a request from Benson McDougall, Myron's earnest colleague and soon to be supportive friend, whose Scottish brogue increased exponentially with the amount of alcohol he consumed. Myron got it all wrong, however, and it became a joke afterward. Apparently, the sentimental Scotsman's words were, "Kinn yah play 'Loch Loman,' laddie." Myron, obviously on a different wavelength, not to mention soundtrack, said, "Sure," and proceeded to give a less than perfect rendition of "La Paloma." Oliver, though, never missed a beat, bowing along blissfully. Happier times indeed…

Even the unexpected presence of Orville Wishert that night didn't dampen the mood — too much. Orville, Myron was told, never attended such frivolous gatherings: the only event he showed up at was the beginning of the year barbecue put on by the board of governors. Nevertheless, there he was. The first hour went well, until he got into the cooking sherry that had been inadvertently set aside on the counter. Orville drank it like pop until fully "corked"; he then became belligerent and maudlin all at the same time. He berated a colleague for his "liberal" political views (communism and liberalism for Orville appeared to be the flip side of the same coin). He had no use for Liberals of any kind, categorizing them "fellow travellers" or "red buddies" who had no place in Alberta or the rest of the country, for that matter.

The response, "Why don't you drop dead, Wishert," Myron recalled, produced a totally unpredictable reaction. Orville's lower lip started to quiver, and large tears slid down his cheeks. Admittedly, his fellow department member had endured a rather vigorous and prolonged harangue from Orville, but still, in retrospect, it was…unkind.

Orville was comforted after his outburst of tears and offered a ride home by another college instructor who had to leave the festivities anyway. Odd what lay beneath the layers of outer epidermis, thought Myron, seeing the little man being led away distraught but docile. Who knew that Orville was really a sensitive guy — at least when it came to what was conveyed to him about him!

∗∗∗

Myron never met Oliver's wife, Helen, at the party. He did know that a short time later she was involved in a serious auto accident that left her in a coma for several weeks. She partially recovered, but when occasionally asked how she was, Oliver said "improving" and left it at that. Not wishing to pry, Myron probed no further. Now, wheeling into the plaza parking lot, Myron wondered about that and how Sheila fit into the picture.

Oliver's home wasn't far from the plaza (Myron looked up the address just to be sure) in Northview Estates, a middle-class enclave developed about a decade ago. Unlike some of the older sections of the city, it was denuded of trees, a black mark against the builders who levelled every growth in sight in their rush to erect dwellings for eager customers during the boom period. The economy had slowed considerably, and most of those companies had long since gone belly-up, but their handiwork was still evident in the lack of indigenous trees.

Relatively speaking, Oliver's house was modest, a split-level of brick, siding, and stucco. As Myron rounded the corner, he spotted Sheila pulling away from his driveway in her beige Volvo. He slowed and watched her motor off in the opposite direction. *Definitely something going on there...*

Myron didn't know exactly how to approach Oliver. "Hi, I'm here helping the police investigate Dworking's death," didn't seem quite the right tack to take. On the other hand, he didn't want to be there under false pretences. As he stopped by the curb, he decided simply to play it by ear and see how Oliver reacted to an unexpected visitor.

Oliver came to the door wearing a plain white shirt, baggy brown corduroy pants, and scruffy slippers with the toes beginning to pop through. His face was strained, puffy, and it appeared that he had forgotten to shave that morning. *Rough night, judging by how unkempt he is,* Myron surmised.

"Myron!"

"Hello, Oliver." There was an awkward pause as Oliver held the door open, letting the frigid air rush in. Myron finally filled in the breach. "Ah...was out and about in the neighbourhood — thought I'd pop in — see how you were doing." *Not really a lie; only a half-truth.*

"Well, do come in. The coffee pot is still hot." Oliver took Myron's coat and hung it in the hall closet while Myron slipped out of his toe boots and followed Oliver into the den. "Good of you to stop by in my time of troubles," he said as Myron surveyed the cozy, dark-panelled room. "Have a seat." Oliver gestured to a black leather armchair. "I'll get the coffee."

"Thanks."

Once the coffee was served and the obligatory discussion of the weather and the faltering fortunes of the Edmonton Oilers were dispensed with (Oliver had no interest in the Super Bowl), Myron sought to steer the conversation toward a more meaningful if contentious direction. "Driving up I saw Sheila leaving…"

"Yes… She paid me a visit this morning." Oliver licked his lips and set his cup and saucer down on the coffee table between them with a clatter. "Wanted to bring me the latest news. She's decided to apply for the acting president's position, you know."

"Good for her. I hope she gets it." And Myron meant it.

"She agonized about throwing her name into the hat for the last couple of days. Decided only this morning. The competition deadline, as you know, is tomorrow. I don't think she's going to change her mind…" Oliver trailed off.

"Why should she?"

"No reason, if that's what she wants to do. I…" he sighed thoughtfully, "I don't want her to plunge into this on my account."

Myron saw his opening. "I know this may be none of my business, but are you and Sheila involved?" Normally, Myron would not have been so blunt, but here was the opportunity to ascertain the state of affairs, so to speak.

Oliver solemnly studied his hands for a moment clasped together in his lap. "Helen never fully recovered from the accident, you know?

"I'm sorry…"

"It was one of those things," Oliver continued. "The brain is a delicate instrument…" He shook his head. "She came out of the coma all right, but she really didn't get better. Couldn't remember things, got confused easily — left water taps running, the stove on — almost burned down the place. I tried to take care of her when she came home, but she couldn't be left alone for any length of time."

"I understand," Myron said uncomfortably. He was not sure he could take an outpouring of someone else's grief at that moment.

"Anyway, Helen is at a long-term facility in Edmonton, where my son lives. She's receiving the best care available." Oliver cleared his throat. "That's when I got to know Sheila better. She had been a nurse, you know. I asked her for advice. She was caring. Came over to be with Helen on occasion and gave me...solace. It became clear that Helen needed to be institutionalized. I just couldn't handle it on my own. My son, Richard..." his eyes strayed to a framed photo on the mantle above the unlit fieldstone fireplace, a family shot of a beaming Oliver with one hand around an equally cheerful woman with a soft face and streaked grey hair and the other around a gangling teenager. "He agreed we couldn't help Helen, and with him off to university — well..." he spread his hands out in an empty gesture. "He visits her often, and I come on weekends mostly, when I could find the time, which is something I have plenty of now."

"Terribly sorry about what's happened and the circumstances you find yourself in," Myron said sincerely, not knowing what else to say.

"Yes, well... You can figure out the rest," Oliver said resolutely, straightening up in his seat. "Sheila and I...hit it off. She's a widow, you know — husband died some years ago. I guess," he cleared his throat again, "Sheila and I are about the worst-kept secret in the college. We tried to be discreet with Helen still in the background."

Myron nodded sympathetically. Actually, it was a well-contained relationship; certainly, he didn't know about it and hadn't heard any gossip around the institution. Charles, though, seemed to be fully aware and homed in like a hawk on its prey. In any case, his personal woes seemed minor compared with Oliver's unfolding Shakespearean drama.

"And, of course, it's become much more complicated," Oliver continued, "now that I've run afoul of Dworking—"

"What happened?"

"I was going to ask you that. You were at the board meeting—"

"Actually, I wasn't," Myron interjected. "Sorry I wasn't there — bad timing."

Spinner nodded. "Well, I have been thinking about what happened, and it was a combination of things, I guess," he said with resignation. "I had reservations about the strategy the president was pursuing — cutting certain programmes in order to balance the budget. Not only were they the wrong programmes, but I believed — and still do — not every effort had been exploited to obtain more funding from Edmonton. I can only suppose that I was a little too outspoken for Vanessa. And it was a bit out of character for me, in retrospect, but I was getting frustrated with her unrelenting policy of slash and burn. The college wasn't always run that way, and I sincerely believed — believe — that there was enough flexibility in the system to run a deficit budget. We'd done it before and always found the money in the end. I thought that in my position as dean of Finances and Administration, I had a responsibility to point this out and seek further funding. I made some phone calls. She saw this as a direct threat to her authority and...well...convinced the board to serve my head on a platter. And here we are."

Myron nodded, having read Dworking's angry entry in her journal. "I hope you get your job back," he said with feeling.

"So do I. Boy, that meeting was a bombshell. I got totally blindsided, had no idea that I was going to get canned. Got home in a daze and Sheila...she was livid."

"Sheila? I thought she was in Vancouver?" Suddenly, alarm bells went off in Myron's head.

"Yes...she was. She phoned me from the airport."

"Oh." Myron relaxed.

"When she heard, she could hardly contain herself. Vanessa had done this, you see, behind Sheila's back with, Sheila believes, a great deal of forethought and malice to spite us both."

"Did Vanessa know about you and Sheila?" Myron saw no reference to their relationship in Dworking's journal, which did not necessarily exclude the possibility.

"I didn't think so. I told Sheila that Vanessa's action was probably more about my perceived challenge to her authority than anything personal, but Sheila was convinced that Vanessa was being spiteful —

not sure why. At any rate, she told me not to worry and that she would straighten Dworking out when she got in. And the rest — well, we know the rest."

"Did Sheila say there were problems between her and the president?" Myron asked, trying to get a gage of the animosity that obviously existed between the two.

"Sheila and Vanessa did not really get along, that's for sure, and it was getting worse with the budget cuts, which affected Sheila's area. They were civil, for the most part, at meetings and other college functions, but they instinctively disliked each other — an oil and water thing, maybe..." Oliver shrugged. "Of course, it's all a moot point now since Vanessa's passing. Still, I don't know what happened, exactly."

"No one does," Myron said in an uncommitted tone.

"Police been around asking questions — think it wasn't some unfortunate medical condition or accident of some sort?"

"RCMP have to investigate, cover all the bases," Myron reaffirmed in a neutral voice.

"I suppose..."

"Great shame Sheila missed that special board meeting," Myron said, taking a different tack in the conversation, away from the police inquiries.

"Sure is. Sheila's flight didn't arrive in time."

"Oh, Sheila got to Great Plains that night?" That was significant news that Myron wasn't aware of; he had assumed that Sheila was still in Vancouver.

"Last flight in," Oliver confirmed.

That would have been 12:45 a.m., Myron surmised, relaxing a little. He knew this because he took the same flight a few months before after attending a Learned Conference at UBC. Given that, Sheila had an alibi that was at least as good as his.

"Did you pick her up?" he asked innocuously.

"No. That would have been indiscreet. Sheila parked her car at the airport." Oliver frowned. "Why? Are the police suspicious about

Vanessa's death?" His eyes widened. "There's no possible way Sheila could have—"

"I know," Myron reassured him. "It's just police would want to account for everyone's whereabouts just in case. You told all this to the investigating officer?" *Well, so much for tactfully avoiding the notion that Dworking's death is considered suspicious!*

"No. I didn't mention my involvement with Sheila. Didn't see the relevance or want to drag our relationship into it. But guess it's pretty well out in the open now."

"If it is, I've heard no idle talk about it in the halls," Myron said, trying to be positive. He put aside Charles's snide comment at the board meeting.

"What do you think of Sheila's chances for the presidency?"

Myron told him that he didn't know but thought that Sheila had as good a chance as anyone else at the college. After that, the conversation drifted off and then sputtered. There didn't appear much else to say. Myron told Oliver to keep the faith and quoted a famous twentieth century sports philosopher to the effect that it wasn't over until it was over. Oliver thanked him for stopping by, and with that Myron took his leave.

***

The Super Bowl was a bust. Washington trailed Denver 10–0 in the first quarter; then the Redskins woke up and scored 35 unanswered points in the second quarter. By halftime the game was over, final tally Redskins 42, Broncos 10. It was like that most years, Myron realized, media hype, a great deal of anticipation followed by a blowout.

With a longer evening than he imagined looming, Myron's thoughts strayed briefly to Oliver then, possibly by association, to his accordion, which presumably sat collecting dust in a battered case in a forgotten corner of the bedroom closet. He hadn't played it since the party, with Oliver providing the accompaniment. Maybe he should take it out and tickle the keys a bit.

Myron played in a band every weekend for a number of years in the metro Toronto area, earning his weekly stash to keep him afloat while attending university. He wasn't very good as far as accordionists went; he had a tin ear and couldn't harmonize with a dial tone, but he could read music and muddled his way through — acceptable enough for Bohdan Babich and his Music Kings in a venue where polkas, waltzes, and elongated tangos ruled.

Most Saturday nights, the Music Kings were on stage at some ethnic hall, playing their gig — by and large, weddings and anniversaries. He'd stand with that goofy "this is fun" smile, pulling and squeezing the bellows, exercising the bicep muscle in the left hand, while drunken twirlers, stiff two-steppers, and flamboyant floaters occupied the dance floor.

To be sure, the accordion was the perfect happy instrument, bubbling with merriment and cheer, and Myron had performed his fair share of "Roll out the Barrel" and "Clarinet" polkas. However, he knew if he took it out now, he would only play sad songs in minor keys because deeply embedded within each accordion lay the innately mournful cries of the tragic Slavic soul. As he opened the closet door to reassure himself that it was still there (and not hauled away, inadvertently or otherwise, by Nadia's movers), he instinctively knew that his accordion was the perfect melancholy mood-inducer best suited for the forlorn, dejected, and/or reasonably intoxicated.

The case remained exactly where he had put it almost a year ago (why would Nadia take it? Accordions were not a hot item, rejected even by understocked pawnshops). After a long, ruminative stare, Myron did not open the accordion case — best not to sink into a depressing stupor with some peasant ballad of lost or unrequited love. Besides, if he started playing, no doubt, complaints would be quickly registered with the building manager. Management policy: no dogs, cats, or accordions allowed.

Instead, he sat on the empty living room floor, his back propped against the wall, took out his pouch of Sail tobacco, extracted a plentiful pinch, and stuffed it into his pipe. A quick flick of the Bic resulted in a satisfying cloud of aromatic smoke. He replayed his visit with Oliver, his unfortunate circumstances, and Sheila's involvement. (One thing was sure, Sheila's alibi might not be as tight as first thought!) What he couldn't quite get a handle on was how Charles fit into the equation. He'd discuss this with Freta; also, a more thorough reading of Dworking's journal might yield further clues...

Chapter Twelve

Monday

Overnight, a Chinook came sweeping down through Great Plains. The warm, dry wind descended from the eastern slopes of the Rockies, displacing the cold embrace of the Arctic high. It occurred most often in southern Alberta. Calgarians, in particular, liked to boast to the rest of the province deep in the clutches of a winter continental climate of how these warm coastal winds that swirled from the mountains raised the temperature as much as thirty degrees in a matter of three or four hours, creating absolutely balmy conditions. The downside was that this thaw didn't last for more than a day or two before the thermometer took a rude plunge; moreover, there were high winds, up to a hundred kilometres an hour, associated with this phenomenon.

Myron awoke early, conscious of the whistling outside: flitting wind, the price to be paid for a momentary heat wave. He got up quickly, his mouth stale and his tongue feeling like scorched shoe leather. He had overindulged in his pipe again.

"Once more unto the breach," he muttered, meandering to the bathroom. His first class wasn't until nine, but he wanted to get to the college well in advance, read his lecture notes, and have that all-important first mug of coffee.

Myron arrived at his office by eight. He was surprised that Ted's door was closed; the tax man cum instructor was usually on the scene, ready to talk shop and/or gossip. Shrugging off his parka, Myron yanked out the appropriate set of notes from his world history folder and placed them on the desk. Next, he grabbed his distinctive Great Plains College mug featuring the institution's motto, "Raising the Bar" (there was a Latin equivalent, but Myron couldn't remember it) and headed for the cafeteria. The universe was unfolding as it should...

Today, however, there was a slight glitch in his routine. He had forgotten to clean out the mug from the previous week, and he noticed that added to the emblazoned orange and purple school colours was a bluish mould that had magically materialized at the bottom. Thinking that it could be hazardous to his health, Myron made a quick detour to the washroom. There he encountered Charles Leaper filling up his electric kettle. The dean of Arts and Sciences was nattily dressed in a dark three-piece suit matched to a rich, red tie. His hair was slicked back, indubitably, Myron thought, with that "little dab'll do ya" hair gel.

"Morning, Myron," he said brightly, taking a sneak peek at himself in the mirror above the sink. "A bit of a blustery day."

Myron took up his position at the adjoining sink and ran water into his soiled mug. He saw that his own hair was an entangled mess. Blustery, indeed; maybe he should get some of Charles's gel, along with Grecian Formula while he was at it. "Yeah...sort of blows you away."

Charles laughed good-naturedly. Myron did not like Charles, and he was sure the feeling was mutual. It was nothing personal (in fact, they had never really locked horns over any substantive issue and had generally been quite civilized to each other); rather, it was instinctive and intrinsic. Charles's chief asset was his innate cunning not only for survival but also for advancing his cause — namely himself — at the expense of others. It was a harsh judgement, and perhaps unwarranted, since to a greater or lesser extent, there was a bit of Charles in everyone, including Myron himself.

"You're in early," Myron said, shutting off the tap and vigorously wiping the inside of his mug with a paper towel. Charles usually arrived at nine every morning and worked late if he had to.

"A little earlier than usual today. Can't sleep when the wind howls... never could."

"Well... she sure howled last night."

"Loosened a shingle or two, no doubt... How's it going with you?"

"Comme ci, comme ça," Myron responded. He was pretty certain that Charles was aware of his matrimonial problems, even though he tried to keep it discreet. It was one of those institutional phenomena — that sort of news travelled quickly, providing excellent fodder for the gossip mill.

"Hanging in there is three quarters of the battle, isn't it?"

"I suppose that's true," Myron acknowledged, not sure in what context he should take Charles's remark.

Myron studied the bottom of his mug, now devoid of its organic growth; he suddenly thought of Dworking's journal and her comments concerning Charles's upcoming sabbatical. How did that now fit into the scheme of things? Was there a chance that Charles would forgo a shot at the presidency for a year's leave from the college? Not likely, but he decided to find out, albeit in a circuitous fashion. "How are your sabbatical plans coming along?" he asked casually.

"Ah...funny you should mention that...mulled it over just last night." Charles wrinkled his brow. "I had hoped to begin doctoral work at the U of Edmonton — in fact, have it all set up — but with the unsettled state of affairs here, that might be put on hold for a while, depending..." He shrugged.

Myron understood that Leaper would have a growing desire, if not need, for a PhD for status, as well as professional reasons as he moved up the administrative food chain. In fact, it was a common practice; a number of individuals had taken a similar route over the years. The accepted standard was a degree from the Faculty of Education, University of Edmonton, or, less so, the rival university in Calgary.

No doubt, Charles had his dissertation topic staked out: a qualitative and/or quantitative analysis on some aspect of the college system in the province. It could range from college comparisons, to institutional leadership, to university transfer programmes, to the Faculty Association(s) and collective bargaining rights. Myron could attest to this pattern, having perused a number of these theses penned by colleagues in the college library.

As in the case of Sidney Sage, Leaper was aspiring to enhance his upward mobility in academia with a doctorate added after his name, but unlike Sage, he planned doing it with a bona fide degree.

"You're going for the acting president's position, I take it?"

"Yes. I've applied. With my experience and length of time here, I think I have something positive to contribute. I hope that the selection committee and the members of the board agree," he added meaningfully, a shrewd smile sliding across his face.

Well...that certainly confirms that, Myron thought, and to Charles's credit, it was not an overly overt attempt to lobby him for support. "Those are definite assets," he said.

Kettle full, Charles made his way to the washroom door before pausing in contemplation. "By the way, I saw you talking to Corporal Osprey in the cafeteria the other day. Has she drawn any conclusions yet as to the nature of the President's unfortunate death?"

"Not that I'm aware of," Myron said.

"All sorts of rumours about the police being suspicious, and Corporal Osprey sure is inquisitive."

"That's her job," Myron responded.

"Hmm... I suppose you're right. Tragic the way it happened." Charles waved his free hand in a vaguely dismissive fashion and shook his head. "Imagine getting into your car, strapping yourself in, and freezing to death. What a way to go!"

After Charles made his exit, Myron stared at his own face in the mirror. "Did I detect a note of glee in Charles's voice?" he asked the other Myron.

***

Coming back from his first class, Myron spied Ralph Sorrey hanging around his office door. He hadn't seen the student since that irritating Wednesday afternoon world history session.

"Want to see me?"

"Yeah."

"Come on in." Myron opened the door, dropped his lecture notes on his desk, and sat down heavily, indicating for Sorrey to do likewise.

Sorrey appeared no less belligerent than the last time. "I'm dropping your course," he bluntly declared, placing a standard drop/add form from the registrar's office on the corner of Myron's desk. "Guess I need your initials."

"Okay, no problem, but can I ask why?"

Sorrey shrugged. "Don't like it — it's irrelevant."

"Irrelevant? I'm not sure I follow?"

The youth brushed a stray strand of black curls from his eyes. "I'm just not getting anything out of it. To me it's irrelevant to what's happening today."

"History can be a lot of things — even boring to some — but never irrelevant—"

"So what's the relevance of Louis XIV or all that other stuff we've taken?" Sorrey challenged.

Caught off guard, Myron had to think for a moment. Like most academics, he had made an *a priori* assumption that his discipline was both relevant and important, but he rarely had to actually justify it. Sorrey, obviously in the throes of some personal crisis and/or reassessment of his academic/career goals, had invited his instructor to do precisely that.

A whole plethora of arguments popped into Myron's mind. The usual ones about history repeating itself (did it really?), about studying the past to appreciate/anticipate the future, of coping with new circumstances by discovering and applying analogies from bygone eras, etcetera, etcetera, etcetera. All these arguments (which admittedly were rather esoteric and nebulous) Myron suspected would bounce off Sorrey like an India rubber ball off a concrete wall. He tried a different angle. "How would you change this course to make it more relevant, meaningful to you?"

"I dunno." The kid shrugged again. "Make it more real — like how can I get a job out of this stuff?"

"Well...you probably can't immediately, but down the road there are related jobs to be had."

"Like what?"

Myron refrained from being curt with Sorrey; instead, he gave him his best salesperson pitch. "A history degree is a good springboard into other professions such as law, archival and library work, the civil service, and External Affairs — not to mention teaching. But what you're really asking about is the value of a liberal arts education in general. All I can say is that it's valuable in and of itself."

Myron could tell from the blank expression on Sorrey's face that he wasn't getting through. "You know, Ralph, if you're taking this course expecting to receive specific training for a job, you're probably in for a big disappointment."

"So why go to class or to the college?"

What else have you got to do with your imploding life? Myron thought. He said, "At its best, college — or at least the academic portion of it — prepares you for a lifetime of living, learning, and career challenges. If nothing else, the global history course ought to point out that the only constant in humanity activity is change."

"So?"

"So...in practical terms there's a brave new rapidly evolving employment world out there, which you can't be trained for, because neither you nor I will know what to train for by the year 2000. Jobs existing today will vanish tomorrow, to be replaced by ones not yet conceived off. You've got to be prepared. The college may do it badly, but what else is there? A liberal arts education will hopefully make you more complete and adaptable, with the ability to think and to articulate your thoughts so that you will have a job in the next century."

Having exhausted his John Naisbett repertoire as a futurist, Myron concluded, "Of course, the choice is yours."

"Are those jobs you listed the only ones a history degree will get me?"

"No," Myron said evenly, trying to hide his exasperation. This kid needed a career counsellor, not a history instructor. "What do you want to do?"

"I dunno — something exciting."

"Well...with a history degree you can always try to join the CIA."

"Huh?"

Myron pointed to a yellowing advertisement cut out from the *Miami Herald* tacked to his bulletin board. The CIA, it announced, was recruiting recent graduates with history degrees from campuses across the United States. The ad (at least three years old) was sent to him by a colleague as a joke, and Myron for some reason thought it humorous enough to save and display. Now, it served as a facetious illustration of the variety of opportunities that could be had by those with historical knowledge and training. "Is that closer to what you had in mind?"

Sorrey didn't appear impressed. "Why'd you take history — to teach?"

"No, because I like it!"

Win some, lose some. Myron lost Sorrey. Evidently, the young man found nothing enjoyable, enlightening, or practical about Myron's course or academics in general. Myron finally initialled the drop course section on the form, and Sorrey made his escape.

***

Early afternoon rolled by, and Myron was still in his office, wrestling with student essays. Statements like "John A. caught a cold and died of death" or "the Ukrainians were expelled from Acadia" were easy enough to deal with. However, there were those students with syntax issues that proved a little trickier to diagnose and explain.

Myron always knew when a sentence was not quite right, but ferreting out why in precise grammatical terms sometimes proved elusive. "Technically, what's wrong with this sentence?" he muttered rhetorically to himself. He read it through again in his mind. *On December 1, 1869 McDougall issued a proclamation to the empty land filled with Buffalo which was illegal because it had not been consummated.* He, of course, knew what the author was attempting to convey, but the sentence just did not compute, especially since those that preceded and followed were equally convoluted and obtuse. Myron rubbed his eyes; he had been reading too many essays of questionable quality on Louis Riel and the northwest to the point of brain numbness. He had to stop for a while before he started to become indifferent to the prose or actually believe some of the material written. He slashed a double red line at the side of the margin and wrote "awkward wording — meaning obscured" and left it at that. It would take him longer to correct this one paragraph than it took the student to write the whole essay, he decided. He eyed with a growing apprehension the accumulated pile he still had left to mark.

At that moment, he had a welcome diversion when Sheila appeared at his open door. "Got a minute?"

"I sure do." Shoving his essay pile aside, he gestured to the empty seat.

Sheila was dressed in her no-nonsense business suit: dark-green jacket and matching pants with a jabot down the front. Her body was tense and her face drawn. She got right to the point. "I understand Oliver unburdened his soul to you yesterday?'

"I wouldn't quite put it that way, but yes, he told me a few things."

Sheila nodded. "I hope you can appreciate our...situation."

"I think I can."

"And be discreet about it?"

"Of course, I—"

"It's important to Oliver…and to me." There was a sense of urgency in her voice, a controlled yet palatable hint of panic in her eyes.

"I know this must be distressful…"

"Yes…yes, it is." She collected herself. "Look, Myron, I know Oliver appreciated you popping by — I just don't want things to turn out badly…" She trailed off.

"In what way? Surely your relationship—"

"I'm talking about Dworking's death and the police investigation." She cut him off. "Oh, I wish that this business was all over with — these hanging clouds over our heads."

Myron was still puzzled by Sheila's rather imprecise comments but set that aside and said, "You have the least to worry about."

"Do I?" She gave him a crooked smile and let it hang. "I just wanted you to know that Oliver wouldn't — couldn't hurt anyone. He's quite distressed about Dworking's death and the suspicions that have been cast on him."

"You've heard the rumours?"

"Yes — nasty rumours."

Myron nodded. "I'm sure the police investigation will be concluded soon and everyone can move on."

"I–I hope so."

Myron could sense that there was something else bothering the dean. "Sheila, what is it that you're trying to say to me?"

She sighed. "You're well meaning, I know—"

"But the road to hell is often paved by well-intentioned people."

"No. That's not what I meant. Oliver talked too much about us and our situation. I'd hoped to avoid all that."

"It would have all come out eventually."

"I suppose you're right. I just ask you not to mention it to anyone."

By "it," Myron presumed his conversation with Oliver, which seemed innocuous enough — at least to him! "Well, as you said, I'll be discreet," he assured her. It wasn't exactly a promise, but that was the closest he was going to come. He hadn't planned to relate his conversation with Oliver to anyone else except Freta.

"Thank you." She seemed relieved.

Myron changed the subject. "Oliver told me you were going to apply for the presidency?"

"I submitted my resume this morning. Got a call from the board secretary — I'm on tomorrow, 8:30 a.m. sharp. Blythe and Hoar are in a hurry. I think all the candidates will have their interviews tomorrow, probably one after the other."

"Undoubtedly, since they're to make a recommendation to the board for approval Wednesday night."

Sheila sighed heavily. "I wouldn't bet on my chances — especially after the last board meeting. Came on kind of strong. They really pissed me off!"

Myron tried to be optimistic. "You never can tell. All you can do is give it your best shot." *Too bad that the third member of the Selection Committee is such a dud*, thought Myron. The perennial Mackay would most assuredly go along with Blythe and Hoar in support of whomever they choose.

"So will Charles." Sheila broke into his thoughts.

"You and Charles don't get along?"

"That's putting it mildly. Long story — dirty water under the bridge now." She didn't elaborate.

"Well, may the best woman win!" Myron declared with a wan smile, still processing the "dirty water under the bridge" comment.

CHAPTER THIRTEEN

Monday night

It had been a long Monday, and after his last class, which ended at four, Myron decided to stick around the college and have dinner: a cheeseburger with lots of fries (the cafeteria was noted for not sparing the spuds) covered in gobs of ketchup. It was quite tasty, actually, and at the moment he wasn't worried about calories.

Through the day, he kept an eye out for Ted, but his office door remained closed, and he was nowhere to be found. The same was true of Freta; they agreed to let the hot-as-Sahara stir they created after their weekend liaison cool down a bit, but he did want to let her in on his meeting with Oliver and receive an update from her end. He'd phone her later when he got home.

Myron took his "square meal deal" to the concourse, a large open area where students congregated and relaxed in industrial-strength sofas grouped in judiciously spaced units around industrial-strength coffee tables. The place was quite deserted now, with most students having gone home or to their favourite bars. The evening class rush wouldn't start until about six. Chewing on his patty, Myron wearily gazed through the large, triple-glazed window into the rapidly darkening night. In the forefront, he saw his own reflection, a strangely detached figure staring back at him.

"Ruminating, are you?"

Appearing beside his reflection was the heavily bundled form of Harold Wisenburg, philosophy instructor and chairperson of the Humanities and Social Science Department. Wisenburg was in his midfifties, a thick barrel of a man, harbouring a long bushy beard with an abundance of wizened grey streaked throughout. He had protruding cheeks and deep-set eyes, black as coal. It was those eyes, Myron believed, that gave Harold the Rasputin look: soulful, irascible, with a tinge of animal wildness.

Harold was an ideological misfit, a humane Marxist who renounced his American citizenship during the height of the Vietnam War and fled to the untainted nirvana of Northern Alberta. The college became his refuge, where as an experienced savant with a ready young audience, he could denounce Uncle Sam's capitalistic corruption and imperialist nature.

"No, just finishing my dinner. Can't chew and think at the same time," Myron responded, cranking his neck around.

Harold sat down on the edge of the battered coffee table, facing the historian. "I'd hardly call that dinner," he said, eyeing the ketchup-smeared paper plate with distaste.

"Beats my cooking. What's up? You're hanging around rather late. Got a night class?"

"No, not till Thursday," Harold responded, setting his briefcase down beside him. "Just finished a hastily called meeting of departmental chairs and those in the president's office, formed a committee to plan a farewell tribute for our late president."

"Was that initiated from the board?"

"Probably. It was Charles, though, who wrote the memo to all of us suggesting a college-wide goodbye to Vanessa combined with an introduction and welcome to the new president. I guess the board will make that decision on Wednesday."

Myron nodded. "Big of Charles, also shrewd, since in all likelihood he will be our next acting CEO."

"Quite possibly," Harold agreed. "Anyway, after considerable debate, I daresay it was finally decided to hold a posthumous tribute this Friday evening."

"You mean there was less than enthusiastic endorsement of the idea?" Myron couldn't quite manage to keep the sardonic tone from his voice.

"Not that exactly. Most chairpersons agreed that a suitable send-off was appropriate. But some worried about sufficient numbers showing up and/or having anything complimentary to say."

"You're kidding!"

"Actually, I am being a bit facetious. Still, a couple were serious — spent three quarters of an hour debating the point. Finally decided to go ahead with a few safe speakers — the chairperson of the board and, ah, Charles volunteered and maybe a community member from outside the college who knew Vanessa well — not sure about that yet. A couple names were mentioned. Also, we'll encourage anyone attending who feels moved to say a kind word or two. As a backup, I and at least one other chairperson could fill the breach." He paused. "Did you want to speak as past president of the Faculty Association?"

"I'd rather not," Myron said firmly. For a myriad of subliminal reasons he'd have to think about, he didn't want to speak. "It would be more appropriate to let Jeffery do the honours." Jeffery Pierce was the current Faculty Association head, and Myron could always say, if pressed, that he didn't want to step on Jeffery's toes.

"Fair enough. I'll ask him." Harold paused, giving Myron a pensive look. "You know, I didn't mind Vanessa at all. She was a straight shooter with me. I...well. Never mind." Harold checked himself. "She's dead, and I'm sorry. By the way," his voice took a brighter tone, "as an added incentive to attend, the committee decided to provide free food, the catering costs to be shared by the board and Faculty Association — and have a cash bar open. That way not only can we drown our sorrows for the passing of the old but also celebrate the selection of the new."

"I suspect I'll just be drowning my sorrows."

"Your choice, but you don't think that's too gauche, is it? There was some argument over that point."

"What — the cash bar?"

"Yes."

"No, Vanessa would have appreciated the gesture. She liked a drink or two at any function I'd seen her at. Certainly, most of our colleagues will. Good idea. Glad the committee went ahead and resolved to do it."

"Well, among academics I'm not sure anything gets resolved — just suitably reworded." Harold laughed. It was an old joke but with a germ of truth. "I'm sure that—" He stopped abruptly, and Myron followed his eyes to the third person who had suddenly materialized, casting shadow over them.

Nadia stood there, a sudden apparition, flitting eyes that didn't quite make contact, her hair noticeably dishevelled and her face flushed. She had the wanton look of a woman who had hurriedly jumped out of someone's bed, Myron reflected later. Certainly it was a different Nadia than the one who had confidently marched into the apartment a few days ago and stripped it of "her" possessions.

Harold, catching the sudden charged atmosphere, got up and excused himself. "I'll probably see you tomorrow," he said.

"Right. Thanks, Harold."

The philosopher patted Myron on the shoulder, gave a curt nod to Nadia, and made his exit.

There was a throat-constricting pause that could have been a couple of seconds or an eternity before she bluntly informed him, "I'm in trouble."

"Oh?"

She fished into her handbag and produced a pack of Du Mauriers. With a shaking hand she lit one and blew the smoke through the side of her mouth. "Let's go for a ride. My car is parked just outside."

Myron nodded. "Let me just grab my coat from my office."

Nadia was a striking woman, not beautiful in the classical sense but attractive, with many ephemeral qualities both in her physical presence and personality. For Myron, one was part and parcel of the other. Dark complexion, raven hair, expressive eyes, full lips — all set comfortably in place. The only genetic blemish was a slightly ennobled nose, "a Mona Lisa with a Barbara Streisand protuberance," he once remarked in a moment of levity. The rest of her was slim and long-legged, and even in her winter apparel, Myron thought she too had lost some weight.

"So where are you living now?" Myron asked, trying to break the tension as they walked to her vehicle. "You left no forwarding address."

"At Sally Barlow's place for the time being," Nadia answered tightly. "She works at the paper. I think you met her once."

Myron nodded.

After that, a screaming silence prevailed between them until they got into the car. He'd been in it only a few times since the day they picked it up from the dealership. He tried another innocuous question. "How's the Rabbit running?"

"Fine. Hard starting for a while. Needed adjustment — something about the fuel injectors."

She pulled out onto the main road, a rigid river of ice and encrusted snow with patches softened into slush courtesy of the Chinook, and accelerated smoothly through the gears. In the greenish light of the interior, her eyes straight ahead, she appeared preoccupied. Her life was unravelling in an unexpected way.

"Where are we going?"

"Nowhere — anywhere," she responded cryptically. "Look..." She bit her lip, determined to say her piece. "I've been having an affair."

Myron knew that he shouldn't have been caught by surprise. Unhappy women sometimes had affairs, and Nadia had clearly indicated she was unhappy. Still, hearing her say it was a shock, and he reacted to it. If nothing else, it had a therapeutic benefit for the reptilian part of his brain.

"Damn." He hit the dashboard a little harder than he wanted to. She flinched but kept looking straight ahead. They were now heading northwest toward the airport on the same highway he and Freta had traversed on their expedition to Dworking's residence.

Myron calmed himself and tried to be objective and reasonable. "How long?" he asked quietly.

"Does it matter?"

"Yes, it matters," he hissed behind what seemed to him clenched teeth. It *did* matter, actually. How long was he floundering about attempting to understand what was going on in their marriage while was she screwing about?

"Three...four months," she said softly.

"You met regularly?"

"I didn't keep count, if that's what you mean," she answered with a tinge of defiance.

"Who is he? Do I know him?"

"Look," she gave him a sideways glance, "I didn't come to play twenty questions. I had an affair, let's leave it at that."

Myron held his tongue for a moment, letting his anger subside as they drove in silence, his thoughts racing. In terms of maintaining his faithfulness, he had taken the higher moral ground — until a couple of days ago. In the end, a moot point maybe. But damn it, she most definitely set up a self-indulgent scenario, one that had much less regard for him than he had for her. Nadia had been calculating and systematic in the way she had gone about her cheating. But even that wasn't the point; she seemed hardly contrite about it all and in her dramatic appearance not overly forthcoming. Given his state of mind, perhaps he wasn't thinking as clearly as he should. Something was up; he didn't know what. Hopefully, she would enlighten him.

"So...why have you decided to tell me now?"

"Because..." she hesitated, "you were bound to find out sooner or later, and I wasn't sure how you would react."

"What'd you think I would do...go after him...you? Become unhinged?"

"I–I wasn't — am not sure." She pulled into the terminal lot, stopped the car at a parking meter, and turned to him. "What are you going to do?"

Myron honestly didn't know at that moment. It was as if he was having a surrealistic conversation with a stranger in an alternate universe he once knew intimately. He ignored her question. "You said you were in trouble?"

She sighed. "Things have become a bit messy," she said vaguely.

"With your...lover?"

She put the idling car into gear and proceeded out of the airport parking lot. "Yeah, with him and this whole town."

"Care to explain?"

"I'm...I'm not ready to do that — yet." Her hands tightened on the steering wheel as they headed back to the main highway. "I need some time...to sort a number of things out."

Myron shifted toward her in his seat and frowned. Those were close to the same words she used when she walked out — the harbinger of a broken record?

She gave him a nervous look and continued, "I haven't stopped thinking about you, you know."

"What do you want me to do?" Myron asked, suddenly feeling deflated and very tired.

"Be patient. I've got an investment in you that..." she searched for the right words, "is hard to let go because of...mistakes."

"We both made mistakes," he acknowledged. To be sure, he was far from the perfect marriage partner.

"We...we might have to leave this town. Maybe go back east — start all over," she said barely above a whisper.

Myron had no response. He couldn't quite fathom it. Were they to cross the Rubicon together, or was he just being taken for a ride?

Nadia let him off at the main entrance to the college. As he got out, she leaned over with glistening eyes. "Be patient," she repeated, "I'll call you."

For a long moment his eyes held hers, searching the features of the face he loved, his mind flashing memories of what they had together. Then, abruptly, he let them go and nodded. He stood watching, none the wiser than before, as the car sped away, its taillights disappearing in the distance.

***

Albert Einstein believed that pipe-smoking contributed to calm and objective judgment. Ensconced in his apartment, Myron set about to test Einstein's theory in a deliberate and methodical fashion. He reamed out the bowl of his best Brigham, thoroughly depositing the carbonized curd in the garbage, gave it a quick drag to make sure it wasn't plugged, and carefully filled and tamped down a couple of layers of tobacco. This was followed by a flick of his Bic and a slow intake and expulsion of contemplative smoke. He felt too mentally drained to call Freta, or anyone else for that matter. And after relighting for a second time, he relaxed, taking solace in his thoughts.

They were a bit askew. Never mind that what he was doing or not doing seemed quite irrelevant to Nadia and to whatever issues beset her. She didn't ask about him; but then, equally, he was too shocked really to ask about her. It was a conversation in the stratosphere, as fleeting as a jet stream; there was an understanding of sorts and a promise, and he felt better that they had talked. But nothing had changed, and he was still on hold while she made up her mind whether he was worth keeping. Never mind, he realized; even if she made her escape, he would always have feelings for her — tarnished momentarily by outbursts of anger and emotion and, no doubt, diminished with time, but never extinguished. *Receding tail lights*, he mused bitterly, *something like that but not quite — ever increasing distance but not quite beyond the pale.*

Finally, in the wee hours of the morning he fell asleep and had a dream so intense, it bordered on a spiritual experience. It was as if he was floating, bed and all, toward a white, shimmering light. The light at the end of the tunnel? Then Nadia appeared beside him, stroking his brow. "Everything will be fine now," the mirage soothed, "just fine…"

Myron woke up with a start, his pulse racing. Did Nadia's sudden woes have anything to do with Dworking's demise?

Chapter Fourteen

Tuesday

By Tuesday morning, all evidence of the Chinook was gone. The Audi started a little less freely and rode a little more stiffly on the hardened streets. Back to a normal continental climate: crisp with snow flurries in the air. Myron too felt a little more hardened after his encounter with Nadia; the cold light of day expedited the process. On his way to the college, he realized that nothing had really changed between himself and his wife — she was just keeping her options open. The ball was still in her court, and it was up to her to make a play.

The day began well with a couple of morning classes and a departmental meeting where course changes and workloads for the following year were discussed. Myron got his course on the Soviet Union approved for the next academic year; he looked forward to teaching a topic that had been his "minor" field in the doctoral programme. Enrolments seemed to be growing, everyone's jobs were secure, as far as could be determined, and despite the ever-present threat of funding cutbacks in a time of government restraint, it appeared that more instructors might be needed to accommodate the projected student increases. Wisenburg's announcement of the scheduled Dworking wake/coronation of the new president received a muted response, but most indicated that they would respectfully attend.

Back in his office, Myron decided to tackle his ominous pile of student papers, get as much work done as he could, and take the night off. He'd planned to pay Freta a visit, see how her investigation had progressed, and possibly nurture their growing relationship. His rapidly warming thoughts about Freta were rudely interrupted, however, when Sidney Sage suddenly showed up at his door.

Sidney had been absent from the departmental meeting, but here he was, dressed in his best Don Cherry costume: a midnight-blue three-piece suit hiding a mostly pink, high-collared Pierre Cardin shirt (*monogrammed?*) with a flashy tie wedged firmly in place by a conspicuous golden pin. He looked uncomfortable as hell.

He seemed flushed; maybe the collar was cutting off his circulation. "Like to take a few moments of your time, if I may — pass on some information and perhaps have an exchange of views," he said, wetting his lips with the tip of his tongue.

"Oh? On what?"

Casting a furtive glance around, Sidney literally tiptoed in, carefully closing the door behind him. *Shoes on too tight?* Myron wondered. Sidney sat down and gave Myron his infamous eyeball-to-eyeball stare.

"Let me start off by saying I have applied for the presidency. In fact, I had my interview about a half hour ago."

Myron kept his face an indeterminate neutral, but the little voice inside him let out a loud guffaw. *Is this guy for real?*

"Now, I know," Sidney said in a rush of words, "that I'm a dark horse — the unknown — but I am confident that I haven't over-reached on this — that I can do the job and provide the kind of creative new initiatives this institution needs."

In other words, you want to lead us all straight up your arsehole until we're in so much shit, we'd need a year's worth of laxative to blow us out. Myron, however, kept the thought to himself.

"I believe," Sidney continued, "that the committee was impressed."

"I'm sure they'll give you due consideration," Myron said with his deadpan face still intact.

"Quite. However, as the faculty representative on the board..."
Here it comes, thought Myron. "I would certainly appreciate any
supportive input on my behalf that you could provide."

"Well, Sidney, I too would give you due consideration if the
Selection Committee puts your name forward as their candidate of
choice." (*God forbid.*)

"Yes, yes, but should there be some question or perhaps dispute
as to the best choice...ah, board members would then have a
contribution to make to the selection process, I should think."

Myron frowned. "True, but as I understand it, the Selection
Committee is mandated to bring forth one candidate for the board as
a whole to vote on. Have you been led to believe otherwise?"

"No, I'm only thinking of possible contingencies."

"Well, never hurts to look at all the angles."

"Precisely," Sidney exclaimed. "All I ask is a good word on my
behalf should a suitable occasion arise in the deliberations of the
board."

"Now..." Myron cleared his throat, "now that I'm aware that you
are running, ah...I shall endeavour to be judicious in that regard if,
as you say, the opportunity presents itself."

Myron was engaging in diplomatic double-talk, but it sounded
good, and for all his smarts Sidney was incredibly dense when it came
to what people really thought of him. He had to be, or he wouldn't
have run, Myron reasoned.

Sidney was obviously seeking an ally on the board, but not this
time; he had burned Myron once, but not twice. Rather than spurn
him outright, which was not Myron's style — character flaw or strong
suit, depending on one's point of view — Myron would play Sidney's
game in the knowledge that he didn't stand a pup's chance with the
Selection Committee — he hoped!

"If you would, that would be much appreciated," Sidney said
earnestly. He wet his lips again. "On another matter...I normally
don't prattle..."

I bet!

"And I hope that I'm not being too personal or out of line here, but some news has come to my attention — totally unsolicited," he emphasized, "that I presumed you'd like to know about."

"Oh?"

"It, ah…concerns your wife."

"Yes?" *Now what the hell is this about?* wondered Myron, suddenly perking up.

"I of course don't know what your situation is, but my neighbour works at the *Great Plains Daily Reporter*, and he related to me a rather distressing story yesterday that I would not have given much thought to except that names were mentioned. Your wife," Sidney's voice took on a hushed tone, "had a fight with a fellow employee, and some heated words were exchanged."

Myron didn't say anything but waited for him to continue.

After a lingering pause, Sidney plunged ahead as if now that he was in for a penny, it might as well be a pound. "George, my neighbour, thought it a lover's spat but…" He gestured upward with his hands and shrugged as if to say *who knows…*

"When did this…spat occur?" Myron asked calmly.

"Late last week — I'm not sure. George was working after hours when he overheard them yelling at each other. They ceased abruptly when they realized they weren't alone. She stomped out shortly thereafter, very agitated."

"Did George say what it was about?"

"Not exactly, only that it was a dilly with a lot of name-calling. He had the impression that they had been, ah, involved for some time before this row. I hope this is not too unseemly of me telling you this, but as a colleague, I thought you should know for what it's worth."

Myron nodded. "A heads-up is what you are saying."

"Precisely."

One good turn deserves another, Myron reading between the lines. *Quid pro quo. You put in a good word for me in my quest for the presidency, and I'll tell you about your naughty wife and her escapades.*

"Did George mention the name of this individual?"

"The guy writes a weekly column — Streuve, I think he said."

Myron nodded. Conrad Streuve indeed had a column on local events and personalities.

"Well, Sidney, thank you for sharing."

***

After Sidney vacated his office, Myron leaned back on his swivel seat, put his feet on the desk, and started to laugh. He laughed so hard, he almost fell over backward. It was one of those bittersweet laughs one has about the ironies of life. It dawned on him that Streuve's melancholy behaviour at the Co-op Mall was the result of his falling out with Nadia. He was her mysterious lover, and she dumped him! And he, in an enigmatic way, was telling Myron about it. Myron had suddenly become a kindred spirit of sorts for Streuve. It was so funny, it hurt.

"Enough of this," he muttered, glancing ruefully at his stack of essays yet to read. "Better get on with it!"

But before he did, he gave Freta a call at the RCMP Detachment Office. They were to get together that night after a couple days off to catch up on the case and "other" things but hadn't arranged a time.

"I'll be running a little late tonight," she informed him, "but I do want you to come over — say about nine. I've got a surprise for you."

"A surprise? What kind of surprise? I've had a couple already today."

"Oh, you'll like this one. I can't tell you, can I? Won't be a surprise then."

"Okay, rendezvous at nine." Myron hung up, pondering his "surprise."

Myron's contemplation was abruptly interrupted by a knock on his door. It was Ted.

"These walls aren't that thick — thought you'd gone mad. Listened to Sage too long or something. You didn't open your door."

"Ted! When did you come in? Didn't see you earlier or yesterday. Took the day off?"

"Of sorts — attended a state of Alberta and the world economic conference with some of my students at the Great Plains Inn. Quite enlightening — a couple of interesting speakers." Ted plopped himself into Myron's extra chair.

"And what did you find out?" Myron asked, dismissing the essays as a lost cause for the rest of the afternoon.

"That Alberta's economic slowdown will continue with the falling of energy prices; that we have about an $11 billion deficit; and that Don Getty is a better quarterback than premier. Globally, the Russians are getting a shit-kicking in Afghanistan and are ready to withdraw — not that it counts for anything, financially speaking — and that Perestroika and Glasnost aren't going to solve the Soviets' productivity problem. Too much central planning and drinking on the job."

"Maybe I should have attended this talk. I'll be giving a night course on the Soviet Union next year. I didn't realize the Russians were such an economic force globally."

"They're not," said Ted, "quite the opposite. I'm just giving you the highlights of our witty speaker's comparison of large countries' economies, of which the USSR is the butt end. Maybe, I'll take your course, find out what's wrong with them."

"To really understand the Soviet communist system, the most important thing is to learn alternative facts," said Myron with a smirk.

"How's that?"

"Oh, it takes a bit of preparation. I'm working on it. Come to the first class for a demonstration."

Ted raised an eyebrow. "Pray do tell, what do you plan to do?"

"I haven't worked it all out yet but it involves a few basics..."

"Like?"

"Sitting in the dark to create a feeling of anxiety and tension. Make comments like students will be targeted for failure if they ask too many questions or not correctly phrase them or don't believe that black can be white if the occasion requires. They'll get the drift of how things work in the Soviet Union as the course progresses."

"Wow! Can't wait."

"I knew it'd turn your crank," Myron said in a bemused tone. "Tell you everything you wanted to know about the Russians."

"Speaking of knowing, what did our illustrious Poli Sci prof have to say?"

"Ah, let me tell you a tale of my day so far." Myron proceeded to inform Ted about Sage's bid for the presidency (Sidney never mentioned anything about confidentiality — probably because he never practised it himself) and the latest tabloid on Nadia.

Ted shook his head. "Very funny on both accounts, if it weren't so sad."

"Yeah, ain't it…" Myron glanced at his watch. The afternoon was wearing on. "I think I've had enough of this place for one day."

They both got up. Ted, a towering lump over Myron, put a hand on his shoulder in a fatherly fashion. "What you need is a good stiff drink. I'm finished here as well. Say I meet you at the Corral downtown — quaff a couple."

"Sounds good. I'll meet you there shortly. Gotta hit the can…"

It was there that Myron came upon his last unseemly revelation before exiting the college. Orville Wishert had his back to Myron, facing the urinal. His pants and boxer shorts were wrapped around his ankles, two wrinkled buns exposed. Myron stopped dead in his tracks; no way was he going to stand cheek to cheek with this strange little man. He made a 180-degree turn out the door, deciding that he could stand the pressure until he got to the bar.

CHAPTER FIFTEEN

Freta greeted him wrapped comfortably in a full-length mauve bathrobe with a pair of matching slip-on slippers. He gave her a casual hug and modest kiss, a far cry from their torrid session together over the weekend. But then having known each for only a few days, Myron didn't have a feel for what was an appropriate greeting between them. She disengaged herself and ushered him into the living room. He staked out his favourite love seat.

"Coffee, tea, or something stronger?" she asked from the tiny kitchen.

"I'd go for something stronger, as long as it isn't a drink of any kind," he said teasingly. (Two hours and three beers with Ted had put him in a jocular mood.)

She poked her head around the corner. "Hold that thought — for later." She gave him a wink.

"In that case, tea would be nice." He had coffeed himself out and didn't want an alcoholic beverage at that moment.

Freta came in with a tray of cheese and crackers. "Something to nibble on if we get hungry. So, let's get caught up. What have you uncovered the last couple of days?"

"Not a whole lot," Myron admitted. He told her about his visit with Oliver and his chat with Sheila.

Freta mulled that over. "She was agitated about you speaking to Oliver and the ongoing police investigation?"

"Seemed to be, wants to protect him, I think, in any way she can."

"Don't know why she would be overly concerned."

"Sordid rumours are floating in the college to the effect that Oliver did Dworking in for firing him."

"How do these things get started?"

"Very easily, believe me."

"Well, I talked to him again. Told me pretty much the same thing he told you regarding why he was fired."

"When was that?"

"Monday morning — the first person of interest I managed to reach. He didn't mention Penny's telephone call, though."

"No, he wouldn't. They both want to keep their relationship discreet."

"Well—" She was interrupted by the kettle whistling in the kitchen.

Myron got up. "Relax, I'll make the tea."

"Thanks…the tea bags are on the second shelf in the cupboard nearest the fridge."

"Right…you were saying," he called from the kitchen.

"I'm going to do what I should have done much sooner."

"What's that?" He brought in a brown teapot and two mugs.

"Confirm Penny's story through airline and telephone records." She poured her tea into a mug. "Want yours now too?"

"No, let it steep a while longer."

She settled back into her chair, sticking her feet underneath her. "If it checks out, I'll forget about her and drop Oliver down a notch on my list as well."

"It'll check out," Myron said. "Sheila arrived in Great Plains after midnight."

"How do you know?"

"I guess I forgot to mention this part. Oliver told me that she was on the last flight in, and that was 12:45 a.m."

"Well, that's good to know," Freta said, surprised with a touch of annoyance. Myron couldn't be sure whether it was because he forgot to mention it or that Sheila's stature as a suspect was suddenly greatly reduced. "I'll have to confirm that," she added.

"That sounds reasonable to me. Oh, before I forget, there is a tribute to Dworking Friday night. I'm sure all the suspects will be there. Might be worth attending — get some impressions. Sugar — can't drink tea without sugar."

"Same cupboard, bottom shelf."

"Right! Don't police usually attend wakes and funerals of homicide victims?" he asked, making his way to the kitchen again.

"Potential homicide victims," she corrected him. "Unless I get a break soon..." She shrugged as he came back. "We haven't proven conclusively that she was murdered, although I can't shake that feeling, just intuitively, you know... And there's nothing in the RCMP procedural manual about attending funerals or wakes. Ugh! How can you drink that?" She eyed Myron with mock disgust as he put two spoonfuls of sugar in his cup before pouring the tea.

"I like a little tea with my sugar," he said, settling back and taking a tepid sip.

"Each to his own, I suppose. But you're right." She returned to the business at hand. "It might prove productive to attend this tribute/wake/whatever. Rob and I are quickly running out of leads and ideas. What time?"

"Seven. In the concourse area. Free food, cash bar."

"Nice touch. Oh, wait. I will be a little late. I'm meeting Dworking's sister, Sandra. She's flying in from Toronto Friday night at seven fifteen, I think, to make arrangements after the release of the body."

"Releasing the body? That mean the coroner's work is done?" asked Myron, a bit surprised. The unthawing process sounded complicated and lengthy to him when Freta first mentioned it.

"No, far from it. She will have to wait for that, but there's lots to do, I'm sure, in terms of dealing with her sister's possessions and assets and eventually funeral arrangements — she did mention cremation."

Myron nodded. "Seems appropriate somehow. I suspect that's the way Dworking would have wanted it. Probably stipulated as much in her will."

"What'd you mean?"

"To be quietly cremated, ashes scattered." Myron waved his right hand as if spreading seeds. "Seems her style somehow."

"I wouldn't know," said Freta, helping herself to a cracker.

"So there's nothing new on the corpse front?" asked Myron, changing the focus of the discussion.

"No developments, no — or at least nothing really new. Only odd note was what I mentioned the other day. Dworking sustained a bruise at the base of her skull, forceful enough to possibly kill her, but it gets a little too speculative after that. Maybe she slipped, fell, managed to get up, climb into the car, and passed out and froze. Problem is I don't buy that," Freta said in a grim tone.

I think we've covered this already. "Neither do I," he agreed. "Someone whacked her and placed her in the car — arguably it's just as, if not more, plausible."

"The blow to the back of her head had a very definite shape to it like it was made by a rounded blunt object. Forensically speaking, that's clear, but how it came to be inflicted, not so clear, and there it sits. If we could just find the object that bruised her skull, that would help immensely, but no such luck." Freta paused, exasperated. "At any rate, I'll meet you at the college after I pick her up from the airport. Maybe she'd like to attend."

"Okay...so what have you learned from Dworking's journal?" Myron asked, curious about the names mentioned and any bits of other information it contained. Freta had kept it for further perusal.

"Talked to those on her naughty list. Let's see... I didn't get very far with Leaper. Yes, he was well aware of the Primrose incident. No, there was no personal animosity between them — Primrose was let go as part of the college's downsizing, to use his words, in certain areas where there was an evident redundancy. Yes, Dworking spoke to him about his initial handling of the dismissal, but for clarification purposes, and no, she did not chastise him for doing his job. Yes, he was granted sabbatical — he hadn't decided whether or not to take it, and no, he was not aware of any pending reorganization with or without him. And why was I asking these questions anyway?"

"In other words, he said nothing — totally stonewalling."

"Something like that. Next was Wishert…" She paused and shook her head. "How can any institution let a man like that loose on unsuspecting students? He's a psycho. First, he raved on about Dworking as some sort of demented monster literally foaming at the mouth; then he started on me. Why was I bothering him, asking stupid questions. Was I accusing him of killing her? Was I out to pin it on him? Really, on and on he went. Pretty weird reaction. I left him threatening to sue me for false accusations!"

"That's about par for Orville," Myron commented, thinking about his last rear-view of the mathematics instructor. "What about Sidney Sage?"

"Bit of a pompous ass — said that his degree was widely accepted in institutions throughout North America, that it was perfectly legal and he didn't see what the fuss was all about, other than a few of his so-called colleagues trying to discredit him for reasons related to professional jealousy. According to him, Dworking had not talked to him about it at all."

"That figures too," Myron said with a sigh.

"The most embarrassed was Blythe."

"Oh, yeah? How does he fit into the picture?"

"He did some investing for Dworking, about $80,000 worth that she had to play with."

"Must be nice."

"Maybe she won the lotto. Who knows, but she found out that Blythe was under investigation for an alleged misappropriation of funds — at least his licence was under review. He told me that it was all a misunderstanding and that all the charges were dropped. I checked, and essentially, that's half true. Although no criminal activity was established, contrary to a client's wishes, he redirected some funds into a questionable venture. It wasn't so much a breach of trust, apparently, as negligence or incompetence. He did end up making restitution and paying a hefty fine. Dworking found out and had a chat with him about her portfolio. Maybe that note in her journal was just a reminder to herself to do that. According to Blythe, Dworking had complete confidence in his ability to manage her money and chair the College Board of Governors, and that was that."

"Hmm...but it does give Dworking quite a hold over Blythe. After all, she needed his compliance both as chairperson of the Personnel Committee and the board to get rid of Oliver."

"True, but it still doesn't lead us anywhere. You know," she said with a note of exasperation, "as of this moment I'm not any further ahead in this case than I was last week!"

***

They continued to talk about the investigation without any further insights or ideas. After a while, Myron excused himself to use the little boys' room. Freta put the teapot and mugs on the tray and carried it to the kitchen. When he came out, she stood in the hallway, her eyes bright.

"What?" he asked, looking down. "My fly undone?"

"Try again."

"Ah...you promised me a surprise!"

"And here it is," she said, smiling mischievously, untying the cord of her bathrobe and opening it up.

"Wow!" Myron exclaimed. Revealed was a lacy black bra with a fancy frill around the edges, which although supportive, didn't exactly hide Freta's endowments. Also very evident was a red garter belt connected to long, sheer black stockings that almost reached the top of her thighs. All in all, a most enticing display that at the same time left precious little to the imagination.

"And I got something for you," she said in a sultry voice. From the pocket of her robe, she pulled out flashy red briefs. She twirled the merchandise around her index finger and threw it at him, turned around, and slowly walked down the hall. Myron stood mesmerized for a few seconds — just her hip motion seemed to have rarefied the air.

Minutes later, Myron entered the bedroom with nothing on but the briefs. Freta was lying on the bed, turned sideways toward him with one leg raised provocatively in the air, waving her toe at him. "Not bad," she remarked. "A bit of a tight fit, I bet."

Myron pounded his chest. "Me Tarasyn, you Jane!"

With that, he bounded across the room, leaped onto Freta's bed, and almost fell off the other side.

"Very clever, but don't hurt yourself, or Jane will be disappointed."

Undaunted, Myron recovered his balance, raised himself up to his knees, and took a hold of her foot. He gently began massaging as Freta lay back. "I'm going to work from the bottom up...slowly stopping at all the right spots," he promised, letting his fingers do the walking.

Almost an hour later, they were both under the covers, quite spent.

"Tell me," Freta murmured, her eyes half closed. "Did you and Nadia indulge in such sexual frivolity?"

"Why?"

"Oh...just curious." She moved up against the headboard.

"Well, we did stay in one of those theme rooms in the Fantasy Hotel at the West Edmonton Mall once."

"Really! What room did you pick?"

"The Polynesian room, I think it was."

"How was it?"

"Just an ordinary hotel room with a high price tag. The main attraction was a huge hot tub decorated like a volcano. You could create your own steam via one of those humidifiers. The bed was themed too. Supposed to be one of those Polynesian reed boats, but it looked more like a gondola to me, with all sorts of ornaments sticking out the sides. Actually, come to think of it, our night there was a bit of a comedy of errors."

"How's that?"

"Well..." Myron realigned himself, moving up so that he would not have to continue speaking into Freta's bosom, "to begin with, I filled up the tub with too much hot water. Guess I wasn't paying attention. I couldn't get it to drain, so we waited for it to cool — watched some romantic comedy on TV. Took some time to cool but I still felt like a lobster being boiled after I got in. So did Nadia. The real killer was the bed, though. I stubbed my toe on the ornamentation and then proceeded to bang my knee on the sideboard getting in. Hurt like hell."

"It sounds like you were lucky not to have injured another vital part of your anatomy," Freta mused.

"Yeah, I think the hot water shrivelled it enough that it didn't get in the way of anything. Oh, and did I mention the ceiling mirror above the bed?"

"Was that exciting?"

"Could have been. I didn't have my glasses on. Couldn't make out much of what we were doing."

"You know," Freta chuckled, "you're such a card."

"Nadia called me a klutz."

"Speaking of which," her tone became a little more serious, "Nadia is in the clear. Her appointment with the president had been cancelled; she didn't see the president that night. And besides, she has a solid alibi — you and your friends and someone else. Want to know where Nadia went when she left your apartment?"

"Either Sally Barlow or Conrad Streuve," Myron stated flatly.

"How'd you know? She and her helpers dropped off the stuff she collected from you at Barlow's place, after which she visited Streuve. According to Rob, he lives some distance from the city in a mobile home trailer park and — short answer — time frame doesn't work, Nadia didn't leave till after midnight."

Myron nodded. "Great. Takes her off the list."

"Are you being sardonic?" Freta asked. "Your tone—"

"Yeah, just a bit..." He proceeded to tell Freta about his unexpected encounter with Nadia and Sidney's subsequent clarifying addendum.

Chapter Sixteen

Wednesday

Myron didn't leave Freta's apartment until about 2:00 a.m., but then he was normally a night owl, and he still obtained sufficient sleep to get through a couple of morning lectures without dragging. In fact, his energy level was quite high.

However, by mid-afternoon he could hardly keep his eyes open. It wasn't his late night escapade that was doing him in but rather the wretched essays he was reading. He'd start one, but almost imperceptibly, the words would begin to run into each other, and then the next thing he knew, his head bobbed, his eyes popped open, and he hadn't the foggiest notion of what he had just read.

Maybe he should take the afternoon off. His apartment needed cleaning, he was down to his last pair of Stanfields, and the fridge was getting mighty empty. While he was at it, it wouldn't hurt to shop around for some furniture and maybe a stereo. The college was getting to him; besides, he'd have to come back for the big board meeting that night.

He laboriously completed reading the essay he had started three times before, assigned a grade, and scribbled a couple of comments about how it contained the germ of a good discussion that unfortunately never came to fruition because of content errors and the inability of the student to write a sentence. He tossed it on the finished pile, which to his dismay was only approximately half of the "to-do" stack.

"That's it," he muttered to himself, "I'm outta here."

But before he could make good his escape, Ted ambled in and plopped himself into a chair, dropping with a thud his *Canadian Tax Law* text (23rd edition) on the corner of the desk.

"Got ten minutes before class," he announced, scratching his bulbous nose. "Just received some news hot off the hall waves that you might be interested in. This is a scream."

"Okay, so lay it on me." Myron leaned back in his chair, stretching.

"It's Wishert — he's gone off his rocker."

"That's hardly news. He's been off his rocker for years!"

"Yeah, but this time he's really done it. He's gone AWOL!"

"I don't follow."

"Get this. According to a couple of students I just spoke to, about midway through his class he lay down on the floor, yelling something about police harassment and that he couldn't take it anymore. He then quite calmly told one of the students to call an ambulance. And it took him away!"

"What?"

"I kid you not!"

"When did this happen?"

"About an hour or so ago."

"Well, that's just…peachy!" said Myron.

Ted blinked at him. "You, who has studied for years, who has read books, who has a PhD, and that's all you can say — peachy."

Myron shrugged. "What else is there to say? Somehow, I'm not surprised."

Ted shook his head. "I've got to go, but don't say I'm not keeping you informed."

"You're a regular news bulletin, Ted."

***

Myron had just gotten his toe shoes and parka on when the phone rang. With a sigh, he sat back down and picked up the receiver. Freta was on the other end. "We may have gotten the break we needed in the Dworking case," she said excitedly.

"Oh?"

"Penny lied. I checked with Air Canada. She took an earlier flight from Vancouver. It landed in Great Plains at eight thirty, not twelve forty-five. She phoned Spinner, all right, but not from the Vancouver Airport, as I assumed. It was from the Great Plains airport when she got in on the early evening flight!"

Myron had a sudden lurch in his stomach. When Oliver had told him that Sheila phoned from the airport, he got the impression that it was after her late arrival. What did he miss? Was he misled? Or did Oliver not know? Sheila was one of the good guys, as far as he was concerned. "Why would she lie?"

"Because she did it?" Freta prompted.

"She lied to Oliver then," Myron said, frowning into the telephone.

"Did she? He could be covering for her."

"That doesn't make sense. Why would he even mention the telephone call to me? Why not let the alibi stand on its own? It just doesn't make sense."

"Slip of the tongue? You said she was upset that he mentioned it to you."

"Yes, but we could be jumping to conclusions."

"Well, I'm about to go and find out," said Freta with determination ringing through the line. "It's about time I had a serious chat with her."

"Yeah," Myron said, disheartened. "Oh, before you go, a bit of news that will probably catch up to you. Wishert had a mental breakdown — I think." He told her what Ted had related to him complete with Wishert's comments about the cause of his distress. "I wouldn't be surprised if the RCMP got a call from his lawyer and you from your superior. Just a heads-up."

"Great!" she exclaimed. Myron could almost visualize her rolling her eyes.

Myron's office was on the third and top floor, one of a dozen enlarged cubicles along a relatively narrow corridor with an expansive view of the college grounds and the city beyond on one side and dead space on the other, where one could lean on the railing and look down on the to-and-fro movements of the Lilliputians on the main concourse level. He had inherited C 308 from his predecessor and couldn't think of a better location, even if given the choice. It escaped the usual human bustle of the floors below, replete with numerous classrooms, was centrally located to the stairs and elevator, and strategically positioned just above the deans' and departmental offices on the second level.

The only drawback was that with a vast cavern of open space, an echo chamber was created where bits of distinct conversations on the first floor could often be heard intermingled with a constant general din. Myron had gotten used to it, and if he really wished a quiet zone, closing his door usually did the trick. He liked to keep his door open — not as claustrophobic, especially when he worked alone late at night. At those times, with the concourse emptied of its jabbering humanity, he could hear the faint, vibrating sounds of the edifice's mechanical soul providing for its own regeneration — an entity that was somehow unto itself hermaphroditic.

However, at that moment his attention was on activity on the second level. As he made his way down the stairs, pondering the ramifications of Freta's phone call, he spotted Sheila leaving Leaper's office. The dean of Career Studies wore a very grim expression, and if looks could kill... Leaper came out seconds later with a smug smile; he walked in the opposite direction into the men's washroom.

What was that all about? Myron wondered. He was tempted to catch up with Sheila and ask her but thought better of it. The lady appeared extremely cross and undoubtedly upset. And Freta was hot on her trail. Best not to press — at least at that moment.

Instead, he went into the men's room and parked himself beside Leaper in front of the urinal.

"We meet again," the dean quipped.

"It must be the pressure," Myron retorted. "Sheila looked fit to be tied just a moment ago?"

Charles gave Myron a shrewd sideways glance. "Women can be like that," he said, giving himself a vigorous shake before stuffing himself back in and doing up his fly. "But she'll get over it," he added in a nasty tone.

"Over what?" Myron asked.

"Oh, you'll have to ask her." He gave Myron a twisted smile, washing his hands. "You know, Myron...you're a very inquisitive fellow."

But...Myron waited for Charles to elaborate. Leaper, however, seemed to change his mind about finishing the sentence. Instead, he said, "Don't forget about the board meeting tonight." And he was gone through the swinging door.

***

Myron neither went shopping nor did he clean his apartment or do his laundry. When he entered his abode, he took off his winter wear and his rumpled tweed jacket, marched straight to his bedroom, and fell into a deep sleep infused with a bizarre dream...

Myron/Alice was in Dworkingland, with Dworking the Queen of the Kingdom. She adorned a velvet throne at the head of a huge table, around which were gathered some very familiar subjects drinking tea.

"Welcome to the Mad Madame's tea party. Care for some?" The speaker was Ralph Sorrey, dressed in a butler's uniform.

"Ralph! What are you doing here and dressed like that!"

"Hey — it's a job!"

At the end of the table sat Orville, Sheila, and Sidney.

"The queen's a bitch," whispered Sheila.

"She's a witch," corrected Orville.

"It's all a matter of degree," explained Sidney.

Opposite them were Streuve and Nadia. He had her in a choke hold, while she battered him with a cup. "What could I do? She threw herself at me. Now she doesn't like me," exclaimed Streuve.

"I just need time to sort out my life," wheezed Nadia.

"And I protest!" shouted Oliver. "I did not see this coming."

"What?" the queen bellowed, incensed.

"I protest!" repeated Oliver.

"Off with his head!" commanded the queen.

Charles scurried forward in a black academic gown and bowed low before her. "Yes, Your Majesty — right away… Guard!" he shouted.

Blythe appeared, replete in conquistador garb. "Take the protestor away to the scaffold." Charles pointed at Oliver.

"She can't do that!" wailed Sheila.

"Oh, yes she can," pronounced Charles.

"Tea! Give me some tea!" shrieked Dworking.

"The queen wants some tea," ordered Charles.

From a huge copper kettle, a cup was poured, and a multitude of hands hurriedly passed it on to Charles, who delicately placed it before her. "Your tea, Your Royalness."

She took a slurp. "It's cold! My tea is cold!"

"The queen's tea is cold," came the hushed chorus from the crowd. "How can that be?"

"You did this to me." She pointed an accusing finger at Charles. "You've cooled my tea!"

"Oh no…not me." He quivered.

Dworking shivered violently. "I'm cold…so very cold."

"The queen's cold…so very cold," they all chimed in.

"I'm freeeeezing," she declared, getting up from her throne at the head of the table and stretching her arms out. "I'm freeeezing."

Her breath swirled in the air, and she turned into an ice statue.

Timidly, Charles moved closer and gave her a nudge with his hand. She did not budge. "I think the queen is dead!" he said.

"The queen is dead?" they asked.

He nudged again with more force. "Definitely dead."

"The queen is dead," they sang. "Long live the queen."

"We need a new monarch," someone shouted.

"Precisely," said Sidney.

"Yes, the kingdom needs a new king," Charles averred. He hugged the throne, and others rushed toward it.

Meanwhile, Myron/Alice began to fade away. His last image was of the frozen queen toppling over and shattering into a million, Technicolor pieces.

He woke up with a start; that was about as weird a dream as he could ever remember having. He couldn't even begin to interpret it or assign any meaning other than his stressed brain rerunning a collage of events through the prism of *Alice in Wonderland* — and he didn't even particularly care for Lewis Carroll! The subconscious psyche was a funny thing, he decided, and let it go at that.

Getting up, shaking the cobwebs of his dreamland experience, Myron checked his watch, noting with relief that it was only five thirty. The board meeting didn't commence until seven (an hour later than usual; presumably it wouldn't take long to dispose of the one topic on the agenda), which gave him plenty of time to freshen up and grab some supper. He lit his battered Brigham and pondered whether he should settle for a burger at the "Golden Arches" or try something more exotic. First, though, he wanted to get a hold of Freta and see if she had tracked down Sheila. When he got no answer at her apartment, he tried the cop shop. He was put on hold while someone located her.

"Osprey," said an officious voice.

"Freta… It's Myron."

"Oh, hi. Won't be home for a while yet."

"I won't be either. Board meeting tonight, remember. Did you talk to Sheila?"

"Hang on a sec…" she said. "There, don't want this conversation recorded, do you?"

"No…"

"Okay, I interviewed Penny less than an hour ago. A woman under tremendous stress, I'd say."

"Yeah. I think she had a rough session with Leaper today. Don't know what it was about, though."

"She didn't mention it to me, but anyway, she admitted that she took an earlier flight than the one she was scheduled on. Arrived in Great Plains at eight thirty or thereabout. Said she never mentioned this because no one asked her. In my initial interview, like you, I certainly got the impression that she was in Vancouver or in the air when Dworking died—"

"Then she didn't actually lie," he interjected.

"A very moot point, Myron. Deliberate omission is almost as bad as commission. She misled us into thinking she had an alibi."

"Something doesn't add up. Why didn't she tell Oliver that she got in early?" Myron asked.

"Why indeed! If he was telling the truth, that is."

"I'm sure he was."

"Her story is that she phoned him to tell him just that — that she managed to get on an early flight and would stop by. But before she could, Spinner, of course, told her about his being fired. After that, the conversation turned to his woes and what she should do about it, and, according to her, she simply forgot to mention that she was already in town before she hung up. She then drove to the college to pick up some papers from her office for a meeting next day. She also admitted that she stopped by the president's portable on the off chance that Dworking was still around."

"And?" Myron held his breath.

"No, she didn't confess." Freta sounded disappointed. "Apparently, Dworking wasn't there."

"What time was that?"

"A little after nine. Then she decided to go home rather than bother Spinner. End of story."

"Well, it could be the truth."

"Weak, Myron, weak. She's my prime suspect. Look, I've got to go. I probably won't see you until that tribute Friday night. Remember, I'll be late."

"Okay. I better get going too… Oh, by the way, thanks for those sexy briefs — very timely; all my other shorts are in the laundry."

CHAPTER SEVENTEEN

After his dinner "chez McDonald," Myron drove hurriedly to the college. He had enough time to hustle up to his office, get rid of his winter wear, and grab a pen and notepad — a psychological if not always necessary item, he discovered, for any meeting — and retrace his steps down a floor to the boardroom.

He made it at seven on the dot, and it appeared that so had everyone else. The room was buzzing with conversations as members spread themselves out in little groups around the large conference table. Bowell was saying something about his "great Bowell movement" on skis to Prybiewski, the "grocer king," and Chorney the sleazy lawyer. Prybiewski seemed distracted, while Chorney expressed interest in acquiring a new pair of cross-country skis, and what kind of deal could Bowell give him? Blythe and Hoar were quietly conferring in a corner with Cecil Mackay hovering nearby, coffee in hand, studying his shoes. Sarah Libalsmith, the newest member of the board, was chatting with Whitford, while Stanley Piech, the soft-spoken Employees Association rep, and Mona Radcliff, the student rep, looked on immersed in their own thoughts. The two deans were, of course, absent, waiting no doubt somewhere in the wings to see which one the Selection Committee favoured.

Blythe glanced at his watch and made his way to the table; as if by radar, the groups broke up and individuals zeroed in on their preferred sitting places. Myron found a vacancy between Stanley and Libalsmith, directly across from Blythe and Hoar.

Blythe, seeing that everyone was accounted for, promptly brought the meeting to order. "We all know why we're here, but before I get to tonight's agenda, I'd like to make an announcement concerning a tribute for our late president." Blythe went on to state that he, on behalf of the board, had agreed to sharing with the Faculty Association one half the expense of putting it on. It was an executive decision, and he trusted that there were no objections. Noting none, he then strongly suggested that board members attend and perhaps even partake, with a few appropriate words about how Dworking may have influenced or impressed them.

"Mull it over for Friday night," he urged. "Now, for the main business at hand—"

Mona Radcliff shot up her hand.

"Yes... Ms. Radcliff?"

The student representative was a large, bespectacled adolescent whom Myron had in his Canadian history class. She wasn't exactly an A pupil, but she wasn't shy about speaking her mind in Myron's class, and evidently she had something on her mind now.

"I have a procedural question. Will we be presented with a list of candidates?"

Blythe looked puzzled. "A list of candidates?"

"From which to vote on," Mona prompted.

"Er...no, Ms. Radcliff. There were a number of candidates from which the Selection Committee has made a choice, and which we will submit to the board for ratification."

"Is that fair, I mean, shouldn't we know those in the running?"

Blythe favoured her with a "say cheese" smile. "You weren't here at the last meeting, but it was decided then that the Selection Committee would be responsible for inviting applications, interviewing, and selecting a candidate to be brought before the Board as a whole. That process is now complete, and we are now ready to proceed."

"I don't think that's fair," Mona persisted.

Blythe stirred uncomfortably in his seat. "In what way is it not fair?"

"I think we all should know who the candidates are and vote on who we think is the best. I mean — isn't that fairer?"

Myron leaned forward, hands clasped together. Mona was audacious, he'd give her that, but where was she coming from? She seemed wound up tighter than a cork.

"By agreement with the board as a whole," Blythe explained tersely, "it is the prerogative of the Selection Committee to bring forth tonight one name. The committee, after all, interviewed the candidates and made their best choice based, in large part, on those interviews."

Blythe was beginning to sound exasperated and redundant. He hadn't anticipated a challenge — least of all from the student rep.

But Mona was unrelenting. "I should like to know who the candidates are, not just the one who is to get voted on."

The board chairperson glanced at the faces around the table, perhaps assessing them for direction or hoping that someone would interject, help him out, and straighten this female out. Most were perplexed; the rest appeared both puzzled and slightly amused, Myron noted. He considered himself the latter; certainly he wasn't overly distraught with Blythe's obvious discomfort.

Hoar took up the challenge. "The Selection Committee hadn't intended to release the names of all the candidates, just our choice. There may be an issue of confidentiality here. They applied in strict confidence and may wish to remain anonymous if they aren't successful."

Mona remained petulant and unconvinced by Hoar's rather feeble argument. "I don't see why we can't be given the names."

"Well…" Hoar ran a hand through his silvery locks. "If that's a real concern, and feeling around the table and the other members of the Selection Committee agree, then I suppose we could provide the names — as long as it is understood that this is provided strictly in camera."

Like most board members, Myron was mystified about this strange wrinkle thrown in by an obstinate student, who, Myron was sure, the board chairperson believed should have been seen but not heard, at least on this matter.

Blythe cleared his throat. "That's fine by me. Cecil?"

"I'll go along with the committee," Cecil responded as if by rote.

"What is the wish of board members?" Blythe asked, clearly annoyed by the turn of events.

"I don't really see any harm in naming the candidates," said Bowell. "Probably general knowledge in the college community by now."

Myron couldn't argue with that. News in an institution leaked out through telephones, vents, cracks between the doors; it scurried along the floors, darted across ceilings, and hovered in the air. Indeed, it could be found in just about every area where the human voice could penetrate.

"Is that the consensus around the table then?" Blythe asked.

Board members either nodded or shrugged. It didn't strike most of them as a major issue. Certainly, it wasn't for Myron.

"Very well then…" Blythe conceded. "I will release the names, but as agreed to by the board as a whole, I will insist that board members vote only on the candidate recommended to it by the Selection Committee. We had three…er worthy candidates: Charles Leaper, Sheila Penny, both of whom you are all familiar with, and Sidney Sage, instructor in the Department of Humanities and Social Sciences. After due—"

"I vote for Dr. Sidney Sage," Mona announced, cutting Blythe off in mid-sentence.

Bingo! Myron suddenly understood in the momentary silence that followed. He wasn't the only one Sidney had lobbied. Myron was willing to bet a year's supply of Sail pipe tobacco that Sidney had approached Mona. She was probably taking a course from him. She'd be an easy mark for him; a little chat after class was probably how it started. He wondered what inducements Sidney had offered to the impressionable, most certainly naïve student representative. Whatever it was — flattery, flatulent rhetoric on his own behalf, offer of a better grade, perhaps (he hoped it didn't go to that) — it raised serious ethical questions. Myron wondered how many others sly Sidney had attempted to influence…

"Ms. Radcliff, you are out of order," Blythe stated indignantly. "The Selection Committee has not endorsed Mr.…er, Dr. Sage."

"I…I object!" Mona's voice quavered slightly. Her steadfast resolve was showing signs of faltering.

"Your objection has been duly noted and ruled against from the chair," Blythe snapped back. "Now, can we get on with the meeting?" Giving her a hard look, he waited.

Having apparently shot her bolt on Sage's behalf, Mona clammed up. Her eyes moistened but her repose remained defiant, arms folded across her chest. Myron felt sorry for her and angry that she had been put in such a position.

Receiving no further response from the wayward board member, Blythe continued, straining to keep his voice normal. "It was a difficult choice, but in the end, the committee recommends Mr. Charles Leaper as its nominee for acting president. The decision was based on his experience, his administrative skills, and his overall knowledge of the operations of this institution. The committee felt that, on balance, in this interim period of stress and uncertainty, Charles will provide prudent management. Now, I will entertain comments, discussion at this point and then put it to a vote — a simple majority."

The discussion that followed was perfunctory. Chorney summarized the feeling of most around the table when he remarked, "I don't see any need for a lengthy debate. The board mandated the Selection Committee to make a choice — they have. I therefore move that we accept the committee's nominee and thank them for their diligent work."

"I second that," said Prybiewski. "And call for the question."

For his part, Myron remained mute. Whatever his feelings about Charles, he could not logically object, and he wasn't about to engage in spurious character innuendos. His reservations aside, he recognized that this was not the hill he wanted to make his last stand on. He was still disturbed by Mona's misguided attempt to promote Sage. She seemed deflated now, head down, eyes reddened.

"Question has been called," Blythe said, casting a wary glance around the table. "All in favour of the committee's recommendation."

Five hands raised. Blythe looked at Whitford, who made a note on her steno pad.

"Those opposed." Myron's hand went up, along with Mona's and Stanley's.

"Abstentions."

One — Sarah Libalsmith. "I'm too new to cast an informed vote," she said apologetically.

"Do you wish to have your opposition recorded?" Blythe addressed the question in Myron's general direction.

Myron shook his head. That would be counterproductive. The vote had been taken; he had registered his protest, and there was no point in belabouring it officially.

Stanley also said no, while Mona whispered a yes. At least she was consistent to the end. Myron gave her credit for that.

"Mr. Leaper is Great Plains' new acting president," Blythe announced with finality.

The rest of the board's business was anticlimactic. Blythe indicated that Charles would carry on with his dean duties as well as acting president for the time being. (He apparently agreed to this in the course of his interview with the committee in the event that he was chosen.) Furthermore, Blythe informed members that the first item on the acting president's agenda was to resolve Oliver Spinner's case one way or another so that a dean of Financial and Administrative Services would be in place as soon as possible.

With that, the meeting adjourned.

Thereafter, Myron turned to Stanley and in a low voice said, "I noticed you voted against Charles as well—"

"Not my favourite, that's for sure," affirmed Stanley, a small man with a rough face seeded by greying stubble. He worked in maintenance — an electrician by trade. "A bit of a prick," he added in a whispered aside. "Been proving that in his negotiations with the Employees Association."

Deans were obligated to sit on the administration negotiations team, of which there were two: one for the Faculty Association and the other for the Employees Association. Leaper was on the latter, while Sheila was on the former. Apparently, Stanley and the Employees Association negotiating team were not happy with the progress to date.

"I heard about that," Myron said, making a mental note to ask Ted for details. He would be up on all manner of collective bargaining at the college. "Something about rewriting a number of clauses in the collective agreement..."

"More like gutting them in the name of management rights. We're arguing over definitions and workloads. Haven't gotten to the salary grid yet. Probably end up in mediation."

Myron nodded. The college–faculty negotiations were coming along more amicably, but then they were not as far along as the employees. "Charles can push the limits of reasonableness," he said diplomatically.

"Treats our side like we were some union thugs to be cajoled and controlled, and I don't trust him to negotiate in good faith as far as I can chuck him."

"I hear you," said Myron, appreciating that both the Faculty and Employees Associations were loathe to be treated as unions, regarding themselves as professional bodies with all the nuances that went with that. Myron suspected that to Charles and indeed most of the board and the late president, the distinction was mostly moot.

***

Myron caught up with Mona in the hallway, thwarting her attempt to disappear unobtrusively. He had to confirm his suspicions about Sidney's influence on her behaviour at the board meeting.

"The selection process didn't go quite the way you would have wanted?"

"No," she said weakly, not meeting his eyes.

"But you certainly said your piece, and that's commendable under rather intimidating circumstances. Are you taking a course from Mr. Sage?" Myron couldn't quite bring himself to addressing him as "Dr."

"PO 201— Canadian politics," she said a little more spritely.

Myron nodded. "Did he, ah…encourage you to speak up on his behalf at the meeting?"

"Well, he mentioned it," she said.

"He talked to you about his running for the presidency and perhaps suggested that you promote his cause?"

"Dr. Sage is a wonderful prof and would have made a great president," she offered with renewed enthusiasm. "He outlined some wonderful plans for a student-oriented college."

"I'm sure he did," Myron said. "And as the student rep, he counselled you to support a student's candidate?"

"Y–yes, but I wouldn't have if I didn't want to. I mean — I just think he would have made a super president."

Myron left it at that. He had learned all he wanted to know. Down the road, Sidney would have to be held accountable for his sleazy exploitation of Mona. He filed that thought away; an appropriate moment would arise, and he planned to be there to do it.

CHAPTER EIGHTEEN

Thursday

After his class that morning, Myron kept an eye out for Ted. Ever since Sheila marched out of Charles's office the day before, he had been curious about the source of the obvious animosity between them. Indeed, it had been evident at the board meeting a week ago, but Myron had let it slide to the back of his subconscious. Now, with Charles in charge, a confrontation of some sort was probably in the air — over Oliver's job, if nothing else — but the crosscurrents of dislike, particularly on Sheila's part, seemed to have deeper roots anchored somewhere in the past. Ted was the self-appointed rumour guru of the institution, and if anyone would know, it would be the intrepid tax expert.

Ted finally arrived at his office midmorning. Myron let him get settled in (the rustling of paper and the banging of file cabinet drawers usually signalled that preparation for a class was in the works) before stepping out of his office and entering Ted's. The big man was seated at his chaotic desk, strewn haphazardly with files and books; he looked harried and dishevelled.

"You're a little late today," Myron said, leaning against the open door frame.

"Yeah. The trials and tribulations of being a parent," Ted answered, rifling through some notes in an attempt to put them in some manageable order. "My eldest son just got his learner's permit, and the first thing he does is go for an unauthorized joy ride with his buddy in my car — the same car that, according to him, fell off the road and ended up on its side in a ditch!"

"Was anyone hurt?"

"Fortunately, no, but the car sustained over a thousand bucks worth of damage. The police want to charge him with sundry offences including careless driving, and the insurance company isn't too happy either — of course, they'll simply jack up the rates!" Ted shrugged. "What can you do? Told him he's grounded for a month, and hopefully he'll learn from experience."

"Well, thank heaven he and his friend survived intact."

"Yeah. I would have killed him if he really got hurt. So, it's official — Charles is our boss."

Myron nodded. "News travels fast."

"Heard Blythe on the radio," Ted said by way of explanation.

"Well, it was to be expected," Myron said, resigning himself to the decision.

"President Leaper." Ted let that roll off his tongue. "Does have a ring to it."

"Acting president," Myron corrected. "And it's a foreboding ring, I fear. I know you're busy getting ready for your class, but since you're the deep throat in this college, I need to ask you a quick question."

"Deep throat, eh…" Ted seemed to like the sound of that. "Okay — shoot."

"Sheila and Charles don't like each other, I've noticed, and that's putting it mildly. There's definitely a strain between them. Do you know anything about the background? With Charles in charge — well, wherever is going on between them is bound to escalate."

"Hmm…. Almost forgotten about that," Ted scowled. "They were close friends once upon a time, if you get my drift."

"Really?" Myron was more than a little surprised.

"There you go again, dazzling me with your verbal profundity."

"Well, elaborate?"

"That's it. Don't know much more. They were a hot item a few years ago — before your time, I guess."

"Charles and Sheila — an item?" Myron asked, his eyebrows arching.

"That's the story. Charles's wife left him and took their two boys to Calgary, I think. Sheila either eased the pain or contributed to the breakup, or both! I'm not sure…" Ted shrugged. "Never heard much after that, but it must have been a short fling. I vaguely recall hearing that she dumped him."

Only later to take up with Oliver. "So 'ole Charles is batting below average with his love life," Myron quipped, immediately realizing that he wasn't exactly a winner himself — although his prospects had greatly improved of late. That would explain both Charles's unsympathetic attitude toward Oliver and the nasty interplay between himself and Sheila.

"This is all rumour, mind you," Ted said. "And that's all I know. Why? Is there something else I should know?"

"No, not really," Myron assured him. "Just vibrations, bad vibrations I'm picking up, which are about to get much worse, I think."

"Well, I wouldn't be surprised, but they've managed to stay out of each other's way, or at least I haven't heard anything since."

"Until now. Thanks, Ted. Your reputation as the source of impeccable rumours is well deserved."

***

Back in his office, Myron decided to tackle the essays for a while, but his thoughts were ajar and diffused with this latest revelation. What did it all add up to? Or was it a non sequitur to what was really going on, like the sentence in the essay he was reading: "Louis Riel was mentally unstable, so he went to Montana and taught school." Myron sat up with a jolt; his mind made a sudden leap like grease across a hot griddle. Non sequitur, or was it an incongruity — a detail that shouldn't be there? Myron's adrenaline shot up a notch. It may be nothing — or the key to solving a murder!

However, he needed to check out a couple of things before he could get too excited. The first necessitated a trip to the college's Learning Resource Centre (aka the library).

Great Plains College was most fortunate in possessing its library. For a small community college, it had an impressive almost 40,000 volumes. Much of the credit, at least as far as Myron was concerned, went to Anne Balatok, the head librarian. She could be crusty and not always easy to get along with, but she liked Myron and was good to him when it came to obtaining books for his subject area.

It helped immensely that he was helping Anne with her major project: the establishment of a regional archive. She was adamant that besides the local museum, the city and its vast hinterland needed a professional archive to preserve the historical record of the area. What better place to house it than the college, where collections could be properly catalogued and preserved under "environmentally correct" conditions?

Myron agreed; archives were necessary grist for the historian's research mill. As part of the college's "master plan," he had advocated that "significant archival space and resources" be included in future expansion planning of the Learning Resource Centre. In promoting such ambitions, Anne and Myron met with the long-time MP for the northern constituency with the goal not only of gaining his support in general but also of obtaining his papers when he retired, which, it was rumoured, would be at the end of his term two years hence.

"It would be a coup," Anne emphasized to Myron en route to a luncheon meeting with the long-serving politician, "if he deposits his papers at our archives rather than the National Archives in Ottawa…" Of course, this was all predicated on getting an archive approved.

Being an ally had its rewards; Anne always found the money, even after the history books budget was used up, to fill Myron's often lengthy requests for titles and journals, no matter how esoteric.

Today, however, he didn't need an obscure reference or a computer search; what he wanted was more straightforward: local newspaper accounts of Dworking's death and the follow-up stories.

Two sources, in fact: the *Daily Reporter* and the *Great Plains Weekly Standard*. Back copies of both, he knew, were stacked in a small room off from the microfilm readers on the main floor. The library policy was to store newspapers, local or otherwise, for three months before disposing of them.

He made it to his destination unmolested — almost. Two students stopped him at the turnstile, making sundry inquiries about their essays and the upcoming midterm test (when would he hand them back, and what did they need to know?). Myron was succinct: the essays would be given back in due course, and they needed to know everything, thank you very much.

It didn't take Myron long to peruse the stories in both newspapers and confirm at least part of his suspicions. He made note of Merle Morgan's name; that was the grounds maintenance worker who discovered the body. In a crucial way, Merle was the key to affirming Myron's suspicions, although, of course, he didn't know it. Fortunately, Myron had a passing but friendly acquaintance with Merle, which could facilitate an amicable chat.

Coincidentally, Myron couldn't help but notice his wife's stories scattered throughout the pages of the *Daily Reporter*. She began her journalistic career as Nadia Tarasyn; that became hyphenated to Karpovich-Tarasyn, which in turn metamorphosed simply into Karpovich in the latest issues. Not an encouraging omen, he decided.

Back in his office again, Myron quickly scanned the college's directory tacked to the bulletin board above his desk. He dialled the Maintenance Department number. "Can I speak to Merle Morgan, please?"

"Ah…hang on a minute," said a very pleasant female voice. "Sorry," she said when she came back on. "Merle's off for a few days. Wanna leave a message?"

"No, that's all right. I'll catch him later," he said and rang off. He decided to phone Merle at home and arrange to meet him at Tim Horton's the next day; he really needed the details of Merle's memorable discovery of Dworking's corpse.

***

Aside from his phone call to Merle, before the day was out, Myron took care of one other piece of unpleasant business. He was not a confrontationist by nature or style, and he really hadn't planned on any specific belligerency, but the opportunity presented itself when, walking down the hall, he noticed that Sidney's door was ajar. *Might as well strike while the iron's hot.*

He walked in and helped himself to a seat.

"Can't win them all, eh, Sidney?"

The Poly Sci instructor was sitting at his desk, his shirtsleeves rolled up, red pen in hand, also engaged in attacking student essays. Unlike his own, Sidney's desk was very tidy, devoid of the usual academic debris that littered Myron's workstation. Even his pink message slips were neatly stacked and impaled on a pointed spindle beside his telephone.

Sidney laid his pen down and offered Myron a weak smile. "I tried."

"That you did," Myron agreed. "And in about the only way you knew how."

Sidney's face took on a quizzical expression, but he didn't say anything.

"For you it's always been not how you play the game but that you win — hasn't it?"

"What do you mean?" With a squeak, Sidney swivelled his chair toward Myron while pushing it out a little from his desk.

"Look…I don't particularly mind you playing your insidious charades with your colleagues — most can see through them, although I must admit getting suckered. Getting me to write you a letter of reference for a degree that came out of a Cracker Jack box was innovative, but using your students for personal aggrandizement — that's really stooping low."

Sidney's face darkened; Myron could tell he had scored a hit. "I don't know what you are babbling about," he said in a tense but controlled voice.

"Sure you do. What inducements did you offer Mona? Never mind, I don't really want to know. I just wanted to inform you that it was a slimy thing to do."

"I never offered any inducements, as you put it," Sidney croaked. "I merely pointed out to Mona my candidacy — and she was free to exercise her rights as a board member."

"Sure she was."

"And I resent you marching in here and insinuating some impropriety on my part." *Sidney has definitely lost his accent*, Myron noted.

"Save your indignation for a more worthy cause. You fucked up royally on this one."

Sidney's eyes narrowed. "I'll file a grievance with the Faculty Association for character slander."

"I don't think so. The ethical committee of the association wouldn't take too kindly to your exploitation of your students. Your name is mud among the faculty already, and you wouldn't want that to turn to total shit."

Sidney's jaw dropped. Myron got up and without further ado walked out. There — he got him good where it hurt, not only in his enormous but delicate ego but also his Pavlovian need to be accepted and recognized by his peers. Sidney, of course, would remain Sidney, just like a leopard couldn't change his spots. Of that Myron had no doubt, but this exercise was for Myron's benefit. Dishing it out instead of taking it made him feel better.

***

It was illogical, had no practical purpose, and was just plain stupid, but Myron did it anyway. After his confrontation with Sidney, he drove straight south along Main Street out of Great Plains until the road narrowed into a two-lane highway. Urbanization gave way to white fields on either side, with stunted shrubbery encased in ice and snow acting like scattered sentinels guarding the desolate landscape.

About fifteen kilometres out, on the right-hand side, he spotted what he was looking for: the forlorn, winter-beaten sign read "Country Living Trailer Court," beyond which a suburbia emerged, composed of about twenty-five mobile homes spaced in more or less an orderly fashion along a main road, augmented by a number of intruding side lanes.

From the air, Myron imaged they looked like elongated shoeboxes with Dinky toy cars in between. He had been out here once before to visit a colleague who temporarily rented in this "blue-collar" district (as his colleague called it) because of the low vacancy rate in town.

As Myron recalled, one entered a narrow hallway that opened into a modest kitchen, replete, he had noted, with 1950s décor, including one of those chrome-legged tables, complete with matching chairs that had yellow plastic materials on the seat cushions. The small Arborite countertop was some sort of faded beige/brown, like the cupboards and walls. The living room relieved the imposing claustrophobia by appearing slightly sunken, if not wider (at least in his mind). Farther down the hall, a few steps beyond the ubiquitous bathroom, one would find two undersized bedrooms.

There wouldn't be much variation, Myron thought, in these prefab homes. It was to one particular address and one particular nondescript bedroom Nadia found herself drawn. He slowly drove by Conrad Streuve's undistinguished abode, located midway down on the main drag, his tires ominously crunching the crusty snow. An older Dodge pickup was in the laneway, and a feeble light penetrated through the kitchen window. No red Rabbit — nor would there be, he presumed, given their apparent falling out.

He rolled a little beyond and parked, leaving the car idling. *Now what? Go bang on the door? Confront him? Act outraged?*

Myron took out his Brigham and stuffed it with aromatic tobacco; he slowly lit it, producing a blue haze of smoke, the escape of which he quickly facilitated, rolling his window down a couple of inches. The pipe gurgled on his draw; he needed to change the cherry wood filter…

He sat there puffing and debating, but it wasn't a serious debate. The whole trip had been a cathartic exercise for himself and his spirit. Deep down, he knew that he had to let go — that's just the way it was. Nadia had found her bed, satisfactory or not, and so be it. He was there simply as a confirmation of himself and his being. He felt more saddened than angry and experienced a sense of loss rather than anxiety or any urge to sudden action. He would, he realized, move on, or as Nadia would say, "plod on," and eventually succeed. Still, here he was...

Darkness had set in, and it was time to return to his apartment. Whatever obtuse logic literally drove him had passed, and he wearily called it a night.

CHAPTER NINETEEN

Friday

While endowed with a certain rugged beauty, Northern Alberta was a harsh mistress. Dressed in boreal green, mostly spruce, aspen, pine, and birch, and dissected by a discontinuity of swamps, sloughs, rivers, creeks, and numerous lakes, the land was initially deemed inhospitable and unforgiving for settler activity except the early fur trade.

However, within its scarred and gouged vastness lay a modest area of flattened plateaus, parkland, rolling hills, and inviting river valleys that belied its foreboding nature and beckoned adventurous homesteaders. Within these confines the soil proved deep and rich, on which heartier, short-season crops could be grown. Agriculture ensured settlement and rural stability, but it was what lay beneath — the gas and oil — that brought wealth and urbanity with all its attendant virtues and vices.

Great Plains mirrored the region's fortunes, emerging from being a quiet agricultural town replete with railways and grain elevators to an officially declared city by the late 1950s. With the economic booms (occasionally arrested by short-lived busts), Great Plains had become the administrative and distribution centre of the region. Still, it retained its stoic prairie grit and the "plain Jane" appearance of a typical Alberta town erected serendipitously, it seemed, in the middle of nowhere. The key was the grid pattern: two major streets, both inordinately wide and straight, intersecting to create the embryonic core. Main Street ran north–south; the significant other east–west.

Myron was on the latter route, the one that began at the Edmonton turnoff a few kilometres to the east and ran like a plumb line past a string of motels, car dealerships, the quintessential mall, into Great Plains proper, continuing on until it dropped off literally into the river valley and provincial park where the road suddenly narrowed and turned twisty. The hinterland lay beyond.

While the weather had turned relatively mild and the streets were clear, except for the odd patch of ice and snow, the traffic seemed congested and unusually slow. *Is there a traffic light out or are they badly synchronized?* Myron wondered. He had hit five red lights thus far, and there were only about nine on the whole street! He had arranged to meet Merle at 8:00 a.m., and at this rate he'd be late. He was now crawling through the nondescript four corners that marked Great Plains' urban heart. On either side were square, squat, brick and clapboard edifices that even with modernized storefront facades could not escape their unadorned 1920s–30s architecture. *The city centre still has a way to go in terms of attractiveness*, Myron believed, *a challenge, no doubt, for the Downtown Merchants Association.*

By the time Myron's little green Audi turned into the Timmy's parking lot, Myron's thoughts had drifted from Great Plains' core features (or lack thereof) to his own melancholy of estranged existence. The existential question, *what am I doing here?* was brought on in all likelihood by the country song he was listening to on the local radio station — vocalized wailing about pain, longing, love lost, moving on...

Luck was finally with him when he managed to tuck the car into a cozy spot alongside the coffee shop just as the former occupant drove off. He saw Merle sitting at the window. *Good, he showed.* Myron wasn't at all sure, since he really didn't know him that well, and he seemed hesitant on the phone. He caught Merle's eye as he got out and waved. Merle waved back — a good sign.

Myron's familiarity with Merle was based on a single encounter that summer. He literally crossed paths with him while walking through "College Park," a mishmash of little streets bordering on the campus, with tiny, mostly ramshackle bungalows and duplexes and a couple of low-rise apartment buildings thrown into the mix. Modest income, low-rent oozed through the neighbourhood, emphasized by peeling paint, unkempt lawns, and broken down cars in the driveways, now covered with a thick blanket of snow. Myron regularly took this route with Ted (weather permitting), a short cut to Robin's Donuts. That day, Ted wasn't around, and Merle just happened to stroll out of the Maintenance Building, headed to the same destination.

Merle had noticed Myron's Audi, which piqued his curiosity. He launched into a number of poignant questions, like who made it exactly, what were the specs, was it expensive, and where did he buy it? With that point of interest as a foundation, they hit it off, at least for the purposes of that particular occasion.

"I think that's a drug house," Merle noted, pointing to one of the dilapidated houses of College Park. They had pretty well exhausted their car conversation. "I come this way quite often, and I've seen some dodgy dudes making their way there."

"Oh?"

"Yeah. Seen more than a few slink to the door, rap on it. Always opened a crack, then, just enough to enter — followed by a quick exit."

As if to confirm Merle's observation (which for Merle, Myron surmised, became more like a stakeout), a badly painted purple Chevy Impala cab rolled slowly by and then came back after, it appeared, circling the block. It stopped a discreet distance beyond the college parking lot. Four stubbly men with sketchy faces and dark windbreakers spilled out and nervously dispersed, only to re-emerge one by one at that particular door.

"See?" Merle emphasized. "What else can it be?"

It certainly looked like it. After their in-and-out business, they slunk off, heads down, necks compressed, ball caps pulled over the eyes, the tell-tale taxi suddenly sitting at the end of the street.

"Yep," Myron confirmed. "Something fishy is definitely going on..."

Later that summer, Myron pointed the abode out to Ted on their walk, but they spied no lurking dudes or clandestinely developing queues. The bungalow appeared abandoned, empty, with the dirty blinds gone. A small sign in the window beckoned them forward.

"Can you make that out?" Ted asked, squinting.

"An announcement of some sort — printing's too small," Myron responded.

"Maybe your drug house moved — new business location?" Ted wondered.

They kept moving closer until they got within range.

"Nope," Myron replied. "Nothing like that..." And he shook his head. Talk about curiosity killing the cat...

The notice read: "Smile, you're on camera." It was signed: "RCMP."

I'll have to ask Freta about that, Myron thought as he finally procured his coffee and settled into his seat across from Merle.

"Sorry I'm a little late. Can you believe the traffic?" Myron said, setting his cup of java down on the table.

"Not a problem. Just got here myself."

Merle Morgan was a scrawny, scruffily shaved man in his early thirties with nervous hands busily molesting the coffee mug. His rheumy eyes took in Myron without questioning the obvious. *Why did you phone and what is this meeting about?*

"So..." Myron hesitated; he needed to ease into a conversation and ask the critical question (at least in his mind) in a way that invited an honest, unfettered response. The profundity that came out was, "How are you?"

"Better now. I was shook up, that's for sure, but getting better now. I've been given some time off to help get over this."

Myron nodded sympathetically. Good; they were on the same wavelength intuitively. Merle seemed to want to talk about his gruesome discovery without prompting. "It must have been awful."

"That it was," he said, leaning forward and lowering his voice. "Sat there stiff as a board, staring straight ahead. In that fur coat and furry cap, she looked like one of those babushka dolls — you know — like from Russia.

"Right..."

"Don't think I'll ever forget it, that's for sure."

"I can imagine. I read about it in the *Daily Reporter*."

"Yeah, the paper got that from the cops."

"No one interviewed you?"

"Well, sort of. I couldn't say much, because there was to be an investigation, and the cops didn't want any of the details out in public. Said they'd handle the press, give the official statement. An *Edmonton Journal* reporter phoned and left a number of messages, but I haven't called back. I was told not to talk about what I saw until they could figure it out."

"And you didn't?"

"Nope."

"So the RCMP are the only ones you gave your statement to."

"Yeah, got asked a lot of questions about what I saw, did I see anyone else, what time and all of that. A young, pretty cop went through all that — why?"

Merle's eyes narrowed as a light bulb suddenly flickered in his brain. Myron could see that Merle was getting suspicious about this meeting, which Myron had passed off as "long time no see" and "heard you had a nasty experience... How about doing coffee..."

Myron decided to be as honest as he could possibly be with Merle. He needed to gain his confidence, and being upfront seemed the best way. He explained that he'd been enlisted by the same lady officer whom he'd talked to. She wanted help to gather information because he knew the institution and the people involved. He appreciated and respected the fact that Merle was instructed not to discuss the case with anyone, and he didn't want to pry unnecessarily, but if he could go over it one more time — just to hit the check marks...

Merle seemed to accept Myron's verbiage at face value and simply nodded. "No big deal to me. I really didn't see anything useful after I found her. And that's what I said to the corporal — had a funny name... Freda — Freda Horsey or something like that. Seemed kinda young to be in charge..." Merle trailed off.

"Freta Osprey," Myron corrected. "And yes she's young, and I just wanted to follow up."

"Can follow up all you want, but like I said, didn't see anyone and really don't know anything other than there was the president of the college frozen stiff behind the wheel of her car. By the way, what'd you think is going to happen to that Olds of hers?"

"Er...I don't know," said Myron, thrown off by the question. "I could ask around."

"Could you? That'd be great. I'd be interested if the price is right."

And you might get it, once the forensic people are finished with it. After all, how many would want to sit in the driver's seat previously occupied by a dead person? People were funny that way; apparently Merle was not...

"Will do," he replied. "Now, I don't want to compromise you in any way, so I won't ask for all the details. I'm sure Corporal Osprey has got all those. I have just one important question. If you can answer that, I'd truly appreciate it."

"Fire away," he said.

***

Driving to the college, Myron digested what Merle had confirmed for him. If Merle indeed had told no one but Freta, and now himself (and there was no mention of it in the newspapers), then a certain person had some serious explaining to do. It was an intuitive feeling, a bit out there, but he believed he was on to something. He wondered if homicide detectives had similar feelings in their cases and the sudden rush of excitement that went with it. This was the equivalent of a smoking gun — circumstantial but concrete. Of course, he had no absolute proof other than a verbal exchange that could easily be denied or dismissed. But he had heard what he heard, which should focus the investigation in a particular direction.

First and foremost, he needed to talk to Freta and go over the official statement Merle gave to the RCMP. However, that would have to wait he realized as he parked the car, rushed into the college, and hustled up the stairs to his office. There were notes to read for his ten o'clock class.

The rest of the morning proved uneventful. The only awkward moment came in the corridor after class — not with the students, but with Sidney who did an abrupt about-face and walked the other way when Myron emerged from the classroom.

Childish but if that's the way it's going to be — so be it!

Back in his office, he closed the door and phoned Freta. Alas, the call went straight to a message machine, and he hung up, not wanting his voice recorded. He couldn't say why exactly, but it seemed the prudent thing to do, and Freta had given him a heads-up that incoming calls were recorded. In any case, he would see her later that night at the Dworking tribute, and afterward, he hoped.

Ted wasn't in, and there wasn't anyone else in the office on the other side to distract him. Not that there normally was. The psychology instructor who had access to the space was rarely there, and when she was, she kept to herself, or at least her door was always closed. Dr. Brewdly didn't seem to keep office hours — at least at times when Myron was around. She was a strange one. The few times that he did interact with her were somewhat disconcerting; she tended to hug walls and never made direct eye contact. A bit of an introvert, Myron surmised. He did overhear two students talking about her in the hall one day. They were intrigued by the fact that she had given a lecture, all the while stroking a lab rat presumably brought in for experimental purposes. The students did not elaborate. Different strokes for different folks, he supposed.

No excuses, then; Myron resolutely picked up an essay staring up at him from the pile and began to read. It proved the source of his only genuine levity that morning. The epistle, entitled "Fur Trade," was less so about that than a rather imaginative story about the plight of the poor beaver. They were victims, this pupil insisted, victims of fur trappers and traders' persecutions. Hunted by the coureurs des bois, Nor'Westers, and short, stumpy Hudson's Bay company Scotsmen from the Orkney Islands, they were chased across the continent all the way to the Pacific, where in order to escape, the essay seemed to imply, they emigrated! Myron laughed and then sighed as he wrote a few pithy comments about an interesting thesis, but *what was the kid smoking?* Of course, he couldn't put it quite in those terms…

Two more essays (not nearly as amusing) later, Ted showed up, a big binder under his arm with bits of paper sticking out. He was a little harried, explaining that he had given the tests back and was besieged by students unhappy about their marks. The discussions spilled over after class into the hall before he could extricate himself.

"Sheesh," he exclaimed. "They were ready to draw and quarter me!"

"That tough, huh?"

"If they spent as much energy learning the tax cases that they were supposed to…" Ted trailed off, plopping down onto a chair with an exhausted sigh. "By the way, do you have ESP or something?"

"Why?"

"You asked me about Sheila and Charles yesterday."

"Yeah?" Myron's interest perked up.

"Saw Sheila in Charles's office on my way up — a bit animated, or at least she was."

"About what?"

"Saw — didn't actually hear. The door was closed, but she was standing at his desk, as I said — animated. She looked tense — anxious. I don't think she was there to congratulate him on his new appointment."

"And you didn't hear anything?"

"Other than the slam of the door when she left?"

***

As much as he was tempted, Myron couldn't share with Ted his suspicions about Dworking's death and who he thought was responsible. If he blabbed to Ted, it would be all over the college in a flash. He had to keep his own counsel — at least until he talked to Freta. The other, perhaps more difficult trick was to maintain his composure and an unassuming, straight face when speaking to the person he believed was the murderer.

Meanwhile, he continued to be intrigued by Sheila and Charles's relationship, past and present. The troubled waters between them ran deep but had remained relatively still until now; suddenly, the current between them was roiling. He should stay out of it, he knew, but he couldn't help himself. He had this compulsive, illogical need to pry.

Sheila's office, along with Charles's, was on the second level, with a large general office separating them. Normally, Myron would have checked with Janet Fere, Sheila's exceedingly friendly and competent executive secretary, before visiting, but he decided to make an exception. According to Ted, she had just met with Charles, and it was therefore unlikely there was anyone else in her office. Bypassing the main office, he lightly knocked on Sheila's door.

There was a momentary pause before the door tentatively opened, with Sheila peering out looking dishevelled and red-eyed, as if she'd been crying.

She let him in, and he settled in a beige leather chair off to the right of her large and neat desk (a feat Myron found impossible to achieve). She wheeled her ergonomically correct chair from behind it closer to him as he glanced at the bookcase behind, stocked with what looked more like bound reports than academic tomes. They too seemed neatly arranged.

"We didn't have a meeting scheduled, did we?" Sheila enquired in a perplexed tone.

"No...I thought that I'd take a chance and pop in — to commiserate." Myron explained lamely, shrugging. "Sorry that it didn't work out for you," he added sincerely.

"Me too, but it was no big surprise; he had the inside track," she said bitterly.

Myron didn't know exactly how to take that comment. Certainly, Charles had cultivated members of the board, more so than Sheila, who could be somewhat austere and crisp in her language, but he didn't think there was a conspiracy to elevate Charles to the presidency. When would there have been time? Still, given what he was discovering of Charles, he could forgive Sheila for being suspicious of an inside job — if her comment was to be taken literally. The cards did seem stacked against her.

"Charles will make life miserable for me," she stated flatly. "And make sure that Oliver never sees the inside of this college again."

"I suppose you would know Charles better than I do." While aware of their past relationship, Myron didn't want to sound too flippant or that he already knew, hoping that Sheila would volunteer further information.

She sighed. "I do, and no doubt you've heard about our past, along with the nasty rumours."

"Only that you and Charles were..." He searched for the proper word.

"An item?" she filled in. "Well, that part was true for a short while."

"I don't think it's common knowledge. I only learned of this in the last couple of days."

"We have stayed out of each other's way — at least I stayed out of his. Now, that'll be impossible. He'll make sure of that!"

"Surely he'll respect—"

Sheila cut him off brusquely before he could go on about professional boundaries and institutional policies. "Not Charles!" she emphatically stated. "You don't know what he is capable of."

Myron caught a measure of mounting fear and anger in her words. He could see it in her panicked, tear-reddened eyes and her fingers gripping ever tighter the side arms of her swivelling chair.

What was he capable of? The thought popped out involuntarily. However, Myron did not voice it. Instead, he nodded sympathetically and waited for Sheila to say more. And she did. A mini torment of loathing rushed out.

"It was a very corrosive and corrupting relationship..." She paused, thinking, her mouth twisted in distaste. "Charm — he could be charming, you know — and obsessive. I have no doubt he will try to destroy me, from the inside out, if I let him." She gave Myron a sour smile. "Our relationship did not end well."

An understatement, if ever there was one. "That I gather," he said feebly. "I don't totally understand how Charles could—"

"Ah...that was my naïveté, blind infatuation, or fatal attraction. Hard to know now, but I said things...private things that were best kept private. With institutional power behind him, he can undermine me. He'll work at it methodically — first use persuasion, innuendo, tit for tat bribing — followed by humiliation, and finally, when my head is between my knees, dismissal."

Myron frowned. Sheila was weaving a most disturbing scenario, which without a specific context was difficult to grasp. God! Sheila was describing a Stalin in the making — the quintessential pencil-pushing, paper-shuffling little bureaucrat who wielded ultimate power and killed millions! *Enough with the ruthless dictator analogy. Save it for class!*

It was clear that Sheila and Charles meant something to each other at one time, which somehow got twisted into dark and absolute antipathy — at least from Sheila's perspective. But then love and hate were close soulmates, often inextricably connected, the flip side of the same coin. Myron could appreciate the angst, if not the apparent vitriol between Sheila and Charles, given his own ongoing drama with Nadia.

"I don't pretend to understand, but surely Charles will act professionally in his new capacity and carry on in a responsible manner. What could he possibly have over you?" *Might as well go fishing.* Curiosity was getting the better of him.

Sheila didn't bite, exactly. "Enough," she answered cryptically. "He'll do his best to take me down and those around me as collateral damage."

"If it's any consolation, I've found that what goes around has a way of coming around. His closet cannot be skeleton-free."

"To be sure, the bastard that he is, but I did the talking and he — well, not only was he a tight ass, but tight-lipped as well."

Myron nodded sombrely. He was dying to know what Leaper had on Penny other than the usual nasty breakup baggage that made her so angry and anxious, perhaps on the verge of a breakdown. There was something even deeper and more disturbing. She wasn't volunteering, and he dropped it momentarily and tried a slightly different tack.

"Has…has Charles bothered you?"

Sheila visibly slumped into her chair, deflated. "You mean stalking, uninvited attention, unsolicited notes? No, he's too smart for that. He has remained in the background, waiting, plotting, knowing that an opportunity would arise."

"How do you know that?"

"Because that's the way Charles operates, and he told me so on numerous occasions in his own circumspect manner when I left him and ever since."

"When did you leave him?"

"Over four years ago now. I suspect it's been festering on his mind ever since. I have avoided him as much as possible; of course, it's difficult in our current positions. Still, it's been kept within limits."

"Certainly well under the radar—"

"As I said, we've avoided each other, but I knew he wasn't finished. Now he has his chance."

"But you have been communicating more lately?" Myron asked, not mentioning that, courtesy of Ted, he knew that she had been in Charles's office just prior to his visit.

Sheila gave Myron an odd, crooked smile. "He wants a quid pro quo."

"Oh?"

"He'd forgive me if I dispense with Oliver. The implication was, although he didn't quite say it, that he'd even take me back. I was stunned and told him that would never happen. He just smiled and said words to the effect that I'd brought this on myself and that he was providing a way out."

"Charles sounds like a delusional tyrant," Myron remarked, a bit shocked. The image of Stalin popped into his mind again.

"Well, he was giving me a proposition, and if I rejected it then my future would take its course, and it wouldn't be good."

"Surely he cannot control the narrative as iron-fisted as that?"

"Perhaps not — not if I take some decisive actions of my own," she added mysteriously.

Myron was on the verge of asking point blank what event/incident gave Charles such a hold over her but pulled back. He didn't want to push too hard or put Sheila in a more uncomfortable spot than she was already in. He vaguely wondered if she had told Oliver. Perhaps he'd talk to him, but he dismissed the idea as soon as it arose. That would have been stepping over the line, going behind Sheila's back for confidential information. Sheila noted his hesitation and sensed the question he was struggling to ask.

"Please don't ask. I've already said too much — the story of my life with Charles." She laughed bitterly. "It is truly something buried in the past, where it belongs."

CHAPTER TWENTY

Myron went home shortly after his meeting with Sheila. He finally did his laundry and cleaned the place up a bit. While engaged in these happy homemaker activities, he tried to find a flaw in his logic regarding Dworking's murder. He couldn't. He was certain that he knew who did her in; proving it, however, was another matter. He would discuss it with Freta later that night, see what she thought of his sudden, insightful recall. Was it conclusive and convincing enough, or not?

A change of clothing was in order for the tribute. He discarded his paisley green shirt and well-worn tweed jacket and put on his last clean white dress shirt and blue blazer. Luckily, his grey trousers still retained their recently ironed shape. A little added panache to his appearance was in order, he decided; although somewhat on the large side now that he had reduced his waistline a couple of inches, the refreshed attire suited the occasion — not overly formal but not too shabby either. He'd let himself get a bit careless in his dress code in the last few weeks, he realized; maybe it was time to retailor and/or add new apparel to his wardrobe.

So, more spiffed up than he had been recently, Myron arrived about half an hour early for the Dworking tribute/wake/Leaper coronation. He was mildly surprised to find a good portion of the college community already there. The cafeteria was nicely decked out with white cloths on its round tables, where decorative candle lighting rested in crescent-shaped holders. Three long tables placed end to end, complete with a podium strategically plunked in the middle and an elaborate PA system located farther back, dominated the portable platform. Large bouquets were stationed atop the industrial-strength speaker boxes on either side of the platform. Caterers were just putting the finishing touches to the head table, which included a number of slender crystal vases with single long-stem red rose inserts.

Myron gave the setup a cursory inspection and wandered off around a corner, side-stepping a large potted palm to the bar. It was open, and business was brisk. But it was not a direct route. Realizing that a ticket was needed, he zeroed in on the table off to the side where a respectable queue had formed.

"This may turn out to be one of the more successful functions of the last few years," quipped Ted, suddenly appearing behind Myron in the lineup.

"Hi, Ted… Yeah, a gala event," he retorted with a trace of sarcasm.

"Wonder what's on the menu? I'm starved!"

"Roast beef, probably. Caterers tend to serve roast beef for these sorts of occasions, or, if we're really unlucky, rubber chicken."

"Or a 'cordon bleu' version of it."

"That too," Myron agreed. "Where are you sitting?"

"Haven't decided — far side or near side? Where do you think they'll start the food line?"

"I'll bet they'll start with the table on the near side," replied Myron for no particular reason.

"Okay, then, we'll stake out a table there — that one on the end." Ted indicated with a nod of his head the one he had in mind.

"Martha didn't come with you?" Ted's pleasantly cherubic wife often attended college functions with her husband, but Myron hadn't seen her.

"No, it's her yoga class tonight…"

They bought their tickets and went to the bar to cash them in for beer. The place was beginning to fill up with milling people. Myron caught a glimpse of Sidney, who on seeing him quickly turned his back. Myron had no doubt he was the latest to be added to Sidney's list of miscreants who were out to undermine him at the institution. That didn't bother Myron; he was probably in good company.

"Come on," said Ted. "Let's claim our table before it's taken."

As they made their way across the floor, Myron saw Sheila threading her way toward the head table. Her face wore a tight, grim mask with no penetrating levity. This was not going to be a particularly enjoyable evening for her, he surmised.

"You go on ahead and save a — two spots for me. Someone will be joining us later. I'll be there in a moment," he told Ted.

Myron made his way to Sheila. She was intently surveying the seating arrangements at the head table. There were name tags beside each chair. He noted that Leaper would be on one side of Blythe, while Sheila would be on the other, flanked by Board Vice-chair Hoar and the inconspicuous dean of Student Affairs, Reginald Mercur. With Leaper about to be elevated to acting president and Spinner no longer there, the ranks of top brass at the head table had indeed shrunk.

"Don't like the seating arrangements?" he asked.

"It'll do just fine," she said distractedly, her fingers playing nervously with the clasp on her purse. She was wearing a conservatively cut black dress with a smart grey cashmere cassock and low-heel black shoes. She had a certain gravitas, which Myron couldn't quite put his finger on.

"Sorry again — the way things turned out," Myron offered rather lamely.

"Pardon? Oh...so am I." She was certainly jumpy and tense — *like a cork ready to pop!*

"Well, I wish you the best and hope that Oliver can still be a member of this institution."

"Not with Charles as president," she said, her lip curled in distaste.

They just had this conversation earlier, and Myron did not want to rehash that particular part. Putting on his optimistic smile, he said with an assurance he did not feel, "Don't give up; it's not a fait accompli yet."

"It will be soon," she said in a small, muted voice.

Myron, beer cup in hand, was still digesting Sheila's remark when a voice boomed over the PA system.

"Ladies and gentlemen. We're just about ready to commence. Please, if you could take your seats…" It was Harold Wisenburg, the evening's master of ceremonies, if that was the proper title for such an occasion.

Myron gave Sheila an encouraging smile and excused himself. He found Ted sitting with Benson McDougall and his wife Barbara, a stout woman with a regal bearing.

"Sheila doesn't appear overly happy," commented Ted.

"No," Myron said, watching her proceed to the head table as if she was about to encounter a dreaded abyss from which she could not retreat.

"Would you if you just lost out on the presidency to Charles?" Benson piped in, taking a sip from what Myron presumed was a plastic glass of Scotch.

"You've got a point there," said Ted, observing Blythe, Leaper, Hoar, and Mercur joining Sheila at the head table.

If only it were that simple. Murky waters could run deep, especially if his suspicions about Dworking's death were correct. Until Myron could talk to Freta, however, he endeavoured to rein in his wild thoughts. He needed a second, sober opinion…

Myron was right about the roast beef but wrong on his choice of strategic seating. Wisenburg, after officially welcoming everyone, suggested that the dinner queue make its way to the buffet table, starting from the table on the far side of the podium, and work their way across the room. Ted sighed, resigned to being among the last to be fed.

"So…" Ted said after a while, "who's this mysterious guest we're saving the chair for? Someone we know?"

"You've seen her around," said Myron casually. "Corporal Osprey."

"The officer in charge of the investigation?"

"The very same."

"Why would she come?" Ted persisted.

"I suggested it. Give her an overview of all the suspects in one place and all that," Myron said in a light tone, not wanting to make a big deal of it.

"You've been watching too many cop shows," Ted said.

"They still think one of us knocked off the president?" asked McDougall, clearly surprised at the notion.

"Benson!" his wife interjected. "That's a very crude way of putting it."

McDougall gave his wife a slightly aggrieved look. "Just wondering if the coppers still believe someone gave Dworking a doing — that's all."

"I guess they haven't ruled it out," Myron responded..

"Well, if they haven't uncovered foul play by now, they won't," McDougall said. "The trail will be cold by now."

"Couldn't be colder than it was that night," Ted contributed with a mirthful snort.

"I think that all this copper activity during the last few days is much ado about nothing. It just leads to nasty speculation and gives the college a bad name," McDougall said. "No one had a go at her. She probably had a seizure of some sort and without help froze in her car. She should be given a proper send-off tonight and leave it at that!"

Twenty-five minutes later, it was their turn to serve themselves at the buffet tables. Myron kept an eye out for Freta, but she had not arrived. Too bad, she might miss out on the highlight of the evening, and the roast beef didn't look that bad…

After the guests finished the main course and were working on a variety of desserts and coffee, Wisenburg rose to the podium. He thanked everyone for coming to pay their respects to the deceased and coincidently to welcome the new president. He then launched into a humorous story, presumably to show the human side of Dworking. Having just returned from the call of nature, Myron missed the punch line (which had something to do with Dworking's ability to give and take off-colour jokes). It was effective, since it drew the intended chuckles. Wisenburg then invited others from the audience to make a contribution to the memory of the president.

There was an awkward silence before Bowell stepped in to the breach. Wisenburg gladly relinquished the microphone.

"As you know," the sports goods store owner began, "I am the head of the board's negotiations team this year." He gave a nervous laugh. "And this year has been difficult, with the budget constraints, as those negotiating for the Faculty Association can attest…"

"No kidding!" exclaimed Ted. "We're getting nowhere fast with them."

"After a number of sessions of discussing offers and counteroffers," Bowell continued, "I and my counterpart on the faculty team agreed on a figure — at least it was one we were to present to our respective constituents…"

"But they reneged," commented Ted with a chagrined expression.

"I took it to the president, and I said, well, we finally did it! Now, I'm not one to be easily intimidated but," Bowell smiled nervously, "she could be fearsome…" He cleared his throat. "She raised her eyebrows and asked what did I do? We made a deal, I said. Then, I proceeded to tell her. She looked at me in that stern way and said that I just better go and undo it…"

"And that's why they reneged," Ted uttered, shaking his head. "So much for the board's independence when it comes to negotiations. I can't believe Bowell would be telling us this in public!"

"The point I want to make is…" Bowell glanced uncomfortably out at the seated gathering. *Perhaps he realized that he stuck his foot in his mouth*, Myron thought. "President Dworking was a formidable personality who had her hands firmly on the tiller at all times. She kept us on the straight and narrow for the good of this institution — even if it meant a little short-term pain for long-term gain… er… Thank you."

With that, Bowell hastily retreated to his seat.

"Well, that went over like a lead balloon," remarked Ted.

"I understand his sentiments, if not his choice of examples," Myron said.

Wisenburg regained the stage and thanked Bowell for his "enlightening insight." Somewhere from the back table a stifled laugh could be heard, which Wisenburg judiciously ignored.

"I appreciated his candour, anyway," stated Benson, draining the last of his Scotch. "We all knew Dworking called the shots at negotiations, just as she did with everything else around here. He just confirmed it."

"Yeah, and handed us the ball we can run with," Ted said excitedly. He was already plotting the next session of the yet to be completed contractual negotiations.

"Bet Charles isn't thrilled by Bowell's little reflection on Dworking's style," said Benson, chuckling.

Ted shrugged. "I bet he isn't, but that's his problem."

Wisenburg's tap on the microphone, followed by a sharp electronic squeal, got the audience's attention again; he asked if anyone else cared to offer a memorable Dworking moment. This time there was silence. After Bowell's revealing performance, it appeared that others preferred to hold their thoughts and tongues to themselves. "In that case, without further ado I'd like to introduce the chairperson of the board, Sheldon Blythe, to make a few comments and in turn introduce our next president."

Blythe said a few well-chosen words about how fortunate he had been to work with a professional like President Dworking. He mentioned her sterling qualities of honesty and integrity and the no-nonsense fashion with which she ran the college. He then turned his attention to Charles, "who, of course, needs no introduction." After a few more smooth phrases about how the selection committee believed and the board agreed that it had picked the right person for the job at hand, amid polite applause, Charles took the podium.

Myron was more attuned to Sheila's reaction than to Charles's beaming face. From his vantage point, he noted that Sheila didn't go through the nicety of clapping. She had put her purse in front of her, and casting a surreptitious glance on either side, opened it and took out a wad of Kleenex. Given what she told him, Myron hoped that she could gamely hold it together until what was surely an ordeal was over. Her face seemed serene, though, with a thin, unhappy smile set rigidly in place.

Leaper was in fine form and to his credit gave a rather objective overview of Dworking's contribution to the college. She was, he averred, "a competent administrator who tightened up the institution's infrastructure to allow it to meet the fiscal uncertainties and fluctuations in provincial support over the last few years." (For a moment, Myron thought that Leaper was describing the head of IBM or GM rather than a college president.) And finally, he noted that she didn't so much articulate a new vision of where the institution was going as emphasize where it was and how it could be improved.

On the whole, it was a good analysis but a poor eulogy. Absent was the usual emotional content, the outpouring of sorrow, regret, sense of loss, etcetera, that one expected on such occasions. Indeed, Myron noticed that no one was overwrought, but then that was probably the way Dworking would have preferred it.

Having given his clinical presentation of the Dworking years, Leaper then spoke of his intention to build on her legacy, of taking responsibilities seriously to continue to forge a comprehensive community college with diverse mandates that would meet the emerging challenges to be faced in the 1990s. It too was masterfully done, with all the right buzzwords.

Leaper appeared to be winding down when Myron spotted Freta coming in. Excusing himself from the table, he met her at the back of the cafeteria. She was inconspicuously dressed in a fashionable winter coat and gloves, high leather boots, and tights over what Myron reckoned was a frilly flowing skirt, judging from a peek below the winter apparel. She evidently had gone home and changed.

"Sorry," she said a little breathlessly. "My meeting with Dworking's sister took longer than anticipated — the plane was late, actually."

"She's not here?" he asked, somewhat surprised. He half expected the family representative to appear.

"No. I took her to the hotel room."

"Oh — too bad. I would have liked to meet her, see if she's any semblance of her sister."

"I suspect not. Sandra is quite a bit younger and, physically at least, taller, leaner, with auburn hair. Some sort of executive at a publishing firm in Toronto... At any rate, I don't think that she was much interested in coming. She said she was tired and not up to it emotionally."

"Well, this is hardly an emotional affair. Why don't I take your winter gear and stick it in my office while you grab whatever's left at the buffet table. Join Ted, Benson, Barbara, and I." He motioned to their table. "I have something really important to run by you later, when there's more time and we're alone."

As Myron made his way down the stairs from depositing Freta's winter outerwear, there was a burst of applause. Evidently, Leaper had finished; all smiles, with the practised flair of a politician, he waved his hand in acknowledgement, stepped away from the podium, and made his way toward his seat. That was probably it, thought Myron. Wisenburg would officially wrap up the affair; people would stick around a mite longer to finish their drinks (or indulge in a couple more) and go home. Business as usual on Monday.

He met Freta at the end of the buffet table with a plate full of sliced beef, mashed potatoes, and a combination of greens in her hand. "Could you grab me a coffee?" she said.

"Black, right?" He set a mug under the spout of the urn and pulled the tap, watching what looked like oily goo pour out. *Must be getting close to the bottom.*

"Yeah, thanks."

As he turned, Myron spotted Nadia from the shadows of a massive supporting pillar. She was a solitary figure, replete with a camera swung over her parka and pen and spiral notebook in her hand. She gave him a furtive glare, which captured Freta in equal measure. It quickly turned evasive when Myron nodded in her direction. She suddenly disappeared behind the pillar without acknowledgement. *I guess she decided she didn't see me*, he deduced. No doubt she was there in her official capacity as a reporter. Freta, he noted, gave no indication that she had noticed her. *Just as well*, he concluded.

"So you were saying you had something important to tell me?" Freta broke into his wandering thoughts.

"Right — yes." Myron instinctively lowered his voice and made sure there was no one within earshot. "It came to me out of the blue — something that I heard but didn't connect until this morning."

"What are you talking about?"

"Dworking's killer, I—" Myron was abruptly interrupted by a stifled scream and breaking glass.

The source came from the vicinity of the head table — the acting president, in fact. He appeared to have stumbled over his chair and fell to the floor, pulling the tablecloth with him. Myron saw Blythe reach out in horror and try to restrain Charles's downward plunge. Charles was obviously in the throes of some sort of convulsion, his mouth agape, gasping for breath, his hands instinctively gripping his throat.

Sheila, Myron noticed in that fraction of peripheral activity that his eyes caught and his mind registered, brusquely stood up, and clutching her purse, backed away as if to dissociate herself from the scene. Not the usual reaction for a one-time nurse used to dealing with medical emergencies, which this most certainly was.

Freta, seeing the distressed man stumble and fall, set aside her loaded plate on the edge of the buffet table and rushed forward with Myron in her wake, the mug of sludge left to turn cold under the spout. He wondered vaguely if Charles had a seizure of some sort or was choking on something.

"Stand back!" Freta ordered in an authoritative tone. The shocked onlookers made room. "We need an ambulance!" she shouted, kneeling beside the prostrated man.

"On it!" Myron heard Ted's voice ring clearly from behind.

Myron crouched behind Freta, who now placed two fingers on the side of his neck, checking for a pulse. Frowning, she said to Myron, "Help me turn him over." His face appeared flaccid and clammy, his body inert. She put her ear to his mouth, observing his chest for any tell-tale signs of breathing. For Myron it was impossible to tell. Freta proceeded to pinch his nostrils and brought her face close to his mouth as if to give mouth-to-mouth resuscitation, only to pull away abruptly.

"I think he's been poisoned," she whispered

Myron leaned closer and got an acrid whiff of something he couldn't identify.

"Oh my God — Sheila." The name automatically popped out of his mouth.

"What?"

Myron looked up, and Freta followed his eyes. They saw an ashen but otherwise blank face staring at them from the edge of a traumatized crowd. Sheila Penny held their gaze for a fraction of a second, then, as if suddenly coming out of a trance, turned and hurried toward the ladies' room.

CHAPTER TWENTY-ONE

"I thought I had figured it out, but not this," said Myron, shaking his head and slumping farther into Freta's couch. It was well after three in the morning before they left the presumed crime scene. Paramedics had arrived within twenty minutes, and Leaper was strapped up and whisked away with admirable dispatch, still alive, as far as Myron could tell. Freta spoke briefly to the attendants, called in for backup, and proceeded to secure the incident area.

"Don't let anyone touch anything here," she motioned to the head table, "particularly the drinks," she told Myron. "The forensics people need to go through it."

Then she spent most of her time taking down names and asking questions of those at the head table. Did anyone notice anything unusual? How was Mr. Leaper before his collapse? Did he take a drink after his talk? What did he drink? The questions produced no concrete results. It appeared that nobody — at least at the head table — noticed anything unusual.

Myron noted Nadia amid the other aghast guests. She seemed just as stunned as those around her. For a brief moment, they made eye contact, a viscerally haunting glance that reached his core, before she turned away. *She'll get a hell of a story, with photos if she's discreet about it.*

"Okay, just what had you figured out?" Freta asked tiredly.

"It's a small detail really, but the more I thought about it—"

"It's in the minutiae of details that cases often get solved. That's why Rob and I have been asking questions, and then more questions these last few days, and why I asked for your help — well, part of the reason…" She let the thought trail away. "So, what have you got?"

"It seems a bit anticlimactic now," Myron said. He had been eagerly waiting for the opportune moment to tell Freta that he had solved the Dworking case, but now there was a smidgen of doubt.

"What is?"

Myron sighed and stated without further preamble, "Charles killed Dworking — that's the way it looks to me. Still does, even if he was poisoned — how'd you know he was poisoned, by the way?"

"Burnt almond. Didn't you smell it?"

Myron nodded. "I couldn't quite identify the odour. I just thought Charles had a bad case of halitosis."

"I am pretty sure it was potassium cyanide. It's fast-acting and more often than not gets the job done. But back to your comment. You say Charles killed Dworking. How did you arrive at that conclusion?"

"As I started to tell you earlier last evening, he actually gave himself away, but I didn't pick up on it at the time. It was only when I was marking student essays with my 'what's wrong with this sentence' mantra that it suddenly dawned on me. The other day he said something to me about how tragically Dworking died strapped in her seat. How'd he know that? No one knew that Dworking had her seat belt on. I checked the newspaper accounts and talked to Merle Morgan. He swore he told no one. Said the police — you — gagged him."

"That's right," Freta said, frowning. "We didn't want the details released — we rarely do in such suspicious circumstances.

"And I knew only because you told me. And you certainly didn't tell Charles."

"I broke protocol or worse by telling you, and no way would that have been slipped to Charles."

"So, how did he know if he didn't do it?"

Freta thought about that for a moment. "I don't know — could have assumed it, I suppose," she added unconvincingly. "When did he tell you exactly?"

"It was Monday or Tuesday, before he was selected as acting president. The conversation — more like a quick exchange, really — took place in a washroom with no one present that I was aware of, anyway. So it would be my word against his in the end, but I remember clearly what he said; I just didn't digest it until a couple days later."

"Okay suppose that's true…?"

"As I figure it," Myron plunged ahead, "he went to her office that night after Spinner's dismissal. You already established that Leaper was at the college that night."

Freta nodded. "Said he worked late in his office."

"Right. Well, he paid the president a visit. Must have argued about something — his future employment, maybe. There was no love lost between them, as far as I can tell, and my theory is that he followed her to her car, perhaps still arguing or pleading his case. I don't see him smacking her in her office and then carrying her out."

"No — there's no evidence of that.'

"Anyway, he followed her out and hit her from behind with some object. You said that there was a contusion on the base of her skull."

"That's right, and that's why the death was deemed suspicious, but not conclusively a homicide."

"Actually, come to think of it, I haven't seen Charles's fancy briefcase he always takes to meetings." *Another small but possibly significant detail.* "At any rate, I don't think it was premeditated — maybe a case of spontaneous rage. Dworking fell against the door. He caught her, eased her onto the seat, and in a moment of insight strapped her in and stuck her keys into the ignition. And that's how poor old Merle found the car, unlocked and occupied by our late president. Charles probably thought she was dead and tried to make it look like a natural death. What do you think?"

"We may never know if he dies," Freta said, "but your theory makes sense in a perverse sort of way. At the very least I can get the forensic guys to search his office and home."

"Look for his briefcase," Myron added with emphasis.

"If it is the murder weapon and he didn't get rid of it," said Freta. "Charles did it. I know I'm right!"

"Maybe, but we still need proof. And how does Sheila Penny fit? She was my number one suspect for Dworking, never mind what just happened to Leaper and your theory notwithstanding. She's still in the running. And you practically accused her of poisoning Leaper — why?"

"That was an intuitive deduction. Throughout the evening, she seemed preoccupied — on the verge of some great cathartic moment or breakdown. I can't explain it totally. Spoke with her briefly and observed..." He paused, reflecting. "She seemed far-off, distracted, certainly not herself. I don't know...but when you said poison, it clicked into place, as I said, intuitively. How come you know so much about poisons — that it was potassium cyanide?"

"I read lots of whodunits and took a forensic course at Penhold. It's one of the more common poisons with the odour giveaway I mentioned. But back to Penny."

"Her name automatically came to mind. And my mouth uttered what my brain formulated. And then she rushed off."

"Well, she sure looked like the cat that swallowed the canary."

"You interviewed her?"

"Got a brief statement," Freta said. "She didn't notice a thing. Like everyone else, she thought that Leaper had a heart attack or some other medical condition."

"Odd behaviour for a former nurse trained to react to medical emergencies," noted Myron. "But then she really, really didn't like Charles."

"Not exactly Florence Nightingale, that's for sure. And you're right; I got a sense of dislike between the two, talking to some of your colleagues. It seemed they were close, very close for a brief time."

"There's more to it than that," said Myron. "Sheila and Charles have a history, which escalated dramatically after his elevation to acting president." He proceeded to fill Freta in on his last conversation with Sheila and the apparent hold Charles had over her.

"Sounds like a pair who deserve each other. Looks like I'll have to dig deeper into Penny's past."

"Well, there's some sordid secret that Charles found out and has over her. That's my impression. What did she say about not aiding Charles as a medical professional?"

"Said she felt sick and had to go to the washroom."

"She did appear stressed, and perhaps she wasn't well," said Myron.

"Well, at this point, all I can say that as a 'medical professional,' to use your words, she would know about lethal drugs, and a washroom is a good place to get rid of any residual evidence."

"So where do we go from here?" asked Myron

"I don't know about you, but right now I'm too tired to think, so I'm going to bed."

"Good idea, let's sleep on it," Myron agreed.

CHAPTER TWENTY-TWO

Five weeks later

"You've been holding out on me," Ted declared ruefully as he marched into Myron's office and plopped down into the only available empty chair.

"I have?" Myron looked up from his notes and laid down his pen.

"Yeah, but before I get to that, I need advice on toilets."

"Toilets?"

"More specifically, toilet bowls. Ours cracked and sprang a small leak — went shopping for a new one. You wouldn't believe it—"

"I don't know a thing about toilet bowls," Myron interjected.

"That's the point," Ted said. "I didn't think there was that much to know — boy was I wrong. I need advice."

"Advice?" Myron repeated, mystified.

"Decisions that must be made — round or elongated, dual flush or regular, liner or no liner, tall or regular? Then there's the flush capacity, the brand, and price range and where it's made — Mexico or China? What should I pay for a toilet bowl anyway?"

"I can't help you on any of the above," stated Myron. "I haven't the foggiest."

"Then I'll cut to the chase. Do you know a good plumber? This is not a project I want to 'plunge into.'"

Myron ignored the bad pun. "I know a plumber, but whether he's good or not, I couldn't tell you—"

"I'll get his name, but back to the issue at hand…"

"Which is?" Myron prompted.

"This." From a pile of papers wedged precariously dangling from his left armpit, Ted produced the most recent copy of the *Great Plains Daily Reporter*, where the largest headline read, "College's Acting President Charged with Second-Degree Murder."

"You've been holding out on me," Ted repeated. "You knew this was coming, right?"

"Wow!"

"Wow? Is that another of your learned comments?"

It wasn't that Myron was overly surprised. Freta had indicated that the Crown had enough evidence (albeit circumstantial) to charge Leaper. He was, however, still taken aback that it materialized so quickly. Of course, he had to keep Ted in the dark.

"I had only a vague idea, Ted — which I couldn't even speculate on."

The month or so after Leaper's sudden collapse had been a whirlwind of activity on numerous levels. While Freta and her colleagues proceeded — quite vigorously, evidently — with their investigation, Leaper made a slow but sure recovery from his close brush with death. Sheila took a sudden personal leave of absence (totally understandable from Myron's point of view) while the college administration limped along without a functioning CEO — almost. Reginald Mercur, the rather unassuming dean of Student Affairs, was next in the chain of command and became the de facto acting president while Leaper was incapacitated. This was before the revelation that the duly chosen acting president was charged with his predecessor's murder. With this latest development, Myron presumed that he'd shortly receive a notice of another "special" board meeting.

While the police buzzed about the institution, quarantining and searching Leaper's office and conducting another round of interviews, faculty and staff gossip escalated from salacious titillation to frenzied hysteria. Still, the business of higher learning continued. The students showed up in classes, and the instructors, unlike the staff, found diversion or in some cases relief (comic or otherwise) in delivering their lectures.

Myron, not having a chance to read the *Reporter* story, wondered how much detail it contained. He doubted that there was much — a cursory background on Dworking and her years as president, her death, Leaper's long history with the college, his elevation to the presidency and the shocking announcement that he had been arrested and charged with her death. Freta, no doubt, would shed further light on this latest turn of events when he took her out to dinner that evening. They hadn't seen much of each other since that intense night.

"Your wife wrote the article," Ted said in a matter-of-fact tone.

"Well, she sure didn't talk to me!" Myron retorted.

"But you're pretty tight with Corporal — I've forgotten her name..."

"This kind of thing the RCMP — in this case Corporal Osprey — plays close to the vest," Myron said. "Besides, it's the provincial Crown prosecutor that lays the charges."

"So, you don't know any more?"

"I haven't read the article, and I'm sure I don't know any more than was reported."

"Okay, okay." Ted sighed. "I believe you. The story doesn't really say much other than Leaper was at his home recovering from his 'mysterious' illness when he was arrested and charged."

"I'm sure the sordid entrails will emerge soon enough," said Myron, feeling like he narrowly escaped Ted's tenacious scrutiny.

"And what about Charles suddenly keeling over at his inauguration? Rumours are circulating that he was poisoned, and you know by whom!"

"Rumours are just that — rumours. No one has been accused or charges laid — if Leaper was poisoned."

"You knew something was up, though," Ted challenged. "You were mighty curious about Sheila and Charles's relationship. And why would Sheila suddenly take a leave of absence?"

"I have what you have, suspicions, and not much else," Myron answered truthfully, as far as it went. "And that's what everyone at the college has indulged in for the last month or so: suspicion and speculation."

"You're no fun," Ted grumbled.

Time to divert Ted into a scenario he can really run with. "There's a more pressing concern for the college community that nobody seems to have considered."

"What's that?"

"Think about this. There were three candidates for the college's top position. Two are out, which leaves only one left in the field."

"Oh my God!" exclaimed Ted.

"Yep," Myron chimed in. "None other than Sidney Sage."

"They wouldn't."

"To be honest, I can't prejudge the board. It's a real possibility that he will be seriously considered this time."

"Holy lentil farts!"

"Exactly."

***

"I bet this is the first time in any college's history that senior administration did itself in completely. Maybe I should contact the Guinness Book of Records people," Myron mused, popping a stray black olive into his mouth. He and Freta were having dinner at Pietro's, reputedly one of Great Plains' better establishments for Italian cuisine. Of course, there were only two others to pick from.

"Any idea what's going to happen at the college, now that it's leaderless?" asked Freta, occupied with cutting her veal parmigiana into manageable portions.

"It'll probably run better."

"Honestly — be serious."

"All right...all right..." Myron put his hand up in mock surrender. "Blythe will call an emergency board meeting, and we'll be searching for a president and at least two deans. In the meantime, quite possibly there'd be a government-appointed interim chief executive officer to run the show — the second-worst possibility."

"What's the first?"

"That the last applicant left standing should become president."

Freta looked puzzled.

"Never mind, it's a long story and inside joke. Let's hope a viable candidate steps into the breach for the short term." Myron brightened up, sat up, and abruptly changed the topic. "So tell me all about Charles's arrest?"

"He hasn't confessed, if that's what you want to know, but the evidence against him is pretty solid. I do really have to thank you, Myron. Your notice of a seemingly trivial slip of the tongue proved the key — and saved my ass."

"Oh? Why's that?"

Freta paused and laid down her utensils before addressing Myron. "I was in over my head, and the top brass wasn't happy about it. The truth is I stalled — delayed my report much too long and was about to be reprimanded or worse."

"I don't understand," Myron said, frowning.

"I should have called in the detectives without delay. I convinced Rob not to — not until we poked around. He was nervous about not following protocol and said we were jeopardizing a potential homicide case and our own careers in the process. And he was right! It was a suspicious death, and Major Crimes should have been called in right away." She leaned closer across the table toward Myron and continued. "Thanks to you, I — we, Rob and I — missed biting the bullet. As I said, you saved my ass."

"In that case, I was happy to oblige," Myron said.

"At any rate, since the search of Leaper's office and home — well, all's well that ends well. My superiors have been forgiving, if not completely mollified, Major Crimes detectives have taken over, and maybe I get to play investigator another day!"

"I'm glad that I could be useful." Myron raised his wine glass.

"Me too, Dr. Watson. You were absolutely right."

"Dr. Watson?" Myron raised an eyebrow.

"I'm Ms. Holmes, don't you know."

"Exactly what was I right about?" asked Myron. "Fill me in."

"Most of it, actually. While Leaper was in the hospital, we searched his office and found a rather pointed letter from the late president that informed him he'd best take his sabbatical, after which the college would no longer need his services."

"Ouch!"

"The alternative of forgoing his sabbatical would be a reorganization and a re-evaluation of his position at the end of the term," Freta continued, taking a sip of her wine.

"I guess that was her way of giving Charles fair warning and giving him a year to find another position," Myron said, reaching for a crouton on his Caesar salad.

"Motive clearly established."

"Charles would have been absolutely furious," agreed Myron.

"But that's not the clincher. We also searched his home, and, as you suggested, the forensics team looked for that missing briefcase. Surprise, surprise, surprise, it was discovered in a storage box underneath the stairs leading into the basement. And you were right: it is a very impressive silver aluminum hard-shell case with reinforced metal corners and sturdy protective rubber feet."

"I guess he couldn't bear to part with it."

"Or didn't have a chance to get rid of it. Anyway, it has a slight dent in the right upper corner and microscopic blood and hair samples match that of the late president — hence the second-degree murder charge. The Crown prosecutor thought that the burden of proof for first degree was too high." Freta shrugged.

"I would agree. My conjecture is that he argued with her and in a moment of rage — now, no doubt, regretted — he whacked the back of her head as she was opening or getting into her car."

"That's the scenario the prosecutor is going with. Of course, Charles is not talking except through his lawyer, who says his client will plead not guilty."

"What about Sheila and the investigation into Charles's poisoning?" Myron asked before shoving a forkful of romaine lettuce into his mouth. He had ordered pasta primavera, which was good but not as inviting as Freta's cut-up veal.

"Still ongoing," Freta replied with a shrug. "Leaper was poisoned, no doubt about that, but nobody saw a thing, and Penny sure isn't admitting it. She has a good chance of getting away with it."

"Did you dig deeper into Sheila's background?"

"After what you said, I did, with interesting results. Did you know she was a nurse in a large Vancouver hospital?"

"I didn't. Her mother lives there, though."

"She was implicated in a series of suspicious deaths a few years back, the so-called 'euthanasia killings' of very sick patients. Penny was the head nurse on the ward at the time. Vancouver Police investigated, but charges were never laid. Two out of the three were frail and elderly, and the other was quite ill. Two overdosed on their prescribed medication, while the other seems to have lethally ingested non-prescribed pills. Nothing could be proven."

"I wonder if that's her secret and the hold Charles had over her?"

"It could have been, but charges were never laid, which is not quite the same as exoneration, I suppose." Freta frowned and took another sip of her Sauvignon Blanc.

"And Charles hasn't said anything?" Myron asked.

"As I said, he's not talking right now. Probably too occupied with his own troubles."

"Poor Sheila. Oliver's firing and Charles's selection as acting president pushed her over the edge and—"

"Poor Sheila?" Freta cut him off. "Poor Leaper, I'd say. He barely survived by the hairs of his chinny chin chin!"

"I can't help but sympathize — just a little."

Freta shook her head. "All I can say is that even if she confessed the consequences probably wouldn't be that onerous, given our justice system. A good lawyer would argue extenuating circumstance and temporary insanity. She'd receive a substantially reduced sentence — he didn't die, after all. Leaper may be a shit head but Penny's no princess either."

"I guess not," Myron admitted.

***

Two days later, there indeed was a special board meeting, after which Myron showed up at Freta's apartment door. He had with him a large bouquet of carnations and a box of chocolates. He sported a huge smile when she opened the door.

"What's the occasion?" she asked suspiciously.

"Anything you like!" he replied. "Early Valentine's — late birthday — but mostly my good news. Three pieces of good news, actually." He handed her the flowers and chocolates and proceeded to seat himself comfortably in her living room. After cutting the stems and sticking the carnations in a glass vase, Freta joined him.

"Want some of your chocolates?" she asked

"Why? Don't you like chocolates? In sufficient quantity, they're supposed to act as an aphrodisiac."

"Eat too many and you'll get the runs," she retorted. "Now what's your good news?"

"The college has a new acting president: our dean of Student Affairs. He's agreed to stay on until the spring when the new administrative team takes over. He'll act in a most unimaginative and orthodox manner."

"Is that good?" Freta asked, not quite certain.

"Actually, yes, given the alternative." Myron was still irritated that the board spent some time debating Sage's candidacy. Thank God Mercur was prevailed upon to continue as the acting president. "Hopefully, there'll be no surprises for a while."

"So what's your second piece of good news?"

"Your nemesis, Wishert — remember the short, bald man who threatened to sue you?"

"How can I forget? He was…weird."

"He's taken an extended leave of absence, and I don't think he'll come back. The RCMP hasn't heard from his lawyers, has it?"

"Nope, not so far. It's all quiet on that front."

"Good! And finally, last but not least, a nice young man came to my door yesterday just as I was ready to leave for work and served me with divorce papers."

"Nadia's dumping you? And that's good news?" Freta had a perplexed expression on her face.

"Not when you put it that way," he retorted with a hint of annoyance. "But there's another way of looking at it."

"How's that?"

"It's over. She's made up her mind and I guess sorted out whatever problems she had. Until those divorce papers were served, she was still using me as her backup — kind of a safety net if things really went wrong. And I would have let her. Of course, I'm not thrilled that she hired Mr. Slime Bag himself, Anthony Chorny, as her lawyer, but now at least I can move on to something else." He gave her his Groucho Marx eyebrow shuffle.

"What'd you have in mind?" Freta asked, a note of unease creeping into her voice. "You aren't going to complicate my life, are you? Those flowers and chocolates aren't you're way of suggesting some sort of lengthy commitment?"

"Who said anything about a long-term relationship? I've come here tonight to share some good news with you, and a quickie."

"Thank God. For a minute there I thought we were getting serious."

ACKNOWLEDGEMENTS

First and foremost I am grateful to my wife, Diane, who encouraged and cheerfully put up with my writing hibernations and to my wonderful daughters, Alisha and Halyna, who initially vetted the manuscript and gave insightful critiques.

I also thank Allister Thompson and Heather Bury for their careful copy edits/comments. A huge kudo to Melissa Novak for a great front cover illustration. Finally, my appreciation to Meghan Behse and Greg Ioannou at Iguana Books for their support.

Any errors of commission and/or omission are entirely mine.

CPSIA information can be obtained
at www.ICGtesting.com
Printed in the USA
LVHW030629181220
674415LV00005B/372

9 781771 804387